# Runs Like Clockwork

## A Steampunk Anthology

Edited by Mark Bilsborough

**WYLDBLOOD**

This edition published 2022 by Wyldblood Press, Thicket View, Maidenhead SL6 6PX





ISBN: 978-1-914417-08-5

# Contents

# Introduction

What is it about Steampunk that's so fascinating?  Is it the escapism, that sense of adventure in a familiar yet far off place? Is it the larger than life characters? Is it the gadgets, all that clockwork and steam? The mechanical men? The Zeppelins?

All of that, probably. We've arguably had steampunk novels since Captain Nemo set sail in the Nautilus, but the genre only really started to take form with Michael Moorcock's *Warlords of the Air* in 1971, then really took off with Willam Gibson and Bruce Sterling's *The Difference Engine* in 1990, though the term itself originates from the 1980s, used by K W Jeter to describe the strange and wonderful new fiction of steampunk pioneers Tim Powers and James Blaylock.

Now, of course, its influence is everywhere in books (I particularly like Jeanette Ng's *Under the Pendulum Sun* and Cherie Priest's *Boneshaker*), films (who can resist *Wild Wild West?*) and TV (from *Shadow and Bone* though *Carnival Row* with a large dollop of *Doctor Who*). There are societies devoted to it, conventions dedicated to it and aficionados dressed for it.

It's a fantasy subgenre which is more about mood and tone than about a strict set of rules. Not everything is steam powered, and you won't find airships and clockwork people on every page, and sometimes there's magic, sometimes not. It's the ultimate what-if, set in worlds like ours but where things may not always be as we remember them...

These stories don't even have to be set in Victorian London, either, even though that's arguably the spiritual home of steampunk. The wild west, deep space, and the here and now are all in scope so long as the stories *feel like* steampunk. And what does that mean? For me it's sepia toned and slightly eccentric, a bit odd and with a frisson of tension and adventure. But why try to pin down something so new and so exciting in its possibilities?

We've got a varied selection here, because sometimes we need introspective character driven thought pieces and sometimes we want out and out adventure, preferably with cacking bad guys and impossible odds. So the tone here is sometimes light, sometimes dark but always steampunk.

Enjoy the stories,

*Mark Bilsborough*
*Editor, Wyldbood Press*

# The Reality Engine

## *Rose Strickman*

Marina, squinting, made another minute adjustment in the miniature cogs of the sledge's engine, positioning her needle-driver at the exact angle to gently, gently maneuver the pins into position. The light was bad, and she tugged on the nearest aether-lamp cord. The glowing orb drifted sullenly nearer.

"Hey!" Jenny looked up, glowering. "I was using that!"

"Just a minute, Jenny, please..." Nothing illuminated like aether, and its levitational properties were perfect for such work. Unfortunately, they were still expensive enough, even with the current rush on, that the workroom at Moses Maccadam's Miners' Equipment Clock-and-Steam Building and Repair only had three, hovering over the long worktable where the girls labored. Or, at least, so Mr. Maccadam said. Marina scowled.

At last. She smiled as she heard the tiny, neat little *snick* that signaled completion. She laid the box-like engine on the table and straightened, hands against her aching back. "Light's all yours, Jenny."

"*Thank* you," Jenny said pointedly as she pulled the lamp back. Marina smarted a little at the venomous edge to her voice—it wasn't like she hadn't *needed* the lamp—but bent back to work.

Finally. Done. This was her final engine. Just in time, too: the clock on the wall trilled to signal quitting time. The girls all straightened from the worktable, stretching cramped muscles and sighing with relief. A storm of happy chatter arose as they put aside their projects and headed for the back passage, to gather their coats and belongings and head out for the night.

Behind them, Mr. Maccadam sidled into the workroom to make his nightly inspection after the girls left, his perpetual scowl especially pronounced. He had made it clear that he despised having to hire women for the miniature work, but there was no way around the fact that only women had hands small enough and fingers nimble enough to build the engines needed for the extreme cold of the Yukon. So Mr. Maccadam had to content himself with making multiple inspections a day, tutting over their work, and prowling around the workroom after hours, looking for flaws. At least he kept his hands to himself — unlike some.

As she pulled on her coat and picked up her umbrella, Marina scowled as the other major reason she disliked her job hove into sight.

"Hello, Miss Lanham!" It was James, Mr. Maccadam's nephew, flashing his wide white smile as always. He was usually serving out front, bantering with the miners who flooded in to buy equipment for the aetherite mines, but he somehow always managed to be at the backdoor at quitting time, smiling away.

"Hello, Mr. James," Marina returned, entirely unimpressed by that grin. He sure was proud of those teeth, she thought sourly, trotting them out whenever he could. That some of the girls were even now giggling and batting their eyelashes at him didn't help matters.

Jenny opened the backdoor onto a scene of horses and auto-cabs, mud and wet streets: it was always raining here in Siahl. Marina had to close her eyes momentarily. *I hate this city. How did I end up here?* It was a trick question; she knew perfectly well how she had come here. She just didn't like to think about it.

"So!" James was saying. "Tomorrow's Sunday. Doing anything, Miss Lanham?" They were alone in the back passage now, the other girls having filed out into the street.

"Church," she said shortly. This was untrue. Marina didn't feel like she had much to say to the Creator these days, so her attendance at divine services had been sporadic at best.

"Well, church services don't last forever. I was going to go take the boat to Leschi Park. If you wanted—"

"No, James," she said firmly. Just as firmly, she suppressed the memories his offer aroused in her. *Never again.*

He gave her the old sparkly again, not in the least abashed. "Okay. Just remember, offer's still open."

*It'll be a cold day in Hell, boy.* Pointedly ignoring pretty-boy, Marina headed out the door.

Outside it was—surprise, surprise—raining. Marina hunched inside her coat as she picked her way along the stone sidewalk. At her side, coaches, both clockwork and horse-powered, rattled over the cobbled street. Every few steps Marina passed a miners' supply store, full of crates, overcoats, fur-lined boots, shovels, and aetherite detection tools—some of them even authentic. Between the supply shops were plentiful saloons, each one filled with loud, sweaty young men, all boasting, shouting and singing while they awaited the departure of their ships to the north. The sidewalk was full of more such young men, each with the bright, shiny faces and arrogant swagger that aetherite dreams induced.

"Hey, pretty lady!" came the inevitable shout. "Want to help me get started spending my aetherite fortune?"

"In your dreams, boyo," she retorted, to a chorus of guffaws. Marina didn't even look to see the laughers. She was searching for the other men.

The *other* men were fewer in number than the boastful fortune-hunters, and much more self-effacing. They did not enter the saloons; they walked quickly, heads down, hands in their pockets. Far from making catcalls at Marina, they avoided her gaze. Their faces were hollow, their eyes shadowed. These were the men who had returned from the Yukon, not with dazzling fortunes, but with empty wallets and bad memories.

These were the men whose faces Marina scanned, searching. Hoping for a certain one. What would she do if she did see him? She sometimes wondered. But she never stopped looking.

In any case, she didn't find him. Clutching her umbrella, she hurried along beneath the aether hover-lamps, making her way back home.

Behind her, a shadow detached itself from its post and fluttered after her, quick and silent.

"Home" these days was a women-only boardinghouse run by a Mrs. Yesler. Marina admitted that it could have been worse: the house was a reasonable distance from the raucous downtown crowds, the other girls were pleasant enough, and Mrs. Yesler was a fairly nice landlady and a good cook, despite her clockwork automaton hand. (She wouldn't say just how she'd lost the original, leading to no end of speculation among her boarders.)

"So, girls," she said the next morning, pouring coffee while a rare beam of sunlight glinted off her metal hand, "do any of you have plans for this fine Sunday?"

"I'm going on a boat ride," said Lena, a tall, serious seamstress. "After church," she added piously.

The other girls all added their own stories, Marina giving a noncommittal murmur.

"Well, just you all be careful," said Mrs. Yesler. "I saw a stranger hanging around outside last night."

"Man or woman?" Marina asked, diverted.

"Couldn't say." Mrs. Yesler frowned. "But there's all sorts here ever since those no-account aether hunters started pouring in. Nothing's the same..."

Mrs. Yesler continued on her well-worn digression into the troubles and annoyances of the modern world while the girls finished up and breakfast wound down. Marina turned away, mind already straying to her Sunday errand.

Just because it was the Creator's day didn't mean the ships ceased departing the harbor—or arriving. The aetherite miners were all in a hurry, after all. Marina, heading down the hill, could see the great smokestacks and propulsion engines of the ships, gleaming in the sun. Marina lifted her face, enjoying the warmth. It reminded her of home, before everything went wrong.

The harbor heaved with activity, with raucous crowds flowing back and forth in rivers. Marina picked her way around the gyrating mass of merchants, suppliers, surveyors, disassembled mechanical sledges, bulging cases and, of course, miners. Young men craning forward eagerly, older men spitting tobacco juice, all of them waiting to leave...

Through the noise, Marina heard a sizzle, and caught a whiff of frying seafood. She hurried forward.

"Hello, Sarah," she said, arriving at the stand. Sarah was Marina's favorite purveyor of fried clams, who regularly plied her trade at the harbor. A small, round woman, she wore the tall hat and long robe of her Skraeling tribe, despite Skraelings being forbidden tribal costume within city limits. It brought in customers, she said, and was well worth the risk.

"Hi, Marina," Sarah said. "Usual?"

"Absolutely." Marina watched, mouth watering, while Sarah dropped the clams into the pan and ignited the aether-fire inside her cart. "How's business?"

"Very well, as you see." Sarah gestured smugly at the vast crowd. "Those miners can't hardly stop themselves buying real northwest clams from a real northwest Skraeling."

"Not to mention the last woman they'll probably see in months. There's, what, one woman for every hundred men up there? Thanks!" Marina accepted her newspaper-wrapped clams and handed over the money.

Sarah stowed it away. "Won't make it easy to find your man, then." She nodded at the crowd and the ships.

Marina froze. "What?" Her heart pounded: she had told *no one* about Nathan.

Sarah rolled her eyes. "Think I'm stupid? I've seen the way you watch the ships, Marina: all the arriving ships, every Sunday, every evening, you're here watching the men disembark, looking them over. Looking for one in particular, I'd say. Who are you hunting for?"

Marina groped, torn between flinging her clams in Sarah's face and bursting into tears. She compromised by turning on her heel and storming off.

"Marina! Wait..." Sarah's voice barely reached Marina's ears through the haze of grief and fury. She stamped on, past hairy, dirty miners, ignoring the catcalls and improper suggestions, until she found herself at the wharf's edge.

She stared down, into the scum of detritus that covered the water's surface, eyes burning. What Nathan had done to her was unbearable. The only thing worse would be if anyone knew. *Nathan...*She wiped away the tears, but they kept coming.

"Your pardon, miss."

Marina jumped and looked up, blinking. A woman stood on the wharf, white of face and black of hair, dressed in black mourning garb. Her eyes, a startling sea-green, observed Marina from within little crinkled webs of amusement.

"Are you Marina Lanham?" she asked.

Marina hung back. "Who's asking?"

"Someone who has a very favorable proposition for you—*if* you are the Marina Lanham who works at Maccadam's."

Marina nodded slowly. "That's me."

The woman held out a silk-gloved hand. "I am Nixa Apparecida. Pleased to make your acquaintance."

Marina did not take the hand. "What's this about?"

"I understand you are an artificer of some skill, Miss Lanham." The woman—Nixa—didn't seem at all taken aback by Marina's rudeness, her silken voice warm and confident. "A skill that goes unappreciated at your present employ. I assure you, you will not find the same reception if you accept my offer."

"What offer?"

"Of work, of course. I would like you to help me with a little project of mine, after hours at your current job. The pay would be far more than you currently receive, and the work, rest assured, *much* more interesting."

Marina hesitated. This sounded intriguing but…one heard stories. *"Easy work, little miss—all you have to do is lie on your back!"* "If you're trying to trick me—"

"This is no trick, Miss Lanham. It is what it seems: an offer of part-time employment, using your skills as an artificer. You may come with me to view the project, if you wish."

"Go *with* you?" Marina snorted. "What kind of fool do you take me for?"

In response, Nixa reached into her reticule and withdrew a small, shiny auto-gun, which she pressed into Marina's hand. "There. You are now armed—and you may shoot me at any time if you feel the least threatened."

Marina stared at the gun. Unless she was very much mistaken, this was a Winchester Silverfire, capable of piercing body armor, firing underwater, shooting multiple bullets in several directions simultaneously, and a whole host of other deadly little tricks that made this model the heart's desire of militia men and ardent collectors alike. She checked the magazine: it was fully loaded, bullets lined up snugly. Never in her life had she held such power; it seemed almost to vibrate in her grip.

"Well?" Nixa sounded amused. "Do you trust me now?"

Marina looked at Nixa. She looked at the gun. She looked at the ships, at the smelly crowds, the vast lines of men disembarking…

Marina turned back to Nixa. "Just what is this project?"

When Nixa promised to show rather than tell of the project, Marina expected to be led to the edge of the city: a tall townhouse perhaps, with shuttered windows and deep shadows. She was therefore surprised when Nixa led her only a little way from the harbor, up the hill past the marketplace, and ducked into a dark alley. Nixa stepped into an alcove to open a secretive door of splintered wood.

Marina hung back. "What is this?"

Nixa flashed her a white smile. "We're going underground."

"Underground?" Marina had heard of Siahl's undercity: the network of passages, caverns, corridors and tunnels that had resulted when the city had raised its street levels following the great aether-fire ten years ago. But she'd certainly never been there. The undercity was the haunt of prostitutes, cutthroats, smugglers, and shisha dens—not a place any respectable woman would go.

Nixa's smile didn't waver. "You may still leave, should you wish."

The Silverfire hung heavy in Marina's reticule. She followed Nixa through the door and down a narrow flight of stairs.

The stink of mud and salt was heavy down here: the smell of the mudflats mixed with the stench of sewage. Rats ran past the women's boots, squeaking. Light stabbed down from unexpected places, and broken glass crunched beneath their feet. A figure suddenly lurched toward them, breathing alcohol fumes; his pupils were like pinpoints in his pale eyes. Marina cried out, shrinking back—but the drunk suddenly focused on Nixa and stumbled back, eyes wide, gibbering incoherently. He staggered away into the dark.

"I am known here," said Nixa, voice light and amused. "You are safe as long as you are with me. Come."

She stepped on, light sparkling in the sequins of her gown. After a moment, Marina followed, heart still pounding.

On they went, and down, through brick archways and through ruined, forgotten cellars. Once or twice, some distance away, Marina thought she heard voices, raised in song and argument, music, but their path never intersected with the revelers. Marina could only be grateful.

Only once more did they pass another living soul: a tall, thin man in a corner, who looked up from whatever he was shuffling in his hands. His eyes burned a brilliant gold, and under his Han silk coat, a long brushed tail swept the floor. Marina pressed closer to Nixa and he grinned, revealing sharp white fangs. She felt his eyes, following them on their way.

At last, Nixa slowed, and stopped before a shadowed door, which she negotiated in a flash of keys. It swung open and they stepped in.

Marina wasn't sure what she'd expected: a dark room, perhaps, with a single sinister aether lamp illuminating Nixa's terrible "project." Instead, she had to blink and screw her eyes shut against the blaze of light within that room: there must have been six hover-lamps in there, illuminating a *very* well-appointed workroom—Marina's fingers twitched involuntarily at the sight of the beautiful artificer's workbench and all that gleaming equipment. Her eyes ran over a brilliant, dagger-sharp, aetherite-edged saw; a top-of-the-line, brand-new Walgrove aether-driver; hundreds of gleaming perfect circuits—oh, *yes!* Marina tore her gaze away, and looked up to see Nixa's amused glance.

"Does the workroom meet with your satisfaction, Miss Lanham?"

"Oh, *yes*, it—" Marina cut herself off. "Where did you get all this equipment?"

"Never fear, I did so honestly. And it's all the best quality. I wasn't going to risk something of this importance by using second-rate equipment." Nixa moved deeper into the workroom, to a second workbench that had hitherto escaped Marina's attention. This one contained such items as an alchemical alembic, mortar and pestle, bottles and vials of various powders and potions, and other tools that Marina couldn't name.

Nixa removed a large metal object from a high shelf and placed it on the bench. "Here, Miss Lanham, is my project."

Marina examined the object. It looked like a crude, incomplete engine in many ways, but there were differences, the chief of which— "What is *that?*"

Nixa's eyes gleamed. "A piece of aether-wood."

"*Aether*-wood?" Marina examined the star-shaped piece of wood hovering in the center of the engine. Literally hovering: Nixa had lashed it in place with silver cords to stop it floating out. Marina could smell its cedar scent, laced with ozone. "I thought that was a myth!"

"Why, how else did the Skraelings build their flying war canoes? A certain species of cedar draws aetherite from the ground and absorbs it into its wood. Or they used to—there's precious few of them left. But a piece of aether-wood," she tapped the fragment with a long finger, making it bob in midair, "will leach aether for a very long time. It is the perfect power source for my reality configuration engine."

"…Sorry?"

"Reality configuration engine." Nixa was perfectly calm. "When completed, this machine shall have the power to edit reality to match its user's desire. It shall…grant wishes."

Marina looked at the engine. It sat on the bench, small, incomplete and—aside from the aether-wood—perfectly ordinary. It didn't look capable of propelling a sledge, let alone granting wishes. "Is this some kind of joke?"

"No, but you can see why I need an artificer's expertise." Nixa gestured around the workroom. "I am, if I may flatter myself, a more than competent alchemist—but I am no artificer. I have got as far as I can on the hardware aspect of my engine. Now I need someone with greater competence."

Marina examined the engine. Yes—she could see where she might begin working. How it could grow—she yanked her eyes away, quickly. "Why me, though? There are finer artificers and mechanics even in this town. Men who've trained in Londinium, even. I just work in a sledge shop."

Nixa was silent a moment, dark eyes trained on her. "But you do have a wish, do you not?" she said softly. "You yearn for something, terribly. I've seen you. I've seen the hunger in your eyes. You have a wish—and you would give anything to make it true."

Marina swallowed against the sudden pain. *Nathan.* Love. Happiness. Her honor. Her parents, back in St. Francisca, welcoming her with open arms... "So you're saying," she said slowly, "that if I do this—and I'm not saying I will—I'll get a wish?"

"One wish. You may use my engine to edit reality, just once."

Marina looked at the engine again. "I'll have to think about this."

"Quite rightly, too. You may have one week. Then I'll come for your answer."

Marina nodded, still staring at the engine.

The next day, Marina was quiet and abstracted as she entered the shop. James, looking up from re-screwing the coatrack into the wall, gave her that long, insufferable grin.

"Marina! How was your Sunday?"

"Fine." Marina began to edge past him. *Reality configuration. Wish machine.* Could it be true?

"You don't look fine." James's grin faded. "Distinctly peaky, in fact. What's the matter?"

"Nothing." Marina pulled herself together. "Just this blasted rain." She gestured out at the wet street. "How do you Siahlites stand it?"

"By thanking the Creator it's not snow!" James laughed. "Want bad weather, try Callbridge, New Albion!"

"I wouldn't know. I've never been East." Marina reached the door to the workroom.

"Right. You're from Califiya, right? St. Angelo?"

"St. Francisca." Marina swung the door open and stepped into the workroom. Yes, St. Francisca. Land of bright sunlight, gentle fogs, the magnificent sweep of the ocean. Not like this miserable, fragile city in its mud-swamp, on the edge of wilderness, hemmed in by the constricted Salish Sea. She had lived in St. Francisca — where her family still lived. A family she would never see again, unless something changed. Radically.

How *could* she have been so dumb? So dumb to fall for Nathan, to follow him here? To give him her virtue even…Marina's face heated as she remembered those long, boardinghouse and shipboard nights, their senses deaf to the roar of traffic and clank of machinery as they committed their shameful sin…Oh, but they had been in love! And he had promised marriage.

Until the morning she had woken to an empty bed, an empty purse and no note from the vanished Nathan. He was just gone — off to the aetherite fields of the Yukon, she assumed. And she was trapped in Siahl: no money, unable to face contacting her family in St. Francisca, alone and lonely in this unending shame and longing…

*"You may use my engine to edit reality."*

And Marina had her answer for Nixa.


"Yes," she said on Saturday evening. Nixa was waiting for her at the street corner outside the workshop, her face veiled, hands hidden in a muff. She'd said nothing when Marina approached, but merely looked at her from behind the sequined netting.

"Yes," said Marina. "I'll do it. I'll build your wish machine."

Nixa smiled, a perfect curve of blood-red lips. "Excellent."

#

13

Marina's life upended, fluttered, settled itself into a new pattern.

Now, instead of searching the streets for Nathan's face after work, she went straight to a certain street corner a few blocks away from the workshop, keeping her head down, her face veiled. There an auto-cab would be waiting, brass shiny in the evening light. Marina would get in, and its pre-set coordinates would take her straight to the hidden door to the undercity. She would knock, and Nixa would open it, black gown velvety against the darkness. Together they would go down to the aether-lit workroom.

There Marina would work on the cogs and wires of the reality configuration engine, calibrating, fine-tuning, putting together and taking apart, the engine seeming to speak to her while she worked, telling her a story of greater complexity and fascination than she had ever encountered before in any machine. So absorbed was Marina that after a while she always half-forgot that Nixa was even in the room, even as she moved back and forth at the alchemical workbench, measuring ingredients, consulting almanacs and charts. Marina sometimes wondered about Nixa's work, but the alchemist never said.

"Good evening, Miss Lanham." "Good night, Miss Lanham." That was all Nixa ever said. She did not murmur to herself as she worked among her alchemical equipment, and she never asked Marina how her had had been, or struck up a conversation in the workroom. She said never a word about herself, and something about her silence prevented Marina from asking.

And, indeed, she soon found she did not wish to ask. So complex was this engine, so absorbing, that she had no thought for anything else. Even at Maccadam's, working on the childishly simple sledges, all the cogs and gears seemed to echo the reality engine's. Her eyes, resting on the sledge engines, saw only the wish machine's inner workings. On Sundays, when she spent all day working on it, she often forgot to eat and staggered home lightheaded to dream of the project, its shining gears, its fabulously complicated calibrations.

Oh, the wonder of working on such a machine—and for such a reward! Marina hardly noticed her constant tiredness, her aching eyes and shaking hands.

"Marina?"

"Mmm?" Marina looked up, blinking back blurriness, to see James's face peering concernedly at her in the dimness of the back passage.

"Are you okay?" James asked, still staring. There was a slight frown on his handsome face. "You look so pale. And so far away."

"I'm fine." Marina made to move past him, toward the workshop.

"You're *not* fine." James's white-clad arm shot out to block her path. "Marina, everyone's noticed. You don't talk anymore, you've got thinner, you're always so pale and—and it's like you're not really *here* anymore. What's happening? Are you sick?"

Marina was about to deny it. But it occurred to her that if James thought she was sick... "You know, I might be," she said, trying to sound as thin and wan as possible.

"You should go home," James said, just as she'd hoped he would.

"No—I can't let everyone down," Marina said as he ushered her toward the door.

"Nonsense. We can live without you for one day. Go home and rest. I'll explain to my uncle."

Drooping, Marina let herself be pushed out the door into the street. Then she straightened and hurried off into the crowd, unaware of a pair of eyes following her.

It was a good day's work, Marina thought dreamily as the auto-cab rattled through the crowd that evening. An entire extra day had seen tremendous progress. Even Nixa had been moved to speech. "Nice work, Marina," she said, surveying the project. "It won't be long now."

Marina smiled, and found her head lolling back against the seat, eyes closing. At the same time, however, her belly cramped. She was starving.

She thought about the dreary supper awaiting her at the boardinghouse and craned to look out the cab's window. Perhaps they would pass something good.

Ah—there was the harbor. At this time of year the daylight lasted a long time, and it was still crowded. Marina hit the button to pause the auto-cab in its pre-programmed journey. It drew to the side of the road and parked, door opening for Marina to descend.

A familiar scent wafted toward her through the crowd. Belly tightening, she hurried toward it—only to stop as a wave of dizziness washed over her. Maybe she really was sick.

More slowly and carefully, therefore, she walked up to Sarah. "Hi, Sarah."

The Skraeling woman turned with a surprised smile. "Marina! I haven't seen *you* for a while. How have you been?"

"Fine...Got any good clams?"

"Lots." Sarah dropped in the clams and ignited the fire, reminding Marina of the aether-fires that burned in Nixa's workroom... "...Marina?"

Marina blinked, refocused on Sarah. "What?"

"Your clams are ready." Sarah held them out in their newspaper cone. She sounded like she'd repeated herself at least twice.

"Oh." Marina took the clams. She reached in, tried to eat them delicately, but the wave of hunger was too intense. She wolfed them down, standing there before the quizzical Skraeling.

"You all right, Marina?" Sarah asked when Marina had finished the final clam.

"Fine!" Marina tried to give her brightest smile, but her belly rumbled, rather ruining the effect. "Got any more?"

Slowly, Sarah nodded. "Coming right up."

Marina waited impatiently while another batch was fried, and she devoured it as quickly as Sarah handed it over.

Sarah watched, dark eyes narrowed. "You know, I had a rather peculiar customer the other day," she said at last. "A Califiyan man."

"Mm," said Marina, biting through a juicy clam.

"Said his name was Davy Lanham."

Now Marina did stop. "That's my brother."

"I thought so." Sarah nodded. "Said he was looking for his sister. Marina Lanham. I didn't say I knew you—I wanted your opinion first—but I told him to come back in a week. Well, Marina? What should I say?"

Marina stood, mind racing, thoughts jagged—and then stopped. Davy didn't matter. Sarah didn't matter. What mattered was getting back to the wish machine at the earliest opportunity.

"Tell him anything you like," she said. "I have to get on."

She turned and strode off through the streets, leaving Sarah gaping after her. She did not see the tall, slim figure who detached himself from his station at a lamppost and approached the clam vendor.

Marina set down her tools and stretched her arms above her head, working out the kinks. She shook off another dizzy spell. "It's done."

"Oh, let me see!" Nixa was more galvanized than Marina had ever seen her, rushing forward, eyes aglow. Together, the two women surveyed the almost-complete reality configuration engine.

It was a crude object at first sight: a small, squat box on the artificer's workbench, with gears and cogs and wheels exposed, its switch a great metal twist. But a closer look would reveal the ranks of minute clockwork gears, the fabulously complicated web of wiring that channeled the power of the aether-wood galvanizer, the multiple funneled compartments waiting for their loads of aether powder.

"Oh," whispered Nixa. "Oh, you've done wonders, Marina. You have my gratitude." She turned to lift a glass bottle from the alchemical workbench. "And I've distilled the final batch of aether powder. Tomorrow we will load up the aether and turn the engine on, at last."

"Yes," whispered Marina. "At last." At last, at last, she would be able to make her wish. She would reconfigure reality.

Her knees felt shaky. She sat down on the stool, and realized that her head was swimming. She propped up her forehead on her hands.

A glass of water appeared at Marina's elbow. "Have a drink."

"Thanks." The water cleared her head somewhat. Marina eyed Nixa. A new thought, one that hadn't occurred before, had presented itself. "What are *you* going to wish for, Nixa?"

Nixa was silent a moment, turning the aether bottle in her hand, the grains glowing white. "There is a…mistake from my past. One that I would correct." She looked up, eyes black and unreadable. "And you, Miss Lanham? What is your wish?"

"The same," Marina said. She laughed bitterly inside: wasn't that always what it was, really? "Mine involves a man," she added recklessly. "And yours?"

"No man." Nixa was staring at the aether again, holding it close so its light bathed her face. It gave her the look of a corpse. "No man." Her lips peeled back in a sudden snarl. "*A world.*"

Marina jolted back, almost falling off her stool. In her chest, her heart thundered. A world? What did that mean? And Nixa sounded so—*strange*. Savage. Almost…mad.

"Nixa?" she said at last, in a small voice.

Nixa looked up, smiling serenely, face as pleasant as ever. "My apologies, Miss Lanham," she said smoothly. "I may have lost myself a moment there." She gave a delicate, ladylike yawn. "It's late. We should both get some sleep."

Slowly, Marina nodded. "Yes."

Marina fetched her coat, umbrella and reticule, and the pair ascended to the surface world in silence. Outside, the night was still, and oddly quiet. "Well, good night," Marina said after a minute, and started for the auto-cab. Her footsteps echoed loudly.

"Tomorrow night, Miss Lanham." The whisper sounded, loud and harsh, behind her. "Tomorrow night, we shall gain everything we desire."

The hairs stood up on the back of Marina's neck. She whirled around, but the street was silent and the doorway to the underworld empty.

The next day dawned cloudy but with no rain. Marina could hardly believe how calm and unexcited everyone around her was: as though this was just another dull, quotidian day. Every moment stretched unbearably. She couldn't stop thinking of tonight.

The day ground by at the workshop, each minute lasting an hour, until, at last, quitting time arrived. Marina, still slow and weak, was last to the back entrance, all the other girls grabbing their coats, hats and umbrellas in a dash out the door into the early evening.

James, however, was still there, hanging around the backdoor with a worried frown. "Marina!" He hurried forward. "Are you all right?"

"I'm fine, James." She stepped inside and hung up her coat. "Shouldn't you be out front or something?"

"I was waiting for you. Marina, you really don't look well." He paused, licking his lips. "I...I talked to Sarah. She says she's seen you going down into the undercity at night."

Marina's head jerked up. "What! You—you were *spying* on me? Both of you?"

"We're both worried about you. Is something going on?"

"What right do *you* have to worry about me?" A rage Marina hadn't known she possessed surged up, hot and violent. "I'm not anything to you! You don't know a thing about me! And you have no right to interfere!"

"I know," said James unexpectedly. His face reddened. "It's...reprehensible, spying on a woman like that. On anyone. I know that, and I'm sorry. But I mean it, Marina. Is something happening?"

"It's none of your business." Marina shoved him violently in the chest. He stumbled backward, breath knocking out of him in a rush. "Stop your *spying*," she hissed. "I'm going to get my life back, and you can't stop me!"

And, grabbing her things, she ran out the door, letting it bang shut behind her.

#

Marina was careful to look around and make sure she wasn't followed, before knocking on the door to the undercity. It galled her that she had to ruin tonight's triumph with such paranoia, but she couldn't risk James or Sarah spying her out.

Good—she saw no one she knew. She knocked on the door.

It opened immediately, Nixa framed in the doorway. "Miss Lanham." Her voice was as calm as ever, but her eyes gleamed and her face seemed aglow. Anticipation came off her in waves, sharpening Marina's own excitement. "Come."

They nearly ran down the twisting corridors of the undercity to the secret lab. Nixa closed the door behind them while Marina, with trembling fingers, slung off her coat. Together they approached the reality configuration engine.

It gleamed beneath the aether-light, ugly and functional and *ready*. Marina felt their creation was as excited and yearning as they were, reaching for the moment it would be used.

Nixa turned to Marina. "Marina," she said, just the slightest tremor in her voice, "you will have the first wish. Will you do the honors?"

Marina nodded and took up the paper bag of aether powder, sitting ready. She lifted the bag, ready to pour it into the engine.

And stopped.

Inside, a voice was crying out, telling her—something. A shiver of foreboding ran through her. There was something she'd overlooked—something important. And another, deeper doubt ran through her, a doubt about the wish she would make—

"Marina!" She'd never heard Nixa's voice so sharp. "What are you waiting for? Pour in the aether! Make your wish!"

Marina took a deep breath. Taking up the paper bag, she poured in the luminous grains.

The engine didn't hum or ignite—it wouldn't turn on until Marina pulled the switch—but the piece of aether-wood began to glow. Subtly at first, then hot-white, the wood shone silver-white like a captured star. There was an odd flicker, like heat haze, the concentrated power making the air waver above the wood.

"Turn it on." Nixa's voice was hard, intense with impatience and eagerness. "*Turn it on.*"

Marina reached down for the switch. And froze.

Slowly, she turned to Nixa. "You do it."

"You have the first wish." Nixa's eyes were like black holes against the parchment of her face. "You turn it on."

Marina shook her head. "It's your engine."

"Nonsense, Marina—don't you want your wish? *Turn it on.*"

"Why—why do you want it to be me so bad?" Marina's voice quavered, and her knees buckled under a sudden assault of dizziness.

Nixa took advantage of her weakness. She sprang on her, long fingers catching at her shoulders, face thrust into hers. "*Turn it on!*" Marina scrambled for purchase as Nixa shoved her backwards over the workbench, the engine shunting aside, Nixa's face white and desperate and mad—

There came a sudden commotion, the door banging open, voices shouting, and Nixa disappeared with a scream of rage, yanked backward. Marina straightened, scrambling for the other side of the workbench.

It was James and Sarah. James held the struggling, clawing Nixa, keeping her arms pinned to her sides.

Sarah, meanwhile, stared at the reality engine with a horrified expression. "Hell's teeth, Marina!"

"What—what are you doing here?" Marina asked in astonishment. Another wave of weakness crashed over her. Her vision blurred and her knees collapsed, spilling her on the floor.

Sarah hurried over, lifting her up and placing her on the stool. Now that she was sitting, Marina realized just how weak and sick she felt, every joint aching, her muscles turned to water. Even worse than how she'd felt for weeks, since starting work on Nixa's engine…

Sarah turned back to the workbench. She stared at the engine as though it was a live snake. "Hell's teeth, Marina," she cursed again. "No wonder you were looking so awful!"

"You bitch!" Nixa screamed from the cage of James's arms. "You've ruined everything!" To Marina's surprise, her face was streaked with tears.

Marina looked from Nixa to the engine, its aether-wood shard still glowing. "What…what would have happened if I'd turned that on?"

"The engine would have been complete!" Nixa howled. "I would have got my wish!"

"You would have died," Sarah said flatly.

Marina reeled. "What?"

"Yeah. Things like that—" Sarah nodded at the engine. "—Machines made with too much aethereal alchemy, they suck the life out of their creators. Why do you think my people never made that many flying canoes? Because they required a human life."

"That's why you had Marina working on your damned engine, right?" James hissed at Nixa. "So it would eat her instead of you, and you could use it yourself."

"That's right." Nixa had calmed somewhat, no longer struggling, but her eyes still burned with their insane fire.

She flicked a dismissive glance at Marina. "Stupid little girl, wanting her worthless young man back—what a fool. You were a clever artificer, Marina Lanham, but no loss to this world. Well worth the sacrifice."

Marina felt sicker than ever. She and Nixa had never been friends, but she hadn't thought the alchemist had this level of contempt for her. "Sacrifice for what?" she demanded. "What were you going to use that engine for?"

"*Home.*" A wild, savage emotion lit Nixa's face. "*Home.*" And she bucked suddenly, throwing James backward, his head smacking into the wall, and dived for the engine.

Sarah leaped forward, but Nixa's arm lashed out and knocked Sarah to the floor, landing with a sickening crack to the head. Nixa leaped, viper-quick, and, hauling the moaning James forward, thrust her Winchester to his head.

Nixa's eyes burned. "Turn on the engine," she hissed. "Do it, or I kill your friends!"

A hollow ringing filled Marina's ears. Her heart fluttered, like a bird trying to escape—but there was no escape. No way out.

Slowly, Marina reached and pulled over the engine. It was hot and vibrating under her hands. Nixa sucked in a breath as Marina reached for the switch.

Then, before she could change her mind, Marina picked up the engine and sent it flying into the wall.

It shattered on impact, cogs and gears whirling and bouncing away, aether-powder spilling in cascades. The aether-wood flew off, already dimming, as the last cogs spun aimlessly on the floor.

Marina didn't waste any time, but lunged at Nixa while the alchemist was still shocked and staring. The two women struggled for possession of the gun, James slumping to the side as they fought—

There came a sudden crack, and Nixa faltered, a bewildered look entering her eyes as her hands fell away. Marina seized the gun, pointing it at Nixa as she backed away, but Nixa was already slumping to the floor, an egg-sized lump on her head.

Still holding the length of pipe, Sarah stood over their enemy. "White-faced bitch," she growled. "My head hurts."

"Sarah!" Marina hurried forward. "Sarah, are you all right?"

"I will be." Sarah winced, touching her head gingerly. "Tie her up, though, quick."

Marina raided the cupboard for wire to wrap around Nixa's arms and legs while Sarah slumped down beside James, cradling her head. James, Marina saw with relief, was reviving, staring blearily around.

"What, she dead?" he said groggily, peering at Nixa. "Good…"

"No, not dead," said Marina. The alchemist still breathed. "But come on, we have to get out of here, get to the police."

Marina picked up Nixa's feet and began dragging her toward the door, while James and Sarah, still concussed and aching, followed, clutching their heads. As they reached the door, a gleam caught Marina's eye: the aether-wood shard, still glowing faintly, hovering above their heads on the ceiling. She shivered and passed on.

Miracle of miracles, it was a sunny day in Siahl.

The sun beamed down upon the city, upon the streets, upon the houses, upon the waiting ships and the lines of miners heading north, and most of all upon the red-brick, tree-lined Explorer's Square, where Siahlites, dressed in their Sunday best, were out walking on this lovely afternoon.

Marina walked slowly, hanging on James's arm. She still felt a little weak, though a few weeks' rest at the Bell Sanatorium had done her a world of good, especially since she'd had James and Sarah for company as they recovered from their concussions. She sent just one message out, via a nurse, and so her brother Davy had come in to visit, face both anxious and so joyful it warmed Marina's heart to see. The siblings had talked for hours in the ward, Marina telling Davy almost everything that had happened. He'd mailed a letter to their parents for her, telling them he'd found her, and assuring them of her continued well-being.

Indeed, it was just as well she'd decided to stop hiding. Their sanatorium stay had been paid for by dozens of donations from newspaper readers up and down the coast, electrified by the lurid story of underground laboratories, evil female alchemists, courageous rescues, and reality-changing machines. Reporters had practically besieged the Bell Sanatorium, mobbing the Wish Machine Heroes when they finally came out. Even now, people were pointing James and Marina out, but they steered clear of them. Neither wanted to ruin their Sunday.

"There you are!" Sarah hurried over through the crowd, carrying three cones of ice cream. She'd put on a high-necked dress and pulled her hat low, with a veil, so no one recognized her either as a Wish Machine Hero or as a Skraeling. It infuriated Marina that Sarah couldn't even take a Sunday walk without worrying about that, but Sarah just shrugged. "Don't worry," she'd said. "I plan on overcharging every white customer at my new clam bar. Except you and James, of course." She was planning to open her own restaurant, with some of the money left over from the public's donations, just outside the city limits, so she could wear her traditional costume. Not that being *in* the city would have stopped her, of course. The thought made Marina smile, though it soon faded.

Now Sarah handed around the ice creams. "Happy Sunday."

"Happy Sunday!" James laughingly agreed. Marina licked her ice cream and tried to smile.

"What's the matter, Marina?" Sarah eyed her keenly.

"Nothing. Just..." Marina hesitated. "I can't stop thinking about Nixa. What did she want to use that machine *for*?"

"She never did say, did she?" said James thoughtfully. "Even at her police interrogation." It was all over the papers: Nixa Apparecida had remained stubbornly silent throughout her interrogation and even throughout her trial, mouth a thin line, eyes impassive. She hadn't even reacted to her sentence of life imprisonment.

"Didn't she say something about her home?" Sarah licked up chocolate ice cream.

"Yes, but..." Marina shook her head. "Where *was* home, for her?" Nixa's voice echoed in her mind: *A world.*

James was shifting around uncomfortably. "Actually, Marina...I wondered..."

She looked at him. "What?"

"Oh, spit it out, James," said Sarah, rolling her eyes. She turned to Marina. "We spent the entire time in the sanatorium wondering what *you* were planning to wish for. Once the engine was up and running."

"Once the engine was up and running," Marina said dryly, "I would have been dead."

"Yes, but what was your wish?"

Marina bowed her head and took a deep breath. She supposed it was time for it to come out. "Davy told you I ran away from home, right?"

"Yes," James said after a moment.

"Did he say why?"

"No." Sarah narrowed her eyes. "Was it that man you were always looking for at the harbor?"

Marina nodded, gulping. "Back in St. Francisca, I…I fell in love." She found she couldn't look at James. "He promised we'd build a new life together. But all he wanted was the money I'd inherited from an aunt. As soon as we got to Siahl, he took all the cash and vanished."

"Hell's teeth," Sarah said slowly. James nodded, eyes wide.

That nod gave Marina the courage to go on. "So…that was what I *thought* I wanted. Nathan back. My honor back. *Happiness* back." She paused. "But then, in that lab, when I was about to turn the machine on…I realized that I didn't want Nathan back. I just wanted to be happy again. And happiness isn't something you can just *wish* for."

"Is it so bad, here in Siahl?" James sounded slightly hurt.

Marina laughed. "A few months ago I would have said yes. But now…" She thought of Mrs. Yesler's warmth, of her work at Maccadam's, of the taste of fresh clams, of Davy coming to find her. And, most of all, she thought of these, her friends, who had cared enough to come after her, to rescue her, even when she had rejected their love. "No, it's not so bad. And I don't want to go back to the way I was, naïve and stupid. Change isn't always bad."

"There's some truth!" Sarah laughed, and they all went on together, sending a flock of pigeons scattering into the air in a flurry of wings.

"Still," said Marina, returning to her earlier thoughts, "I wonder what Nixa was planning to wish for."

"To go home?" said Sarah. They approached a newspaper stand.

"Maybe. But earlier, when I asked her about her wish, she said something really strange." The newspaper seller was lugging a newly-printed bale onto the table, grunting with the effort.

"What?" asked James. Sarah was watching while the seller undid the string and began stacking the papers on the counter.

"When I asked her what she wished for, she said, 'A world'. And then she said she wanted to go home…"

"Marina." Both James and Marina turned at Sarah's tone. She was looking at the newly printed editions. "Look."

The headline screamed it out:

WISH MACHINE WITCH ESCAPES!

And, in smaller type beneath that:

*Cell found empty — Police mystified*

For a moment they stood frozen, staring at the newspaper. Then, with a slow inevitability, Marina looked up.

Nixa Apparecida — or whatever her true name was, wherever she truly came from — stood on the other side of the square, a streak of black in the colorful day, the cheerful activity. She stood staring, waiting until she had all their attention, horrified and trembling.

Sweeping her skirts, she gave them a low curtsy. She came up with a smile on her blood-red lips. Then, turning, she walked rapidly and decisively away.

As though she had work to return to.

*Rose Strickman is a speculative fiction writer living in Seattle, Washington, a rich vein of steampunk inspiration. Her work has appeared in online e-zines such as Luna Station Quarterly and print anthologies such as Sword and Sorceress 32. She has also published several novellas on Amazon. To read more about aether and alchemy in the Atlantean States, please check out Clockwork Dragons and COLP: Underground. Alternatively, you can connect with Rose at https://www.facebook.com/rose.strickman.3/*

# Late Bloomers

### *K.G. Anderson*

While the elderly *vertaines* chatted over hors d'oeuvres in Master Rem Kardamian's elegant living room, I stood upright by the door, my face a mask of attention and respect.

"Kardamian, I believe your *citresse* are finer than ever." The guest nodded to indicate two young trees in glistening ceramic pots by the full windows overlooking our terraced garden. The Master beamed. Taking up his ebony cane, he made his way over to the plants. The assembled guests fell silent as he grasped a slender branch of the *arancet*. Gentle but assertive, his was the touch of a master *vertaine*, a horticultural wizard. The Master spoke softly and his magick took hold: the shrub burst into bloom, new pink-and-red flowers filling the room with the scents of cinnamon and cloves.

"Exquisite!" The guest raised his hands, fingers spread wide. The man, though a shameless sycophant, was correct: The trunks and branches of Master Rem Kardamian's magickal plants were elegant. The blossom colors, for which he was renowned, striking and distinctive.

I struggled to prevent my lip from curling. *But time and tastes had passed Rem Kardamian by. They'd passed him by years ago. Time to get out of the way, old man.*

"Niko!"

I startled and flushed.

"The bell, Niko. Another guest."

"Ah. Certainly." My silk evening coat rustled as I hurried to the front door. I returned with the guest, a master *vertaine* of my own generation. Rem Kardamian made introductions, then waved a hand to indicate me.

"This is Niko Parr, my apprentice."

I bowed low, which enabled me to hide the fury in my eyes. The Master still introduced me, in my 50s, as he had when I was 18 and had just joined his studio. In truth, I was now creating most of the Master's specimens--as well as developing works of my own. But that was never acknowledged.

As the master *vertaines* resumed their conversations, I gave polite attention. I had no other choice. It is unheard of in our country for an apprentice to leave a Master without permission. I'd expected to work for as many as 20 years before being released. But Rem Kardamian had not retired, nor had he released me after 20 years. I'd labored on as he turned 70, then 80, and then, to my horror, 90. *Would there be no end to it? Had the old man somehow found a charm to revitalize himself as he did his plants?*

I felt a sharp tug at my sleeve. Masha, our cook and housekeeper, whispered that the first course awaited us. I ushered the guests into the dining room and poured the wine.

"An exceptional vintage!" The Master spoke in the plummy tones of false modesty. "A gift from Mayor Pashet when I visited the City."

*That oft-cited visit had been 20 years ago!* I thought uncharitably. I'd surreptitiously sniffed the bottle earlier to make sure the wine hadn't gone sour.

It was late when the last of the guests departed and the Master retired for the night. I helped Masha wash up. When the final platter was dried and stored, I climbed the stairs to my attic apartment, too tired, too bitter, to write my weekly letter to Lily. Guilt stabbed my chest like a shard of glass. How I ached for Lily's knowing touch, the melody of her voice in my ear, and her cozy cottage in Set Petriko filled with silk draperies and comforters. How long had it been since I'd gone to visit?

I hung up my evening coat and glanced at my writing desk. No, I could not imagine myself picking up the pen. For Lily would not want to hear yet another tale of the Master's cruelty. I'd seen the impatient twitch of her lips the last time we spoke of my unending apprenticeship.

I woke early to find my room bathed in soft oyster light from the dormer window. The clock that ticked softly on the low bureau beside the bed would have allowed me more sleep, but it seemed hardly worth it. Soon the Master would be in the kitchen, chewing his austere breakfast of fresh figs. If I hurried, I could avert his acid comments about my supposed laziness. I swung my legs over the edge of the bed and reached for my quilted robe.

Masha's clumsy footsteps sounded in the hallway. "Niko! Niko!"

"Coming." Had the furnace died again? It was cold enough. Had vandals broken a window in the greenhouse? I fumbled with the sash of my robe.

I drew open the sliding door. Masha stood a few feet away, her weathered hands twisting the hem of her gray canvas smock. "He's *dead*," she whispered. "I found him dead in his bedroom."

Her dark eyes glinted with intelligence, with passion-- perhaps with suspicion? Had the old woman guessed how I felt about the Master? Had she been waiting as eagerly, as guiltily, as I had, for Rem Kardamian's death? No matter. It was done.

"Call the doctor!" I said. Masha nodded and lumbered down the stairs to the telephone.

In the tiny attic bathroom I washed and shaved. I donned a gray shirt and black trousers--work clothes, but also appropriate for dealing with the doctor and any other authorities. The house was strangely silent.

On my way downstairs, my gaze fell on a young *citresse* in a glazed pot on the landing. Its near-perfect dark-green leaves and red-rimmed buds glowed in the dappled sunlight. I couldn't resist. I grasped a grey branch and murmured the spell. The plant trembled, then answered me with a perfect first bloom--two rich yellow petals that released a fragrance, first of lemon, then of warm ginger. *The Master will not approve.*

But the Master was dead.

A heart attack, the doctor told us. Masha and I stood staring at the untouched basket of sweet rolls and the red tea pot on the kitchen table. She turned to the sink, muttering something. A prayer? A curse? I took a roll from the basket and poured a cup of tea. Then I headed to library, carrying my breakfast with me--a new, delicious liberty.

In the wood-paneled room that served as both library and office, I set about preparing for the first day of my new life. Of my artistic future--if I still deserved such a thing. I opened the drawer and gazed down, as I did every morning, at the photo of Lily in its bentwood frame. Taken 25 years ago, it showed her hiking at the old Queen Markka Bridge. So sad that the elegant bridge was gone now, damaged in the last earthquake.

*Replaced by a newer, sleeker span.* I shuddered. That was the sort of sneering observation Rem Kardamian would have made. Defiantly, I took Lily's portrait out of the drawer and placed it on my desk. At last.

*Clutter!* I heard Rem Kardamian say.

I wanted to send word to Lily, but my first call was to the Master's agent in the City. The firm would prepare an obituary for the papers and notify the galleries that sold the Master's creations. A new woman at the agency had taken over the account.

"Not many remember Kardamian, Master Parr," she

said cruelly. "I'm sure the galleries will be quite willing to return his works to us. And I'll need a list of the works in his studio."

*Master Parr*, she called me. My apprenticeship was truly over! I hurried to the studio to make a quick survey of the *citresse*. Sliding open the tall veneered doors, I entered, nearly bowing out of long habit.

I found six *limance*, an *arancet*, and a tall, columnar *citrinka*. The *citrinka* was ready now, and I caressed a green branch with the gestures the Master had taught me so long ago. It sprung to bloom, showing pale petals and releasing the aromas of Keylan tea and *cardamace*. This specimen was the Master's ultimate work, and might still be of great value.

I reported all this to the woman at the agency, whose name was Claris Vent.

"What will you do now, Master Parr?" she asked.

At first, I thought she was being merely polite.

"Well, you're a *vertaine*, aren't you?" she persisted.

I then realized that, as an agent, she was wondering if she might want to represent me. A flush of embarrassment burned my cheeks and I was glad she couldn't see my confusion.

"Call me when you decide," she said. "I'd be willing to look at your portfolio."

I set down the phone, stunned. In the years--the decades--that I'd waited for Rem Kardamian to retire or to die, dozens of plans for my own career--and my own life-- had been made, remade, and discarded. Now, all I felt was confusion. And fear.

*I must talk with Lily. Lily will know.* She did not have a telephone in her cottage in Set Petriko, so I hurried to the station and caught the mid-morning train going north up the coast.

#

Lily lived on the grounds of the cooking school owned by her former master, Mettem Patanya, one of our best-known *culinariests*. Freed from her own apprenticeship 10 years earlier, Lily had stayed on to collaborate on Mettem Patanya's final books. She was saving money for the day when she and I would build our own studios.

*At last, we can begin!* I clasped my hands, imagining Lily's delicate features, her dark skin flushed with joy at the thought of our new lives. I envisioned her creating the enchanted pastries, iced sweets, and healing beverages that were her specialties.

I splurged on a carriage from the station. At Mettem Patanya's compound I ran up the tiled steps and knocked impatiently on the carved cedar doors. A soft shuffling of steps, and a woman opened the door. My thoughts filled with the Lily of my dreams, I did not at first recognize the round-shouldered middle-aged woman who stood in the arched doorway, eyes downcast.

"Niko." The soft voice was Lily's.

I stepped into the dim foyer. In the great kitchen behind her, pots clattered. "He's gone. The Master! He died this morning."

Lily regarded the floor, her straight brown hair spilling forward over her temples and cheeks.

"Now I can sell my own *citresse*! I can take commissions. When can you come to Sarvit-Mel?" I put a finger to her delicate chin and raised it. The hair spilled back, revealing her thin face devoid of expression. "Lily, don't you understand? This means we can get married."

Lily turned and hurried away. She wore her customary work costume of dark blue pants and tunic and the dim hallway seemed to swallow her. I waited nervously, relieved when she reappeared wearing her favorite blue silk coat.

"Let's walk to the café." She spoke in a soft monotone.

Puzzled and impatient, I followed Lily out the door. As we did on our customary Sunday meetings, we strolled down the hill to the café in the old hotel at the Dosk Bay marina. I noticed Lily's steps were uneven, faltering. When had that happened? I wondered. Then I realized with a flash of horror it had been not weeks, but some months since I had visited her.

Bile rose in my throat as I choked back my hatred for the Master. Many times I'd asked him for permission to marry Lily, but he'd said there was no room in his household for a couple, that Lily would distract me from my work, and that Masha could not be expected to support the kitchen of a *culinariest* in addition to the work of two *vertaines*. Now I bit my lip in shame to think of how I'd bowed to his will. My commitment to him had stifled not just our careers but our lives.

"Lily," I blurted. "I am so sorry. I stayed loyal to the Master far too long." I squeezed her hand, which lay passively in mine. "I truly believe that we are both late bloomers. That we can cast off the restrictions of our long apprenticeships and find ourselves as masters of our crafts. We will not make the art we could have made at 30 or 40, but I believe we can nevertheless make extraordinary art."

She stopped and looked up at me. A silvery tear scarred her delicate cheek. "I am glad, Niko, that you have not given up your art. Neither have I. I've secured an adjunct teaching position at the Royal Culinary Academy in the City."

"The City?" I gasped. "I'd always thought that we would marry, that you would..."

"Our future together, not my art, is what has gone past," she said. "My time is limited, and the time that remains I'll devote to my craft."

"Don't be ridiculous!" I felt heat on my face. My voice

rose as it never had before with her.

Lily's lips pressed together and her expression hardened. We had reached the marina and now Lily moved away from me to watch the slim black ships as they sailed from the harbor. I felt her heart leaving with them.

Our usual table at the hotel café was occupied by two young women with squirming babies. We walked past it to a less attractive one where we ordered hot drinks and consumed them without speaking. Lily had ordered cocoa. I wondered if this was new, or if she had stopped drinking coffee some time before and I had failed to notice. I dared not ask.

Lily seemed so content sipping her simple beverage that I wondered, with some annoyance, if she had magicked it. For just as a *vertaine* can magick a plant to bloom or to fruit, a skilled *culinariest* can with words and gestures transform the dullest of ingredients into an exquisite dish. Perhaps she was enjoying not cocoa but a Peradinian *kokolasse*! My coffee tasted watery and sour.

Everything had changed--even our café. Now a young man and a young woman in harsh white makeup and even harsher voices served the tables. They laughed in a mirthless manner that echoed the seagulls overhead and perfectly reflected my disturbed mood.

I paid for our drinks and asked the hotel's doorman to find us a carriage. As we waited, I reached over Lily's head to grasp the branch of a common camellia bush espaliered against the stone building. A touch of my fingers and a murmured charm brought the sturdy plant into early bloom. My frown relaxed into a smile as I plucked one of the neat red flowers and presented it to Lily. I thought that her expression softened as she threaded the stem into the buttonhole on her coat, the coral blossom aflame against the blue silk.

In the carriage I brought up Lily's move to the City, hoping to dissuade her with warnings about the complexity and cost involved. She shrugged. The move was already underway. In fact, I'd been lucky to find her in Set Petriko; she had returned only to pack a final group of boxes for shipping.

"I'll come visit you in the City," I stammered. "I mean, if you want me to."

"I hope you'll come to the City, Niko," she said. "I hope your art will bring you there."

I soon discovered I'd lost not only Lily, but my studio. A lawyer summoned me to his office where he revealed the Master had left the house, the studio, and the greenhouse, not to me, but to distant relatives no one had ever heard of. They were anxious to sell to a developer.

"You'll need to vacate the property by--" the lawyer consulted a paper in a folder, "the end of next week. And take all those, those, *plants* with you."

"The *citresse*?"

"All of them," said the lawyer, standing up and indicating the meeting was over. "He left them to you."

A flicker of light amidst the gloom! I rushed home and called Claris Vent. I begged the agent to negotiate with dealers to sell the Master's *citresse* to raise the money I now needed for housing and studio space. She called back the next morning to share her astonished good news: with his death, Rem Kardamian's reputation had revived, and with it the value of his works. There would be money, if not for a move to the City, for a studio in Sarvit-Mel.

I soon found a modest stone-and-beam house overlooking the bay, with room for a small greenhouse. I took on an apprentice. Though I'd lacked the courage to defy Rem Kardamian while he was alive, I was determined to bury his tyrannical approach to our craft along with him. I paid Tamarska a generous stipend and insisted that she spend a day every week creating and tending her own works to show at the small galleries along the coast.

Claris Vent at first marketed me as the apprentice of the great Rem Kardamian, but soon dropped mention of the association. For where the Master's work had been known for refinement and subtlety my blossoms were bold, even coarse. My *citresse* came from within my very soul. Or perhaps, my heart. Often there were colors--deep purples and blues, blue-reds and corals--that reminded me of Lily.

I did not forget Lily. I couldn't have, even if I'd tried. For she was becoming a notable chef in the City. The newspapers and arts journals carried stories about her creations. She worked in the smaller venues of the culinary fantastic, but her performances commanded ever higher prices. She won an Emperor's Feast award.

Whenever business took me to the City, I inquired to see if Lily were lecturing or performing. When she was, I bought a ticket. I always had it in mind that I would ask her to dinner, or out for drinks afterwards, but each time realized once I was there that she and her colleagues moved in their own world. I stayed at a hotel, drank by myself in the bar, and the next morning took the train back to Sarvit-Mel. An unexpected invitation from Claris Vent to stay the weekend at her home flattered me, but I chose not to accept.

At last, I planned a trip specifically to see Lily. We met for lunch at a restaurant near the culinary academy where she taught. She looked much younger than she had appeared that day in Set Petriko. Her step was confident and her dark skin glowing. She wore a flowing silk suit in the deep purple of a Polar Night *rhododendial*. I longed to touch it, to touch her, as I would have caressed a rare *citresse.*

"It is so good to see you," I said. "I am delighted to find you enjoying the successes we had always imagined."

She nodded. "And you, Niko! I went to see your *citresse* in the Baer Nostra gallery last fall. I was worried that they would be influenced by--" with a brush of her hand, she dismissed Rem Kardamian. "But, no, your work is entirely your own. And it is brilliant."

"Creating the *citresse* brings the joy I'd always hoped for. Even though--even though you are not there to enjoy it with me."

She looked down at the plate of spring greens they'd placed before her. "There have been times when I've wondered if I was too harsh. If perhaps I underestimated us, underestimated myself."

"I fear that you did."

We began to eat. She praised the food, as did I. It was particularly fresh and light. Oddly, we did not come back to the topic of our failed relationship until the end of the meal, when I paid the bill and we drank hot Quarvish coffee with *anisekke.*

Lily passed her hand over my glass, and a marvelous scent of liquors and spices spiraled up from it. Her dark eyes twinkled as they met mine. She raised her glass and I brought mine to touch it.

"To late bloomers," she said.

"Two late bloomers," I teased, holding up two fingers.

We sipped. And smiled. I thought it was a promising start.

As I slipped into the cold sheets of my hotel bed that night, I smiled, recalling our repartee. *To late bloomers. Two late bloomers.*

I closed my eyes, trying to ignore an unwelcome voice that whispered: *Too late. Too late.*

#

The tall *arancet* was giving me trouble. The leaves had grown larger than I'd hoped, the stems were perhaps too twiggy. I sighed and took a few steps back to get perspective on the problem. I put a hand back to lean against the potting table and gasped in pain. A pruning knife, left on the table, had gashed my palm.

Tamarska, hearing my shout, sprinted in from the greenhouse.

"It may need a few stitches. I'd better get down to the village." I pressed a clean cloth to my palm and it came away soaked in blood.

Tamarska surprised me. She seized my injured hand, pressed her palm to mine and chanted words I hadn't heard since my childhood. A spell. A charm. The old magick! I tried to pull my hand away, but she held tight, feeding the spell.

"Stop it! Don't be stupid! Let go!"

Tamarska released me. I stared at my wounded hand. There was no longer any blood on my palm, merely a pale pink scar. Before I could speak, Tamarska staggered slightly. I caught her arm and guided her to a bench. We both sat.

"So it still works." I laughed weakly. "Where on earth did you learn the old magick?"

"My great aunt. She lived in the forest."

"My grandmother," I said. The old women tried to pass it on, but their kind of magick had faded steadily as the ways of the City spread into the countryside. "We can't use it anymore, you know. It takes too much from us and gives too little back."

I didn't tell her how the Master had beaten my legs with his cane when he'd caught me trying to use old magick to heal an injured owl. I would never beat Tamarska! But I had to teach her the rules. "It's only for plants now. Plants, and food."

I sent her up to the house to regain her strength with strong tea. I cleaned and sheathed the pruning knife. Then I sat on the bench, rubbing my new scar, and mourning the passing of the magick.

I hummed as I packed my bag to take the train to the City. This time, I would splurge, staying at the Prince Krilto hotel. Lily was appearing at the adjoining State Theater, doing a cooking demonstration as a fundraiser for the State Opera. She had invited me to the event and agreed to stay with me at the hotel that night. The next morning, we'd have breakfast, a meal that would reference the breakfasts in our past and, if fortune prevailed, in our future.

A knock on the bedroom door cut short my daydreams.

"Master!" Tamarska's voice trembled.

I opened the door. My apprentice's round face was slack with panic. *Had frost damaged the new seedlings?*

"I just came from the market. There's been another earthquake in the South. The City...the City is destroyed."

*Lily!* And Tamarska had a sister there.

Our panicked calls to the city did not go through. The trains had been rerouted or cancelled.

"I can drive a Verbiest," Tamarska offered.

So I hired one of the tiny steamcars from the village garage, stocking it with two tanks of water in case the stations along the way had been damaged. The drive to the City, usually a matter of three hours, took us until dusk. The roadway was congested with horse-drawn carriages and wheezing steamcars--most fleeing the City, but a few, like us, heading toward it. Refugees from the quake streamed past us on both shoulders of the highway. At two checkpoints we were stopped by the Guard and warned we could not go much further.

We pressed on until we reached a roadblock at the outskirts of the City. Parking on the roadside, we entered a travelers' café, now teeming with panicked refugees. In a tent in the courtyard officials were compiling lists of the dead, injured, and missing.

"Master Lily Beganda," I said when we reached the head of the line. The officer glanced up at me, her eyebrows raised. "The *culinariest*?"

"Yes," I said. "She is my..." *Why was the word "wife" on my tongue?* "My friend. My very old friend."

"And Vanda Mirital," Tamarska put in.

"And Claris Vent," I added, embarrassed that in my panic I had nearly forgotten my friend.

"Beganda...Mirital...Vent..." The officer shook her head. "No Claris Vent on my list. But Master Beganda and Vanda Mirital are in Varissal Hospital. It's not far, perhaps two miles. But the roadways are badly damaged and there are no lights. You must wait until morning. Next!"

Disregarding the officer's advice, Tamarska and I set off immediately. We soon found ourselves stumbling in near-total darkness. Alarm bells clanged, echoing off the walls of abandoned apartment buildings. The stench of gas from broken pipes hung in the alleyways. We'd gone barely half a mile before we gave up and turned back.

We spent an uncomfortable night in the cramped car, windows cracked open but our breath still fogging the glass. The dawn that woke us was clear, cold, and eerily still. The café had remained open through the night and refugees, bags piled at their feet, filled the tables and overflowed onto the terrace and steps. We waited in line to use the wash rooms and bought strong, bitter tea for our vacuum flasks before setting out on foot for the hospital.

For more than two hours we climbed through culverts

and up and down stone stairways that had been fractured and tilted by the quake. I realized with a shudder that had we pressed on the previous night the night, we'd likely have fallen to our deaths or been severely injured.

Seeing the yellow brick hospital building in the distance, we quickened our pace across the uneven terrain. A creaking sound overhead caught our attention. We looked up to see the bridge we had just passed beneath break from its supports and swing free. With a deafening crash, it shattered on the cobblestone roadway behind us. Tamarska seized my trembling hand. We stood panting and shivering.

If we could have gone back, I might have suggested it. But now there was no path but the one forward. We stumbled through the rubble, now keeping as much as possible to open ground.

It was mid-day when we clambered over a heaved roadway and into the broken courtyard of the hospital. I caught Tamarska's arm. "Keep in mind this is a place beyond magick. Healing magick ended long ago, and it left first from the cities. The small bits that you and I do with our plants...they won't serve us here."

I saw disagreement in her dark eyes. I knew she would try--and how could I blame her? But she nodded, and we entered. The clerks at the front desk sent us to another pavilion where we wound our way through sun-lit, chaotic hallways. Green-clad nurses rushed past with clipboards, barking sharp commands. The bitter scent of blood filled the air. Finally, at a cluttered desk, a nurse, his jacket bloodstained, answered us without looking up. "Vanda Mirital? Surgery." He pointed down the hall. Tamarska's round face lit up, her eyes went wide.

I squeezed her hand. "Go."

She flew off, and I turned back to the nurse. "Lily Beganda?" My voice, held steady for so long to soothe

Tamarska, rose.

"Beganda...Lily Beganda..." The nurse hesitated, biting his lower lip. He ran his index finger down the page of a logbook, turned back a page, and stopped. "Ah. She's up on the third floor. It's quickest to take the stairs."

I tugged opened the heavy door and began the climb, my breath loud in the silent stairwell. These worn wooden stairs were somehow more exhausting than the rough terrain we'd walked all morning.

At the third floor I stepped out of the stairwell and paused, confused. Had I left the hospital? It was so quiet and dim here. At the far end of the hall, a nurse with a clipboard stood silhouetted against a tall window, some of its square panes shattered and broken. Beds, parked head to foot, lined the corridor.

I took slight reassurance from soft moans and stirrings from the beds. I moved slowly among them. Eventually I found Lily, recognizing the delicate hand tucked at her side on the narrow mattress. Her head was bandaged. Wide, thick bundles of gauze wrapped her middle, and they were marked with dark flowers of blood. I was grateful for the dimness of the hallway.

I took her hand in both of mine, hoping, I suppose, to warm it. She stirred but did not awaken. Minutes passed. Aides went by rolling a bed, the still figure on it draped head to toe in a stained sheet. At last, Lily opened her eyes. I breathed her name, and she answered with mine. Awake now, she turned her head from side to side.

"The pain," she gasped. "The pain."

The nurse had returned to her station at the end of the hall. I ran and begged her to come to Lily's bed.

She was a handsome woman with delicate features, stiff silver hair brushed up under her cap. "I can give her something for her pain, but you must understand--if I give it, she may not wake up."

"Yes."

"You have a few minutes."

I ran back to Lily's bed. "They're bringing something for the pain."

"Ah."

I would never know what had happened, where she'd been, or how they'd found her. There was no time to ask.

"I love you, Lily."

She nodded absently. I followed her gaze to my hands, and only then did I realized that I was holding her bare arm, stroking it the way I did when coaxing my *citresse* into bloom. I searched my memory for healing spells but found only the most trivial of palliatives. So I began to murmur the *vertaine's* charm for the end of season, the words to summon a final, spectacular blossom.

Lily's dark eyes met mine and at last her lips relaxed into a smile. It was not the smile I had imagined her giving me in my hotel room or at our breakfast the following morning. But it was a perfect blossom that trembled ever so slightly with her breath as the nurse slipped the final needle into her arm.

K.G. Anderson is a late-blooming speculative fiction author from Seattle where she writes web content by day and pens speculative fiction by night. Her stories appear in magazines and anthologies such as *Galaxy's Edge* and *The Mammoth Book of Jack the Ripper Stories* and on podcasts (*Far Fetched Fables*, *StarShipSofa*, and *The Overcast*). For more of her stories visit: http://writerway.com/fiction

# Clockwork Hero

## *David Castlewitz*

A skilled mechanic, Jasper often drew topside assignments. His small and nimble body gave him an advantage that made him a star. He often relished the idea that his father seethed when hearing of his success. He hadn't seen or spoken to the old man in years, but he hoped that Dad kept tabs on him. The old man shoveled coal into the furnaces that boiled the water that generated the steam that ran the engines of the city. He'd never be anything more than an anonymous coaler, while Jasper enjoyed a life of renown.

Jasper emerged from underground at a cellar door that unfolded from the sidewalk on a side street around the corner from the communications depot he'd been sent to repair. The rattling steel doors shook while a siren sounded a warning to nearby pedestrians to get out of the way of Jasper's steel cage.

A light breeze ruffled Jasper's hair and he pulled his short jacket shut. Last time he came topside, the sun was bright and the day was warm. Now he had to face winter's chill and he knew from past experience that it would take time to acclimate himself. Below ground, the temperature was constant. Neither cold nor hot. Just as the light was a consistent gray, neither dark nor bright.

He exchanged glances with a workman in grease-streaked overalls, and got a sneer in return. He ignored the slight and, with a self-assured smile, waddled off the elevator platform, a large brown canvas bag on his shoulders, kept in place by one hand positioned against its bulk.

A few steps took him into the flow of people walking on the street. The bright sky stung his eyes at first, but he blinked rapidly to acclimate himself. Keeping close to the curb, he tried not to bump anyone. He stayed alert for the sharp tweet of an automobile's horn, the clomp-clomp of horses' hooves, and the tinkling of bells made by cyclists in the street.

Now and then he glanced at the Upsiders strolling all around him. A few, like that workman, gave him looks of disdain. Children pointed and laughed. He pulled the beak of his cap down over his brow, hiding his bushy eyebrows and bulbous eyes as best he could. Underground, he looked much like many of his peers. Underground, he wasn't unusual.

As he left the narrow side street, Jasper peeked at a playbill on a brick wall. The weathered broadsheet advertised a performance by Lady Em and her consort, Captain Tom Rath. Enemies on the field of battle, the poster said.

Even in the faded print, Jasper saw evidence of the affection and courage displayed by these two warriors. With the Great Civil War ten years in the past, and with some of the fighters still harboring grudges over the stalemate that ended the fighting, the fact that two opponents could come together as entertainers was a testament to life's vagaries.

The poster's faded image of Lady Em, a thin sword in one hand and a derringer in the other, diminished none of her beauty. Her eyes sparkled. Her wispy yellow hair curled out from under her narrow-brimmed bonnet. Jasper guessed the poster was from a previous year's show. He looked around at other brick walls for signs of a more current performance.

His disappointment mounting, Jasper blinked away tears. Ahead, a blue and white pole outside a communications depot loomed, a red flag affixed to the top signaling a breakdown. He'd need to be there soon.

They expected him. He had a job to do. That's what brought him topside.

His thoughts flashed on a view of Lady Em's swirling blue skirts and knee-high black boots laced tightly up to the curve of her calves. In the posters she was a daunting presence. In real life, in the Harry Barret Theatre, she dazzled her audience with re-enactments of her feats of courage and strength during the war. To Jasper, she was a blonde haired hellion incapable of defeat.

A thick green kiosk plastered with playbills, petitions and other notices displayed a recent poster of Lady Em, Captain Rath, and the supporting cast of the show. Jasper had been right. She'd be performing this day at the Barret.

He had something special to give her, a labor of adoration and love that he'd brought along in his sack of tools. He knew she'd take it into her heart. Who else but a master mechanic could give her such a gift?

Jasper slowly approached the communications depot. He had a few hours yet before Lady Em's show. He wasn't anxious now. He calmly walked to where several men clutching leather portfolios in their hands stood shaking their heads, looking first to the depot's entrance at the top of a set of marble steps, and then into the street, as though wondering where another depot might be.

Jasper knew. He knew all the locations. Over the past dozen years he'd had occasion to visit all of them. Something was always breaking down. An intricate network of tubes and gears, cogs within cogs, linkages and belts provided the mechanics for the simple process of sending documents and money and even missives of love through the pneumatic tubes that linked discrete sections of the city, and linked the city itself to the rest of the country.

Chaos resulted when a depot broke down. A worn cog wreaked havoc. Rerouting the tubes, a manual activity performed by underground denizens – usually children – took time to complete when a destination depot went out of service. Everything slowed, from important documents to trivial letters.

Walking up the steps to the red-flag waving depot, Jasper stretched his short legs in a comical manner. Inside, he dropped the tool bag, letting it slowly slip from his shoulders. It landed with a soft thud on the polished wooden floor.

"You're from maintenance?" someone asked.

A few people standing against the wall made comments such as "About time. This better not take too long, I've been waiting since morning," The depot manager, a tall man with a shiny silk vest and wild curly black hair, offered smiles and verbal apologies to the waiting patrons.

"Well, come on," the manager said. "It's over there. You know what to do."

Jasper knew, but he thought he might as well work slowly so the manager and the impatient people in the room got some inkling of the seriousness of the problem and the need for a master mechanic to fix what was wrong. He wanted to be appreciated.

Jasper stood in the alley behind the theatre, thinking he'd wiggle his way inside since he couldn't afford to buy a ticket. He'd done this before, but the windows along the basement storeroom had been barred since the last time he snuck in. Standing in the shallow recess of another building's back door, Jasper watched one of the stars of Lady Em's show alight from a hired carriage, a bulky carpetbag handing by its handle from one hand.

His imagination soared as he watched Miss Agatha, a tall and muscular black woman billed as an Amazon princess, stride up the steps to the locked stage door.

During the war, Agatha had been Lady Em's close companion. The two fought their way out of dire circumstances several times. Photographs existed of the two standing back-to-back or side-by-side, Lady Em wielding a sword and Miss Agatha shooting attackers with her bow. Dime novels recounted their adventures. Illustrated books retold the stories of their battles.

The stage show always included the ultimate scene, the grand showdown when the Amazon lay wounded and unable to help Lady Em. That's when Confederate Captain Tom Rath entered, his saber held shoulder high. In the ensuing sword fight, Lady Em smiled and engaged in verbal repartee, using her skill as a swordswomen as well as her beauty to win Rath over to her side.

Jasper's head swam with the scenes he remembered so well, ones he'd witnessed more than a half-dozen times. Life-sized toy soldiers charged, some on horseback. Wagons rumbled in the background. Cannon fired with mock explosions made by black wood chips and booming sound effects. Everything was controlled by a mechanical clockwork, Jasper assumed, though he couldn't see into the two-foot high platform on which the theatrics were performed.

He wasn't privy to the Barret Theatre's mechanicals. He'd never inspected the interlocking gears and pinion arms and slippage joints. But from where he often stood in the stalls, a standing-room only section fronting the stage, he often heard the intricate array of meshed gears and cogs and wheels that kept the performance rolling.

At the end of each performance Captain Rath and Lady Em embraced and kissed. Each time Jasper watched this happy ending to the show, he cheered, as did everyone in the audience. He clapped and stamped his feet, enjoying the splendid reconciliation of two formidable enemies.

"You! Hey!"

Jasper glanced at the source of the rough voice. The stage door was open. A beefy man in a striped shirt stood at the top of the steps. Jasper had inadvertently left his secure place in the shadows, had emerged from the shallow doorway, and had ventured into the middle of the alley, his memories of past performances mixing with his imagination to lure him from safety.

"I got a present for Lady Em," Jasper said.

The striped-shirted man put his thumbs under his red suspenders, as though flexing a badge of authority.

"Give it to me. I'll get it to her."

"Then she won't know it's from me."

Stripe Shirt laughed. "Write a note. Can you write?"

"Well enough," Jasper answered. "Can I come in and write something to her?" He should've come ready with some sort of contingency plan, he realized, though he didn't know how he should've known the windows would be barred.

"Just give it here," Stripe Shirt said. "Tell me your name. I'll tell Lady Em."

Jasper didn't want to do that, though he slowly reached into his sack of tools for the carton in which he'd placed the gift he'd made.

Then the unexpected happened. Lady Em, escorted by Captain Rath, who looked so very much taller in person than in any broadsheet, appeared at the door.

"What present?" Lady Em asked. A thin white veil covered her face, but her beauty shone through, as did her pale blue eyes. Her short blonde hair shimmered in the afternoon light, though much of that light was obscured by the tall walls that cloaked the alley.

"For you," Jasper croaked, and again reached into his sack.

Captain Rath sprang in front of Lady Em. He pulled a dagger from inside his suit coat.

"Tom!" Lady Em squealed, laughing. "It's just a cellar-mite. He's not going to hurt me."

Jasper swallowed the red rash that came to his cheeks. He always responded to derogatory comments with a trace of embarrassment burnished by a modicum of anger, the latter because he could do little about it. But he had to forgive Lady Em. "Cellar-mite" didn't sound so nasty coming from her. Maybe she meant it as a sweet nickname.

"Whatcha got there?" Rath asked, the knife still in his hand.

"A gift," Jasper said, the words stumbling from his lips. He slipped his stubby fingers under thin brown twine and extracted a cardboard box from inside the sack.

"Open it," Captain Rath ordered.

"I swear, Tom. You have the most distrusting soul of any man I've ever known." Lady Em let loose a tinkle of a laugh. She took the box and Jasper shuddered to feel her so close. He looked past her veil into her eyes, and smiled.

Lady Em undid the knotted bow joining the twine, which floated to the floor, and then out into the alley. She opened the box and a single word sprang from her lips. "Amazing."

"I made it for you," Jasper said, pointing at the mechanical model of the stage on which Lady Em performed. Hidden inside the boxy model were cogs and wheels and precision gearing. Cardboard cutouts with pasted-on images from old playbills and broadsheets represented Em and her entourage, including Rath and Miss Agatha, Em's personal bodyguard/servant, and all the anonymous players and horses and cannon.

"Wind it up," Jasper said. "The key's under the base."

"This is absolutely wonderful," Lady Em cooed. She gently placed the replica a table just inside the theatre. She inserted the key and wound the spring-loaded motor. In a few seconds, a version of Captain Rath, Miss Agatha, and herself came to life, as did horses and charging soldiers and soundless booming cannon. They all rose from slots cut into the platform and driven by precision gearing.

Jasper beamed with pride.

Captain Rath grimaced and Lady Em clapped her hands. The mechanical versions of the two dueled, manoeuvring around one another until, in the end, they re-enacted their signature kiss of reconciliation.

"This is the best gift ever," Lady Em said.

Jasper braced for what he hoped she'd do next. Lady Em would hug him now. She'd kiss him. Not on the lips, not as she kissed Captain Rath, but perhaps on the cheek.

She picked up the mechanical replica and walked through the doorway into the back of the theatre. "Gary," she announced, turning towards the man in the striped shirt, "you see to it that our cellar-mite here has a good seat for the show."

The box seat gave Jasper a good view of the stage. Elsewhere in the theatre, ticket holders took their seats, and the stalls directly in front of the stage, filled with workmen and children and prim young women in worn out clothes. The high intensity carbon arc lights across the edge of the stage came to life. A hidden orchestra created a cacophony of sound.

Jasper basked in the scene. The large theatre buzzed with voices and the sound of shuffling bodies. The main floor slowly filled. The balcony – all twelve rows – groaned, crowded with spectators. Other box seats along the left and the right sides were soon occupied by well-coifed young men and women in expensive clothing.

Where Jasper sat, three of the four upholstered chairs remained empty. He didn't mind being by himself. No need to put up with sneers and questions.

The curtain remained drawn. The audience stirred, mumbling questions and voicing demands. A tall thin man in a waistcoat with tails came on stage, his hands in the air and a smile on his narrow face. His nose and tiny ears gave him the look of a bird.

There'd be a delay to opening the evening's show, but the fortuitous arrival of an acrobatic troupe meant they'd all be entertained for now. The creak of the door to his box opening a crack caused Jasper to look back over his shoulder. Large eyes filled the top part of that crack. Work boots filled the bottom.

"You the cellar-mite?"

"I'm the mechanic," Jasper said, bristling.

The door opened all the way, revealing a grease-stained face and a workman in a dirty shirt with equally filthy pants. "They gots a problem and I can't fix it. You want ta take a look?"

Jasper approached the workman. "A look at what?"

"Bring your tools." The workman pointed at the sack on the floor, next to Jasper's chair.

"What kind of problem?" Jasper asked.

"I been crawling around," the workman said, "and I ain't got no clue."

Jasper beamed. They needed him. A warm thrill coursed through his thick chest and he hoisted his bag of tools onto one shoulder and followed the workman to a stairwell behind a door marked "Private." It led to the back of the stage, to an area set between two thick curtains.

"Good!" Lady Em gushed as she rushed from her dressing room, a white towel wrapped the top of her head. Her pale legs flashed at Jasper from beneath the dull brown robe tied closed at her narrow waist. She hadn't yet changed into her costume. Miss Agatha stood nearby, her dark skin oiled and a tiara on her head. She'd be first on stage, Jasper recalled.

The gentleman in the tails approached. "It won't go." He pointed at the large boxy platform taking up most of the space. Four feet high, with red-white-and-blue paper bunting on all four sides, a narrow lip went around the edges and empty grooves in the flooring, some curved and most of them straight, hinted at the Lady Em and Captain Rath performance.

"If we don't get this thing moving…" Lady Em didn't continue. Tears brimmed in her pale blue eyes. She leaned close to Jasper and he inhaled her sweet aroma.

"Show me," Jasper said to the main in tails. "How do you start it?"

The dirty workman who'd summoned Jasper pointed to a lever at a corner of the platform. Jasper followed him to the spot. He pushed on the lever. A five-inch wide strap stuck out of the base and disappeared under the floorboards, connecting the performance platform's mechanics to a steam engine somewhere in the theatre's innards.

The strap hardly moved in response to the lever.

Jasper listened for clues, having learned during his apprentice years that missing cogs or worn gears often made telltale sounds. He bent close to the lever and unscrewed a metal plate near the floor. He peered into the platform's internals, and then signaled for the workman to push on the lever again. The gears groaned.

Jasper climbed in feet first. He walked bent over, a wind-up lantern with a hook at one end providing enough illumination that he could inspect his surroundings. To his practiced eye, the mechanical interconnections made sense. He wondered if that dirty workman understood any of the beauty hidden under the platform.

"Push on the lever," Jasper called out, and then watched for movement behind a set of meshed gears in front of him. Something squealed. One foot in front of the other, he waddled along a narrow wooden plank until he found a bent rod. As he suspected, it linked to the lever. Another end of the rod locked the pulley mechanism attached to the leather strap outside the boxy platform. It was much like any other clutch Jasper had ever seen.

He hurried to where he'd left his tools, retrieved pliers, and then returned to pull two cotter pins so he could remove the bent rod. Moments later, outside the box, he used hammer and the anvil he always carried for such occasions to straighten the rod. He flourished his tools as though they were weapons, thrilled to think that his audience of backstage workers and Lady Em and the other performers watched like adoring admirers.

A few whacks repaired the bend and Jasper reattached the rod and reinserted the cotter pins. A signal to the workman standing at the lever brought results. No complaints of compromised gears. Smooth meshing of steel teeth and the turning of the pulley guiding the drive belt, along with the sound of hammers hitting home greeted Jasper's ears..

Horses rose up. Cannon popped into few. As did foot soldiers. Seconds later, the main curtain rose and Miss Agatha, bow at hand and arrow notched, leapt from a perch at stage right.

The audience cheered and Jasper stepped behind another set of curtains, lured there by one of the stagehands. Lady Em soon came out from her dressing room, a narrow brimmed bonnet on her head, a thin sword in her hand. She wore a plain blue skirt and a frilly white top.

"I must thank you," Lady Em said.

"For you," Jasper said, "anything, m'lady."

Em laughed. She turned to Rath. "Know what we need, Tom? We need a cellar-mite of our own."

Jasper blanched. Again? Cellar-mite? It didn't sound so endearing this time. It sounded like an insult. It always was an insult, no matter who spoke it.

"What do you say?" she asked. "Do you want to work for the show? Be our little fix-it man?"

Jasper shrugged, afraid to let his anger seep into anything he might say now.

Lady Em continued. "I'm certain we can make arrangements. We'd need to give you a name, of course.".

"My name is Jasper."

"You wouldn't need to do much," Lady Em continued. "Maintenance, I'd think. Repairs like you just did. Other than that, you'd be free to do… well, do whatever you like with your time."

Rath poked Lady Em in the side. "We're on now."

"I know you'll say yes," Lady Em said. "What cellar-mite wouldn't?" She exuded a tinkling laugh and traipsed to her stage left entrance. From the other side of the curtain, the audience applauded.

Jasper packed up his anvil and hammer. He lifted his bag of tools onto one shoulder. He didn't want to be someone's cellar-mite. He liked being a master mechanic. He'd been a hero tonight, but if he remained with the theatre, on-call for Lady Em and her show, he'd be no more important than that workman in those filthy clothes.

He wouldn't be special. He'd be exactly what he realized she saw when she looked down at him. A cellar-mite.

He walked out of the theatre by way of the back entrance leading into the alley, past Striped Shirt, who didn't look up from his newspaper when Jasper passed.

He waddled to where he'd come topside. He didn't look back at the theatre building. He didn't think he'd ever look at Lady Em the same way ever again. He pondered what excuse he'd give his supervisor for being late returning to the underground. Most anything would do, he thought. He could even tell the truth, that he'd gone to see a show.

He was important enough that he'd get only a mild warning not to violate curfew. Below ground, he was a master mechanic, not a cellar-mite. He liked that.

He didn't like what he now thought of Lady Em. He chided himself for ever having admired her. Maybe she'd been a hero during the war. Perhaps she and Captain Rath, once adversaries, had reconciled. Maybe it even happened in the heat of battle as depicted on stage, with a kiss that ended their duel.

Or it could all be only a performance.

He lurched as he walked, his bag of tools heavy on his shoulder. If he'd been so wrong about Lady Em, what other errors had he made? Maybe he was wrong about his father, who labored every day of the week at the furnaces that made the steam that drove the engines that made the topside world possible.

A retired techie, David has returned to his first love: writing fiction in all its forms. You can find more of his work here: www.davidsjournal.com

# Insulaphobia

*Rhonda Eikamp*

4 August 186-
Dear Charles,

Today the Pope explained to me how the Wilful Island and its inhabitants managed to survive when we defeated the Reckoner. Wavering outside the magnetic field, far out to sea – your scientific mind would grasp it better than mine – so that the Island remained intact, the enforcers that used it as their base remaining trapped in their metal bodies at the moment all the other intelligences linked to that thrice-damned Reckoner ceased to exist. Dog-men mostly, from reports of the coastal villages attacked by the Island during the war, though other less-hellish metal beings are also rumoured. The Pope has assured me that if we follow the rains we will soon cross the Island's path. Sailing toward storms...the captain and crew of our requisitioned ship think us mad. It seems strange that we humans, once hunted to near extinction by machines, now hunt the hunters. I think only of Atha, asleep back there in the vile Conservatory – I saw her, Charles, saw her chest move, though you would give me no hope, though so many other soul-raved were clearly dead in their strange black beds! What little chance, you said, you of the mathematical mind, that my wife's soul had been placed in one of the few enforcers that survived through the Wilful Island. That if we'd had children who needed a mother, you might understand my obsession with seeking her. But oh Charles, where is your heart? Look at the sky. The stars are flames if we love, and nothing if we do not.

Forgive me, dear friend. This journey wearies me. Lonely feathery days spent staring at the sea. Writing letters that may never reach you. In a way I write to myself, to retain some sense of what we do, and so I rant. Stay well.

Your friend,
   Joseph H.


In the sky above us the clouds spell life and below life burgeons, infant life, succulent; we sail through sea-mists and I yearn, I learn, I would tell you how bodies may be circumscribed. Is it a trap, are bodies traps? A riddle: when is a body a trap? I wish to hold your hand in mine as we often did, my other body, my you, always staid with me and yet tender, but hands are forgotten here. I would show you love outside of bodies. I would tell you I'm free.


10 August 186-


And then it was there! Charles, you cannot imagine! One hour ago – the storm came upon us before we knew, dark like instant midnight, swift with a sound of baying hounds. The Captain called a club haul and we came about. In spite of the danger, we crowded the rails, drenched. I thought my eyes would burst as they sought vain shapes in the rain. Then the mass of the Wilful Island broke through the black – stupendous, mountainous! The thunder we had deemed the storm's rough cough was in reality the clanking of that vast machine base, the howls – we discovered with trepidation – those of the dog-men. The Island towered above us, a spiky helmet moving on the water, closing on us like death, grim reaper of a vessel, only to slow and veer before it could ram us. I'll admit, Charles, I feared in that second. Feared, though the Reckoner Itself is destroyed, that my soul might somehow still be taken and trapped, as Atha's and those of so many others in the resistance were. I could make out the camouflage vegetation, stunted trees, and flitting there – figures, tall and spindly, or crouched – dog-men, ape-women, too far to be sure, but abominable, articulated. Fast. Oh my friend – what will Atha be, will I know her, abhor her? (Will she be here?) A winged thing, a vulture? It's said the Reckoner's cruel imagination was endless. Will she come willingly back to the Conservatory and her body, to the transfer devices the scientists say can still be deployed, or will the cages I've seen below-deck here be necessary?

As the storm receded, we tacked closer, wary of weapons. With no sloping shore to the Island, only a metal core falling straight down, we were able to come abreast of the edge as though it were a dock. The figures we presumed enforcers had vanished, leaving eerie quiet. I thought of traps. I thought of Atha, her soul I've seen to the depths of, brave through life's defeats, the stillbirths, our childlessness. I imagined – unwillingly – that soul having been trapped behind machine sentience, forced to watch as it attacked me, tore steel teeth into me. All along the edge were giant stanchions, made perhaps for attack vessels once affiliated with the Island, and the crew, with fear in their eyes, set about lashing our ship to them.

The Pope had joined us on deck, ecstatic about our find and yet reserved as always. I have not yet described to you the Pope, Charles. She is a severe woman. Formerly Lady Edyth Crayton, whom I believe you famously met at the Queen's coronation – yet little of decorum has remained, filled as she is now with the Church's obsessive hunt for the Island. Fiftyish, tall, tea-brown hair kept short and unwomanly, clad always in thick pea-jackets and the blue biretta of her standing, muscled face always frowning... And yet sad, I feel. At our first meal on board in the Captain's cabin, she was not loath to speak of her family, the well-known tragedy – parents and sister arrested, same fate as my Atha, placed by the Reckoner in enforcer bodies as punishment for their part in the resistance, while only Lady Crayton escaped. Lesser known is what she told us then – that when the Conservatory was opened after the Reckoner's defeat, her family were all found dead, the lights that still blinked over Atha's box and some few others gone dark over theirs, no hope of retrieving their souls. Mrs. Spenlow – Irma – had joined us for supper, another seeker who has been given leave to join our journey, speaking of her son she hoped to find alive on the Island, eloquent though uneducated, and she leant forward over the table abruptly, thin and formidable, and asked, quite astutely, why the Pope had undertaken this mission to find the Island "if yer family ain't there". I had earlier seen the Pope bristle at Irma's working-class manners. The Church of the Machineless World is inclusive, they say, a new kind of institution for our new world, but Charles I have not witnessed that.

These last enforcers are machines, the Pope answered. And shall we not be machineless? (I was struck by her steely gaze as she spoke.) Do you suppose your son will have anything of humanity left? You won't even recognize him.

Bristling, Irma assured us she would, "one of the big hounds, he were", that a person present when her son was placed in his enforcer body had described it to her, "one of a kind, my Alfie", apparently with blood-red forelegs and a white stripe down the canine spine that set him apart. Her confidence buoyed me.

And yet, says the Pope, we do not know that the soul-raved can even be retrieved.

The sautoir, I reminded Her Holiness. We must watch for the neck-chain and jewel, the repository of their souls, take care it is not harmed.

She only gazed at me.

We go now to enter the Island, Charles. I will know soon. Atha, I come for you, I pray and I tremble. I will be strong, no matter what you have become.

The crawling, happy shoddy-mill of life beneath a sky, I am alive I feel the nearness of it all. Light and the sea swirl here, cogwheels turn – is there a difference? I feel the nearness of it all, feel you nearing me, my love, my first, here where I have gained more loves than I knew possible.

Charles,

It is done. The momentous events of this day – I am yet aghast, wonderstruck, but I will try to put them in order.

We entered the Island. The vegetation that had taken hold upon mere metal was astonishing – glasswort, thistle, colourful lupine. Gannets wheeled above us. Further inland grew man-high patches of broom and yellow gorse, perfect hiding places. The Island's surface had been deliberately disguised with soil from the beginning, the Pope had told us, with grooves and tomas in the metal to enhance plant growth. Surface complexity, you once called it. You would have been in your element.

Some intrepid of the crew dispersed before us, although – for a reason, as you will see – the Pope and her contingent remained near the ship. The Captain, a crotchety old sea-hand with a mangy beard and a will for adventure, carried a small pepperbox which he kept cocked and pointed in front of him. I was uncertain what harm a bullet could do to the enforcers' trapped souls.

Venturing forth alongside him through the low grass, I begged him to observe restraint.

As we started up the first incline, the enforcers rose from their hiding spots.

Atha's soul, Charles – it stood here before me. I was certain. A feeling (I hear you scoff). Most were dog-men (dog-women?), wolfish, though I marked an owl, a centaur. A snake, risen like a cobra to man-height. I felt myself at that moment Orpheus, there to snatch my wife from this hell of wrought demons.

In the time since war's end the vanquished machines have become a kind of myth for us, depicted as wholly metal monsters, the fact that they were partly organic somehow forgotten. Here was no clanking. Gum rubber made a skin breathtakingly real; articulated limbs flourished. Fur, scales – an artistry. We had frozen in place, mesmerized, and they did the same. At perhaps forty, they outnumbered us by far.

Yet my mind was ablaze with hope, for they were not attacking.

Then Irma rushed past me, crying out. Tension rippled through both fronts, a tightening wave. "It's him! Alfie – son!" The dog-man she approached so heedlessly had long red forelegs and a white stripe down its hyena-sloped back. I remembered her comment.

Her hyena-son had teeth like a shark. It emitted a hyena giggle that I realized was fear. Hesitation, as it backed away. I could hear Irma murmur, telling him she loved him. Loved it, this thing that towered over her, with its bristling fur and grotesquely enlarged claws, bayonets protruding from its shoulders. If it worked, if they retained any humanity.... In the tense stillness a handful of the other enforcers began to creep near us, almost shy, as if to sniff us out though I doubted they had that sense, and I studied them for a sign of Atha, steeling myself (forgive me) for the worst, my heart if not my mouth shouting out, Where are you?

Then a buzz as of a thousand wasps rent the air. One of the crew screamed. From beyond a hillock rose a flying shape. Hovering above the enforcers on the ground, colossal compared to them, dark wings like sails blocking the sun, a whip tail, uncountable arms that were many things other than arms – pipes, saws, muzzles. Armaments rather than arms. It had a face...Charles, I cannot. A death contraption, yet with a face beautiful, soul-crushing. They say the Devil is beautiful.

I knew it was the Reckoner.

Impossible, I hear you mutter. Because the Reckoner had been destroyed, as It sat on Its copper throne in Westminster. Hollowed out, paraded before thousands in its inert condition before being flattened and melted down.

A second Reckoner, some twin? I fear I moaned, Charles.

The flying shape lighted near us. The crew were falling back, aghast. This Reckoner was smaller than Its dead sibling, though still huge. Steelier, all its organic material burned off in battle, leaving that scorched divine face that pondered us now. Dark wingèd angel-demon. A smoldering smell lived on It, acrid servo grease that wafted to us on the sea breeze.

In that poised second, a sound I had been hearing from behind us penetrated my terror.

The creak of large wheels. Muffled commands. I spun.

From the bowels of the ship, hidden beneath tarps none including I had accounted of any significance (for she was shrewd, knowing we would have protested), the Pope and her small troop trundled out a trim, gleaming mitrailleuse, its multibarrel aimed like a sieve of death at the row of enforcers.

Moments happened in seconds. I shouted No! Irma screamed They're people! The Reckoner – deciding only then, I will always believe – gave a bark like thunder, a signal to attack. The mitrailleuse barked back, its rapid-fire bullets meeting the enforcers who ran at us. Even as they advanced, all teeth and talon and retractable blade, some of the enforcers fought the impulse, I would swear before God, Charles, the trapped human souls in them struggling for control, lurching them sideways, tripping them.

I dropped to the sand. Irma did not. Falling, I caught a glimpse of the Pope's face from where she directed the shooting. It told me what I had intuited about her without admitting it to myself. The expression was holy, sanctified – and perfunctory. The Lady Crayton, forced to deal with troublesome inferiors.

The sanctity of life – those souls in the enforcers – was of no concern to the Church of the Machineless World if there were machines to kill.

It was too much. Irma still stood in the line of fire, shouting abuse back at the Pope. Metal carapaces of enforcers burst apart, riddled by scattershot from the mitrailleuse. Enforcers that made it through the volley ploughed into the crew with tooth and blade. I scrambled to my feet and raced toward the Pope, thinking to stop her, but Her soldiers held me back. The mitrailleuse had been fitted with a swivel, perversely clever – the Pope's doing likely – and they redirected it now toward the Reckoner as it lifted on giant wings toward the weapon.

It was over so very quickly.

A crew member lay dead. All about, chunks of enforcer smoldered, an intermittent howl rising only to break off like a shuttered klaxon. The largest heap was the Reckoner, shot from the air. It lay ruptured in the gorse, a black mott of broken metal limbs.

Irma knelt beside what was left of her son's enforcer body. Its sautoir – that blue jewel – lay shattered, gas still rising from it. Imagine, Charles, watching a loved one's soul ascend, no hope of capture. Somewhere in the gas and smoke – perhaps – Atha rose as well.

The soldiers had no more interest in holding me. I stomped to the Pope, nauseous with rage, sick – oh so sick. I would spew bile onto Her pointed shoes. "You're insane. You lost your mind long ago, I presume, in grief, revenge. Today you've lost your soul."

She only shrugged. "We knew that what we destroyed in Westminster was merely the Reckoner's heart, that some part survived, transferred here to this twin. Like the half of a severed earthworm that goes on living, It might have regained power some day."

"But the others needn't have died! My wife –"

"Machines all."

She gave a gesture and soldiers with needle rifles set out across the Island's protuberances to ensure there were no survivors. The Pope turned back to the ship.

Had I held a weapon, Charles, I would have hanged for murder. As it was, Irma's scream froze me. She'd scrambled to the mitrailleuse, unguarded there between Pope and ship, and she swivelled and aimed. A valiant woman, passionate. If ever there were a contrast between humanity and machine-like unfeelingness, it was there in those two women. Irma spun the firing crank.

And the Pope laughed. She laughed, C. For there was no ammunition left in the thing. They'd spent it all of course on the enforcers, gleefully. Irma had overlooked that.

I saw the future in the grieving mother's look then, revenge unbound, searing her through, as she watched the Pope re-enter the ship. She will try again sometime soon. The Pope's life is not safe from Irma Spenlow, but it is no longer my concern.

For, dear friend, I have something more momentous to reveal to you.

Tapping through that carnage afterward, numb with grief for Atha's soul that might never have been there, I found myself alone as I approached the smoking hill that was the Reckoner. Near death, shredded irreparably, It still hummed. Red eyes watched me. As I inched near, one intact twitching arm pushed aside a camouflaged panel in the Island's steel substrate and thrust itself downward, connecting.

I froze, anticipating some unsuspected weapon. My heart hammered.

The eyes turned green. The hideous rectangular mouth spoke.

It said, "My dearest Joe."

You are wise, you will understand. How even through that mechanical voice I could recognize my wife.

This is the truth the Pope may never be allowed to know, Charles. That my beloved Atha was never placed in an enforcer but in the Island itself. Its mind, its driver, distributed across its structure. No sautoir. Alive for as long as the Island proper exists.

I knelt weeping, listening until the Reckoner died, as Atha told me how she could feel the life growing on her, symbiosis with the foliage, insects, even the nesting birds. That they were – forgive me, I weep yet – that they were the children we could never have. That her soul – far from being raved – had found bliss in the nourishing of this life. Insula mater.

Then she told me she loved me.

"My first love," said that awful mouth. "Always and forever. Sweet Joe."

As I write this, our ship leaves her side. The Pope believes the Island dead material without its Reckoner. Yet, before the last life charge drained from the green-lit eyes, the Reckoner handed me a device from Its chest, with which I may always talk to Atha through the hidden panel. We've made plans to meet again in places where she feels it safe to steer close to land, dark nights along the coast, as the life upon her continues to grow....

They say mercy is a human trait, Charles, but think – the Reckoner need not have done that for Atha and myself, enabled our communication. It could have left me in ignorance of her. A conciliatory gesture? By a machine? I begin to think the Reckoner was not the monster humans deemed It. At odds with us, yes, driven to proliferate. Perhaps the evil we perceived was changed by Its proximity to those trapped human souls, to Atha. In the end, I think, It recognized the superiority of our organic life, the myriad fallible systems evolved atop one another, not structured, not straightforward, our chaos that creates emotion, hate but also love. Our minds are a wilful wild island, Charles, overgrown, unpredictable, and I believe It honoured that.

I will need your help now, your knowledge, as I enrich Atha's life in the truest sense, bring to her new flora and fauna in a mix that will prosper. To all others she will remain the legend, the Wilful Island, appearing out of storms, harbinger of terror and awe, but I will know the truth. Storms make landfall, and I will look to the sea then. Her husband, sailing to meet her where I can.


Your friend in confidence,

Joseph Hooker

Addressed to:

Charles Robert Darwin, Esq.
Down House,
Luxted Road, Kent

*Rhonda Eikamp is originally from Texas and lives in Germany. Her short stories have appeared in Lady Churchill's Rosebud Wristlet, The Dark, Oculus Sinister and Lightspeed, with others forthcoming in Phantom Drift and Nightscript. When not writing fiction, she translates for a German law firm. She has never met a moving island, but would like to.*

# Pinkerton

## *Liam Hogan*

"Movement," Crow murmured, and Red snapped the brim of his hat away from his eyes.

There were four of us up on the bluff, killing time in what little shade there was. I'd been sat half-sheltered by a rock, turning my near empty canteen over in my hands, wishing I'd hadn't been so free with the water earlier in the day's ride.

William Townsend, or Red Bill, or just plain Red, depending on your preference, was in charge of this rump of the gang, at least until Riley and Masterton and the rest returned. He had his back against the only tree worthy of the name, his tattered hat tilted forward and covering his face. He hadn't been asleep though: I'd been watching him dance a silver half-dollar back and forth across his knuckles.

"Don't see nothing," Red said, after a moment's gaze.

"Out by the gulch."

Since Crow hadn't moved or reached for the throwing knife tucked in his boot, Red slowly eased himself over to where the Indian squatted, peering out into the heat haze. Crow says he's part Apache, part Zuni, all devil. Masterton says that makes him a mongrel, but he doesn't say it to his face. Masterton's folks got run off their land a while back, though he neither knows nor seems to care which particular tribe of Indians did that. When he brings it up Crow just laughs and asks what made it *their* land?

Red squinted and rubbed the stubble on his scarred face.

"Runt," he called back to me, "Wake up Doc and bring me my glasses."

I leapt up, eager to help, until Red turned and froze me

with a glare. "Do it *quietly*," he hissed, "And stay behind the damned tree line!"

'Doc' Faraday *was* asleep, judging by the snores. Despite the surgeon's goggles he sometimes wore and the manner he affected, he was no Doctor and his real name wasn't Faraday. The combination suited the air of "learnin' and respec-ta-bility" he said his scams required. Woe betide you if, lying wounded on some lonely dirt track, he reached into his black bag and offered assistance, because that's where he kept his Army issue Colt revolver. And no, he wasn't in the Army, either.

It seemed everyone had a nickname. I hadn't wanted too much probing of the hasty moniker I'd given that day three months back when I'd fallen in with them and so, seeing as to how at fourteen years of age I was the youngest as well as the newest member of the Riley gang, I'd suggested they call me: 'The Kid'.

"More like 'The Runt'" Riley had laughed, wheeling his horse around as he looked down on my shivering frame and don't you just know that's the name that stuck?

I'd been in a wagon they'd liberated on the outskirts of Fort Smith, recovering from a beating that had relieved me of everything I owned. A silver lining, in some ways; the gang would never have taken me in if I hadn't looked the sorrowful stray, if I'd had anything on me that might still tell them who I was.

I'd kept my head down until the gunfire had ceased, until the wagon had stopped bouncing over every rut in the road and then some, until it was pulled to a halt and they'd eagerly snapped back the canvas cover to survey their haul.

No doubt they were hoping they'd plundered supplies, or tradable equipment, or maybe even some whisky. They weren't best pleased when what they found was me, bloodied and bruised and buried in a mound of rags headed for the paper mill.

Masterton was all for shooting me then and there, since I'd seen his face and would be able to identify him, but as Riley dryly observed I wasn't the first and won't be the last, so it didn't signify. "We'll just beat him and set him loose. Be a couple of hours before he staggers back into town, or runs into any posse heading our way, by which time we'll be long gone."

It was my fear of the Law rather than another beating that had me pleading to stay with the outlaws. Once the authorities knew I'd been in the presence of the infamous Riley gang, for however short a time, they'd be asking questions. All sorts of questions. Like who I was and where I was from and what I was doing hidden in that wagon, and no amount of evasion would satisfy them, they'd keep asking, keep digging, until the dreadful truth was unearthed and that... well, that would be that.

My life would be over. Over before it had even begun.

"Can you ride?" Red had asked and I nodded yes.

"Can you shoot?" Doc asked and, after only a moment's thought, I'd nodded yes once again.

"Never mind all of that," Riley grinned, "Do you know how to cook and clean, and brush down a horse, and build a fire, and are you smart enough to keep quiet when you needs to?"

I'd looked up at him, dumbstruck, which thankfully he'd taken as a yes to all of the above, particularly the last. He'd shrugged. "So what do we call you, boy?"

Three months later, as I rooted through Red's saddlebags, I was still 'Runt'. I don't think any of them really expected me to last even that short while, what with how hard living on, or rather off, the trail was. My hands that had been suspiciously soft and pale were now rough-edged and tanned.

And yes, it *had* been hard, and I wasn't used to any of

it; had often thought of escape during the bitterly cold nights shivering under a too-thin blanket. But escape to where? To what? And by then I'd ridden with the gang a couple of times and though all they let me do was mind the horses and do their chores, there was every chance people might start to recognise *my* face. Seemed to me there was only one way to leave a gang like Riley's and it involved a rough-hewn pine box. There's no retirement plan for outlaws.

Crow and Red were still sitting there when I returned with the battered field glasses, a yawning Doc in tow. Red held them up to his eyes and whistled low.

"Thought so. Pinkerton," he said and spat at the ground by his feet, a puff of dry dust whipped away by the wind.

Doc blinked into the sunlight, suddenly awake. "Where?"

"Couple miles out," said Crow.

"Heading?"

"Towards."

"Straight?"

With each question Doc's voice became more strident and I started to get nervous. When the Doc gets like that, it usually ends with bullets flying. For all his attempts at refinement, Doc was definitely the loose cannon in the group. Fear made him so.

"Straight enough."

"Goddamn!"

Doc scrambled over and lifted the glasses from Red's grasp.

"Double goddamn," he groaned.

"What's a Pinkerton?" I asked.

The two of them looked at me with disbelief. Crow kept his gaze out to the distance.

"Hark at the innocent!" laughed Red. "Here." He took

the glasses from Doc and handed them to me.

I squinted through the scratched lens, the outer fringes brown and distorted. It took a moment to spot what they'd been looking at. I found the gulch and then scanned the ground leading from it towards our lofty perch. Didn't see anything on the first pass, then I caught a flash of movement.

It was a man, dark clothed, walking with an oddly stiff gait. Didn't look like the sort of thing that would rile three wanted desperadoes. "Who is it?"

Red took the glasses back. "*What* is it," he said, before answering his own question. "A steam-man. Law enforcer."

I shrugged. "What's it doing out here?"

"Enforcing the Law"

"Do you think it's for one of us?" Doc asked.

Red nodded. "Likely. That or someone who just happens to be in the exact same direction of travel. Only one sure way to tell. Doc, you go left, coupla hundred feet. I'll go right. Crow, stay here, see what happens. You want the glasses?"

Crow shook his head. "He's close. I can see him fine."

"What about me?" I asked.

Red chewed his lip, then thumbed left. "Go with Doc and then keep going another hundred. After you get there, count to fifty and head back."

I walked with Doc, who'd taken the time to pick up his black leather bag, the Colt concealed within clinking as he swung it up. "What's going on?" I asked, still none the wiser.

Doc shot me a glance and shook his head. "A Pinkerton," he said, "is an automaton, a mechanical, tasked with a very particular and single-minded purpose: to track down a man. To track down and to kill him. It is very, very good at this. It always heads straight for its target, however far away, no matter what lies between."

I thought of Crow's tracking skills, but they only told you where someone had been, not where they were now. "How does it do that?"

"No-one knows. You see how it was walking?"

I nodded. It hadn't been moving very fast, more kind of slow and steady.

"That's what it does. It just keeps on walking. It might break into a run, if you're real close, but it don't ever stop. A Pinkerton never sleeps and it *always* gets its man."

I chewed on this for a moment. It didn't make a whole lot of sense. "So who's it after?"

Doc smiled, a thin nervous smile that only hinted at his rotten teeth. "Why do you think we're spreading out like this? This is me, you keep going, boy. See you back by the horses."

I kept going, glancing over the edge of the bluff towards where I reckoned the mechanical would be now. Can't say I was particularly scared of the thing; it was just a tin man and not a fast one at that. But I was awful curious.

I got to what I guessed was a hundred feet and then squatted by a bush listening to some bird of prey call from high above me. Probably a vulture, which made me shiver, so I don't suspect I counted the full fifty before heading back in a hurry to Doc.

He was pretty fidgety himself when I got there and without much to say we walked briskly to where Crow was waiting.

Red arrived about the same time, so I didn't feel too bad that I might have rushed my count. Crow sat, still crouched, immobile.

"Well?" Red asked.

Finally Crow stood and turned to face us. Silhouetted by the sun, the wind lifted his silvering hair towards us, his weathered face impassive. "It's the Runt."

There was a moment's stunned silence. During which I couldn't help notice Doc edging away from me.

"You sure?" Red asked, his voice steady, his eyes narrowed and flitting between us.

"Sure as."

And then Red had me one handed by the throat, reaching for his bowie knife with the other. "You little—"

"Wait!" Doc squealed.

Red turned to him, his hand still on the clasp of his leather knife holster as I squirmed in his grasp. "Why? He's led a Pinkerton straight to us. Give me one good reason why I don't gut him here and now?"

"What will the Pinkerton do if you kill him?"

Red snorted. "I'm not expectin' thanks. Job done, it'll totter off home."

"What if it doesn't? What if it's not after one of us, what if it's after *all* of us?"

"It was after the Runt. Crow said so."

"Yes... it only hunts one at a time. And when it's done with that one?"

"I ain't never heard of a Pinkerton with more than one target."

"Red, you know how much it costs to send a Pinkerton after someone? You really think it's *just* after the boy? Are you willing to bet your life on it?"

The pressure on my windpipe eased and I sucked air that rasped painfully on the way down.

"So. What do we do?"

Doc rubbed his chin, the scratch of the uneven stubble audible over the low wind. "We cut the Runt loose. He heads one way, we head the other."

Red nodded. His hand came off my neck and down onto my shoulder. I could feel the bones grind together as he squeezed.

"Makes more sense it's after all of us than just the Runt. Unless you've been holding out on us, boy? Some dark and dirty secret in your short ugly past? Some *reason* you were so bloody eager to join our gang?"

I shook my head. Stars crowded my field of vision.

"Huh." Red stood there, staring into my watering eyes. Then he reached down and tapped the canteen hooked onto my belt. It rang hollowly. "Doc, Crow; bring me your canteens."

"I'm not giving my water to a dead man!" Doc protested.

"This here's your idea, Doc. We want the Runt to last as long as possible. You can have his pony, if you like."

"I'm... going on foot?" I asked, disbelieving.

"Yes Runt, yes you are. You'll still be just about faster than it, long as you don't dawdle. I don't want you doubling back. On foot, once the Pinkerton is between you and us, you'll *have* to lead it away. That's why we're giving you our water. So you can lead it far, far away, understand?"

Red filled my canteen and then hooked a half-full spare the other side of my belt. "Should last you a day, if you're careful. Don't go drinking it all at once."

I stared up at him, confused. Something softened in his stern gaze.

"You want a gun?" he asked.

"He's not having mine!" Doc blurted out. "And it won't do him any good, anyway."

"Nope, suppose not." He swung me round, pointed a finger. "See the mesa?"

At the limits of the horizon, the hot air making it writhe, a steep sided escarpment broke the otherwise flat terrain. I nodded.

"Head for that. Put it between you and it before you sleep. Pinkerton's may be dogged, but they're none too smart. They don't avoid obstacles, they just... kind of go over them. Or through. It might buy you some time." He threw me my bed roll. "Now get!"

I stumbled a half-dozen paces before coming to a halt, looking back. They'd already gathered the horses, the little grey pony I'd been riding tethered behind.

"Guys?" I pleaded.

Red shook his head and turned away. Doc didn't acknowledge me at all. Crow sat bareback on his dusty white mare, stiffly upright. He stared down at me for a moment. "God's speed, Tom Kelly," he said and then he joined the others as they picked their way along the stony path.

I blinked tears from my eyes. The trio weren't exactly the sort of company you might ask for, but they were still company. Now I was alone, lost in the unforgiving landscape, an implacable foe on my tail. And Crow... Crow had called me by name, when I was sure everyone had forgotten, alternating between either 'Runt' or 'Boy'.

That it was the name of another, the name of a classmate from Winchester College, the least distinctive name I could seize upon while quivering half in shock, the other half in fright, my limbs entangled in rags, well, that hardly mattered. Crow wasn't to know I'd lied with the very first words I'd spoken.

I peered over the edge of the bluff, glimpsing my metal nemesis. It had halved the distance between us since I'd spied it through the field glasses. I stumbled back, not wanting to be seen, or not wanting to see it. Time to go, legs trembling.

The bluff ran roughly east-west, coming to an abrupt end at sheer cliffs to the east, the dirt path Red and Crow and Doc had taken sloping down in the opposite direction. I began to pick my way south. I figured I couldn't straight towards the mesa, not until the Pinkerton began to climb the bluff at my back, otherwise it would have the shorter, flatter, easier route.

And, if I could time it right, and if it was true they always headed in a straight line, perhaps I could drop that mechanical monster over the side of the cliff. See how it took to that! I took a deep breath, bolstered my courage.

After only a couple of minutes' descent, with the wind cut off and the southern side baked by the sun, I caught myself reaching for that second canteen. I forced myself to stop. I'd earn it when I got to the bottom and saw the Pinkerton a-top the bluff.

Although the slope was gentle, it was still tough going. Up on the back of a pony I'd been protected from the sharp, spiny grasses that clung to the arid rock. Now they lodged in the tips of my fingers and the palms of my hands as I scrambled down, as the dry earth crumbled beneath my feet. My progress slowed as I scanned warily for spider or snake. I knew, or had been told, that a rattler is more frightened of you than you are of it, but after my second encounter I didn't see how that was possible.

I was glad when the ground began to level out, became more open. From there, though, I couldn't see so far up the slope. I still didn't want the Pinkerton cutting corners and missing the bluff altogether, so I continued south, looking over my shoulder as I went.

For a short while, I thought the metal assassin was maybe stuck somewhere on the other side, or worse, that it had already crested the bluff, unseen, and was accelerating through the downhill dip towards me. But no, it was just plodding along at its own regular pace and when I'd just about convinced myself that it wasn't following me anymore, that Red and the others had been mistaken, I saw it glint in the afternoon sun.

It was closer now, seemingly not slowed down much or at all by the climb. Close enough that I could see the hat it was wearing was a bowler; black and domed. I don't know why that riled me as much as it did. Maybe because it was a mimicry of civilized behaviour, as if it was trying to fit into polite society, even here, in the middle of nowhere, despite its single minded and deadly objective: me.

I yelled at it for a full minute and a half, colourful curses learnt from my time with the Riley gang, finally running out of steam and gulping that promised reward from the canteen. Metallic and warm, it didn't cheer me any.

Time to swing east. Time to see if I could lure the mechanical to its demise.

I set off at a run. But even so, I could see it wasn't heading for the steepest part of the cliff. I'd been too slow switching from south to east, too busy cursing it. It had already topped the bluff and was going to skirt the worst of the fall.

And then I saw it stumble, lurching forward over a boulder, looking as if it was about to take flight, before succumbing to gravity and rolling, limbs spread wide, the sound reaching me a moment after each impact, a cascade of loose rocks and dirt following sharp on its heels.

A screech of something—whether bird or beast or machine I did not know—punctuated the final clatter and then there was silence, my breath short as I sheltered my brow with my hand and stared to where the thing had fallen, a whisper of wind the only movement.

I was almost disappointed. Once again, I wondered why hardened men like Doc and Red were so easily spooked.

Then I saw it, still replete with bowler hat, walking calmly from the rock fall, so close I could almost see its dimly glowing eyes staring back at me, so close I imagined I could feel the heat from its furnace.

The trickle of sweat running down my back suddenly felt chill. How much time had I wasted trying to trap it? In the hour since I'd first laid eyes on it I'd not gone far, not far at all, and this thing did not rest. Would the mesa still protect me? Would I even reach it before nightfall?

I jogged until I felt the sharp pain of a stitch in my side and then, for the rest of the day, I plodded through the arid scrub. Each time I looked back across the dusty plain I could see the Pinkerton, relentlessly following; but gradually the distance between us grew. Red had been right; at a brisk walking pace I was faster. But every time I stopped for a gulp of water, or had to negotiate a thicket of spiny bushes, or a gulch, or strayed from a straight line, it would begin to catch up.

The mesa was bathed in the red of sunset by the time I reached it and it was dark before I figured I'd gone half way round, putting its ample bulk between me and the Pinkerton. Would it be enough? But what choice did I have? I couldn't go stumbling blindly into the night; my head was pounding, my legs aching and my stomach empty.

I huddled with my blanket round me, thankful for the pieces of jerky that had somehow found their way into its folds, either by accident, or as Crow's parting gift. I almost cried at the thought.

Where were they now, I wondered? Had the gang rendezvoused somewhere west of their original meeting place? Had Riley and Masterton's day been fruitful? Were they, even now, laughing over the day's spoils, a hearty stew bubbling in a pot, a bottle that would have made me cough and splutter being passed around, no thought of the vacant spot I left around the fire?

I knew I needed sleep, but it wouldn't come. I was too cold, too miserable, too frightened. In the dark, every hoot, every scratch in the dirt, every dry leaf brushing against its neighbour, might be the Pinkerton announcing its arrival.

Was it truly unstoppable? Certainly, it was hardy; the fall from the cliff had proved that. I worked through what little I knew about it. It was man-made, from metal. Heavy, then, I guessed. Powered by steam... Did it have an inexhaustible supply of coal and water? If it didn't get its man before the boiler ran dry, would it end up seized, stuck, frozen out in the desert for future travellers to stumble across?

But maybe it was better than I was at finding what it needed. My canteen was nearly dry. I'd discarded the spare, an action I still anguished over. At the time it had felt good, a lightening of the load, but now I could only carry half a day's water. Still, on the bright side, there was no guarantee I'd last that long anyway.

I guess I must have dozed off, eventually. I snapped out of a nightmare of glowing red eyes and sharp metal teeth and unbreakable holds as the first light of dawn feathered the horizon, streaks of red no less dramatic than in my dreams. I shivered as I stood, the blanket still wrapped around my shoulders.

If I'd stopped to roll it up... but it was bitterly cold and I had the thought that a brief burst of motion might warm me. I looked back as I set off and there, barely twenty feet away, clambering down the rocks from above, was the Pinkerton!

I could hear the hiss of steam, the clank of valves and as I stared the silver neck turned all the way round like an owl's until it was looking straight at me. I knew then that I'd only previously imagined the glow in its eyes, because what I saw was so much worse. A deep, baleful red glow, flames that seemed to make its gaze flicker and brighten.

I couldn't help myself, I stumbled away, running into the dim dawn, not stopping until my heart was pounding and my legs burnt.

It was only as I slowed, gasping, and reached down to my belt that I realised the near empty canteen was not there.

That was that, then. How long could I go without water? Not long and not far. Not far at all. Even if I found a fresh source, I couldn't carry it with me. As soon as the day heated up, as it surely would, I would get slower and slower, while that damned automaton plodded ever onwards. My race was over.

I half thought about trying to skirt round the pursuing machine. If I ran, might I not complete a circle, back to where I must have let the precious canteen fall?

But there was no guarantee that I'd be able to find it. There was no fire, no sign of a camp to tell me where I had lain. And the idea of heading even remotely towards the pursuing Pinkerton...

Shuddering at the thought I set my sights on the slowly rising sun and let it guide me.

The line of half-hidden trees emerged out of the heat haze like a mirage. I squinted at the vision unsure if it was real, blinked salty sweat from my eyes. I'd discarded the woollen blanket a while back, another lightening of the load I now regretted, as the sun beat heavily at my brow.

I'd been daydreaming of Covent Garden's Martelli's Ices, trying to remember all the colours and names and flavours. Luxuries from a different world, a different life, a life that I had thrown away with my rash actions. So I could well imagine that what I saw was mere illusion, a figment of my overheated brain.

Until the line became solid and I heard a noise that grew into a roar and there it was, the turbulent flow of a river cutting its way across the flat landscape, coming from who knows where. I ran towards it, clambered down the spray-dampened rocks, scooped up the sweet, cold water and splashed and waded. My whoops echoed between the low canyon walls.

A whole wide river, not just a stone bed creek. A torrent, not a trickle. Deep enough that in a few more steps I was swimming, battling the current. So much water!

But though I might drink as much as I wanted, I had no way to carry a single drop of it with me. Nor could I linger, not for long, not with the Pinkerton hard on my heels.

And the river meant it could refill its boilers and my slim hope that it might run dry would come to naught.

What about its furnace, though? The pool was surely as deep as the Pinkerton was tall; would it extinguish those hateful flames?

I swam to the far side, clambered up the slippery rocks. From the top of the canyon the river had cut, I looked back to see the Pinkerton, plodding methodically away, closing the slight gap I'd eked out over that morning's endeavour. I lined up its path with the plunge pool below and scanned the horizon for some marker that would allow me to keep it on course. A mile away a lone pine stood, half blasted. A little to the left of where I needed to head, but close enough.

I thought about waiting, hoping to see the quenched boiler emit a mighty cloud of steam, watching the Pinkerton drown, but I'd played the waiting game too many times already. I should be trying to keep as much distance between us as I could, for as long as possible. With my clothes dripping and my boots squelching, I set off once again.

My shirt was dry before I made it half way to the pine. The thicker material of my trousers took a little longer, my woollen socks longer still, but by the time I reached my target the river was nothing but a damp memory.

As I skirted the lightning struck pine, standing a moment in its thin shadow, I realised I wasn't alone. A man, a rancher I guessed, leant against the twisted trunk.

"Howdy," he said, as he saw me pull up short.

"I... erm, howdy," I croaked, the first words in almost a day.

He nodded back the way I'd come. "Pinkerton following you?"

"Yes," I said, as I saw the dark figure rise up from the canyon edge. Damn. It had survived the pool. "Yes, it is."

He looked me up and down. "You don't look the sort."

"I'm not," I replied, though I could see no reason why he would believe me. I was running, wasn't I? Fleeing justice?

"Well," the rancher said, after a moment's contemplation. "Town's thataway," he pointed towards a black smudge, a column of dark smoke. "Wouldn't recommend it for a wanted man. Plenty there who'd be happy to claim any price on your head. Wouldn't really recommend it for an innocent, neither. But you..." he smiled, "you might want to take your chances."

"Is it on fire?" I asked, as a puff of the smoke split from the column and drifted its own way into a cloudless sky.

He laughed. "You not been this way before, son? That there's the biggest foundry in the province. Busy making rolling stock even before the railway gets here. Name of Romley Bluff."

I hadn't heard of it. But that it had a foundry was mighty interesting.

"Thanks," I said to the rancher, who tipped his hat in solemn reply, before lowering it back over his eyes and retreating to the shade of the tree. I set off on my new bearings, a glimmer of hope still alive.

It was mostly gone by the time I reached the outskirts

of Romley Bluff. I was limping, slowing up. My damp socks had raised ugly blisters and my throat was nothing but sandpaper, blood spotting my hand whenever I wiped my parched lips. Behind me, the Pinkerton was closing in. I was a few of minutes ahead of it at most.

More than once, I didn't think I'd make it. But each time I looked back and saw its dogged presence, fear had spurred me on, despite the lancing pain.

Even so, I couldn't go much further. This was—it had to be—my last stand.

Something blurred my vision as I wondered if Red and Crow and the rest of Riley's gang would be proud of me. I'd bought them a day. Two, if you counted how long it would take the Pinkerton to get back to where all this had started.

But somehow, I doubted they'd be thinking of me at all.

I got some looks as I stumbled through town, bedraggled, covered in dust, my face raw from the sun. But they let me be. I was just a boy with empty pockets. Looks were all I merited. It was what was following me that got their attention, a flurry in my footsteps as kids were dragged off the street, shutters rattling and doors banging closed, thankful the Pinkerton had other business today.

I limped towards the smoke stack and found a vision of hell. Steam powered pistons slamming down on red hot lengths of iron, sparks flying, small globules of metal glowed briefly on the packed earth floor. A workman, covered in thick leathers, gloves up to his elbows, cuffed me around the ear as he passed. "Ged-out," he hollered over the din, not even bothering to look back to see if I complied.

He headed over to the glowing heart of the building, the mighty furnace. Chains lifted a swinging crucible to and fro, liquid metal splattering from its lip. As soon as his back was turned, I slipped inside, hugging the thick wooden wall away from the chaos, the heat and choking air clawing at my bone dry throat. I slid between disused presses, buckets of pig iron, anvils and hammers with handles longer than I was. Behind me a sharp cry rose above the din; even my brief linger at the doorway had taken too long. I glimpsed the Pinkerton through a hanging curtain of thick metal chains, eyes reflecting the hot metal glow, looking straight at me.

The cry was repeated and through the heat haze I saw a man, black and hairy and wild, strike out with a long metal pole, the end a hooked point. I remembered what the rancher who had picked Romley Bluff out had said. How many of the hardened men living here were fugitives from the law?

I held my breath as the pike shot towards the Pinkerton's back, but whether the cursed thing had eyes in its neck or other senses, it casually reached out a hand, seizing the shaft of the pike and wrenching it sideways and down. The man wielding it, caught off-balance, slammed into one of the solid wooden pillars that held the roof aloft with a sickening crunch. He folded to the ground and lay there dead or insensible as the Pinkerton continued to advance, eyes still locked on mine.

Fear and anger propelled me forward. I'd meant to reach the other side of the foundry before the Pinkerton entered, hoping to lead it under that swinging crucible, directly into the white-hot furnace. But once again time was against me. As I swung around the edges of the building it followed, a curve taking it away from the worse of the fiery obstacles. I cursed. If I could have, I'd have held my position the other side of the press, but I'd tried such a tactic before and with every failed attempt the Pinkerton closed the gap, that gap that was now as narrow as it had ever been. I staggered on, though I was nearly bent double with cramp, faint with exhaustion, though every step was like walking on broken glass, though I could feel the walls close in as I fought for breath.

Ahead, a bright rectangle showed a door on the opposite side of the foundry. Desperately, I made for it. Behind me the steady clang of hammer on steel broke rhythm and I heard another shout. Then the sound of grinding metal, shrill and piercing. I didn't look back, but I hoped for the best.

I broke free of the stifling heat and into a yard stacked high with wooden sleepers and shiny new rails. Riley's gang had chewed tobacco and discussed deep into the night whether the coming railway was a good or a bad thing, mainly with respect to their larceny, but I'd seen nothing to confirm its imminent arrival until now. With horror, as I worked my way painfully through the labyrinth of stacks, I saw that the yard was enclosed. There appeared to be only one way in or out: back through the foundry. I had trapped myself! Cursing, I threaded my way to the rear, keeping the foundry at my back, until I reached the barb-wire fence and could limp no further, hoping and praying for a gate, or just a kid-sized gap. But if there was one, it wasn't where I was, where I had to stay. I curled myself up, grasping my knees as though if I were small enough, the Pinkerton wouldn't be able to find me, and there I waited, utterly exhausted.

A thud shook the dirt where I cringed and there was the noise of a mighty chain unravelling, punctuated by yet another scream.

I prayed to every god I could think of that I'd lined it up right this time.

For the briefest of moments there was silence. Then the hope was stifled in my heart as metal fists smashed through the timber wall two yards to the left of the door. The Pinkerton emerged, clothes smouldering, metal domed head now bare, outlined by angry flames at its back.

I trembled as it clambered over the stacks of rails. Up and down it went when it could so easily have walked around, but it never strayed from its path as soot blackened faces with gaping mouths appeared through the ragged hole in the foundry wall. I should have clambered back to my quivering legs, tried one last time to outpace the metal monster, even tried to scale that damned fence, for all it would have ripped me to shreds. But I didn't have it in me even as I sat, snot bubbling from my nostrils, gasping for breath between my sobs.

And then it was stood over me, my back pressed against the fence, barbs biting into my flesh. Nowhere left to go.

"Vincent Dodgson," it stated in a metallic voice.

It was a name I hadn't heard for five months, a name I had told no-one, most definitely not the Riley gang. It was my name: my real one, the one I had been born with. Whether the Pinkerton's steam powered voice box was incapable of phrasing it as a question, or it never intended it as anything other than a statement, I did not know.

I gulped and nodded, waiting for the end, for the flashing hand that would be the last thing I ever saw. Or did the Pinkerton have some weapon, some gun or blade with which it performed its official duty?

With a speed that left me breathless, it extended a scuffed arm, the jacket torn and trailing smoke, the metal discoloured. I flinched, but instead of a knife the hand held a letter. Through falls and rivers and fire, somehow the envelope was still pristine and shockingly white. What the...?

"Your father says he is sorry."

I took the vellum warily, half expecting a trap, half-expecting some legal document, the formal sentence from a distant judge, a lengthy list of my crimes, to which evading a state sanctioned officer of the law would need to be posthumously added. Tucked in the shadow of the Pinkerton, I read the brief, formal letter contained within, unable to take any of the words in until my blurred vision cleared, until my heart slowed, until the idea that this wasn't, after all, my end caught up with me. Then I read them again, astonished and disbelieving.

There was no anger in my father's words, not even disappointment. I would have expected a sterner letter had I failed to make the required grade in Latin. I wondered if the apology he had the Pinkerton pass on was an afterthought, or deemed too sentimental to commit to paper. In the clipped grammar of an educated Victorian businessman hiring out the British built eight-legged steam devices that create the finest lace, the letter informed me that my father was currently residing in Chicago and that he hoped to see me there. To assist with that re-union, there was a second, smaller envelope, wax sealed.

I hoped for a moment it contained money. But my father was not such a fool. He would not have sent me something that might prolong my adventure.

It held a single sheet of paper, folded twice. Embossed with the crest of the Chicago and North Western Railways, it asked any and all upstanding members of society to aid my return, promising immediate recompense on receipt of a reasonable bill to that effect.

It was signed not only by my father, but also by the Chairman of the railway. In these parts he was bigger than the State Governor. It was a passport, in the old sense; requesting safe passage. Back to the stultifying security of my father's—my family's—business. Back to my future.

There was a small postscript after his careful signature, a couple of thin lines across the bottom of the page. These I will quote:

"I trust sending a Pinkerton to find you did not alarm you unduly. It seemed expedient. I hear these things give hardened criminals a run for their money, so I'm sure it will have no problem locating you, my son. I hope it finds you in healthy and profitable employment."

I laughed at that, a barked release that provoked a cough and sudden, hot, stinging tears. As I lowered the letter, astounded to be alive, the Pinkerton retracted its damaged arm.

"Receipt acknowledged," it said, turning away, task completed.

*Liam Hogan is an award winning short story writer, with stories in Best of British Science Fiction 2016 & 2019, and Best of British Fantasy 2018 (NewCon Press). He's been published by Analog, Daily Science Fiction, and Flame Tree Press, among others. He helps host Liars' League London, volunteers at the creative writing charity Ministry of Stories, and lives and avoids work in London.*

*More details at happyendingnotguaranteed.blogspot.co.uk*

# Just a Story
*Valerie Hunter*

They sat in a row: Althea, Dora, Fenella. Dr. Grimsby's third team, and the only one that was all female.

Fenella had heard Dr. Grimsby speak during her very first year at the Mechanical Institute, when he'd arrived as a guest lecturer. All the girls said Dr. Grimsby was the only one to take women seriously, to give them a chance. He was the one whose eye they had to catch if they wanted to be anyone.

So Fenella had listened to Dr. Grimsby's lecture carefully, all about the melding of medicine and mechanics, though it hadn't lit any fires in her like it had in some of the others. If she could have glimpsed herself sitting here in five years' time, she wouldn't have believed it.

Yet here she sat.

Dr. Grimsby eyed them now, his gaze intense. "The latest Bestia subject arrived today. I'd like one of you to take charge of collecting his personal data. It's most helpful if it's just one person forming a bond with the subject. Your observations will be invaluable."

He turned to Althea first, the senior member of the team. "Althea, would you like to take this on?"

"Perhaps it would be best for one of the others to gain experience with such work, since I've done it before," Althea said quietly.

Dr. Grimsby turned to the middle seat. "What about you, Dora?"

"You know I'm better at the practical side of things." Dora's voice grew bolder with each word. "I was hoping to assist on the operations."

"Were you? Well, then." He turned one last time. "Are you up to data collection, Fenella?"

"Of course," she said. She'd only been at Forestview a few weeks, but she knew what was expected of the newest member of the team. You said yes to any assignment, particularly the ones no one else wanted, and you tried not to wonder why others had refused them.

Fenella started her data collection the next day, after another meeting with Dr. Grimsby. This time she was the only one sitting across from his desk.

"Your job," Dr. Grimsby said, "is to put the subject at ease. Befriend him. He should feel safe with you."

He said it like it was some kind of grand, surprising pronouncement when all Fenella could think was, shouldn't anyone feel safe with her? She was hardly a dangerous person.

But all she said was, "Yes, sir."

Dr. Grimsby passed her a copybook. "You're to take this each Monday from the Records Room. There will be questions each week. You're to record all your interactions accurately, and alert us if you see any deterioration of the subject's mental state. Now off you go."

Fenella walked down to the subject ward in the basement, telling herself she'd do fine. She was good at following directions. She'd prove that to Dr. Grimsby, and maybe next time he'd let her do what Dora was doing, inserting the actual mechanizations.

They were trying to create a better soldier. A melding of man and machine, with reason and courage that could be controlled in battle. This new soldier would be able to win the next war so much more quickly than ordinary soldiers had won the last.

At least, that was what Dr. Grimsby had said when Fenella arrived at Forestview, giving an impassioned speech that hadn't actually inspired her. Not that she'd dare say so, but it had sounded rather silly. Still, when she was given the specs, the minutiae of gears, cogs, and wires, she felt enthused in the same way she always did when she had a project to tackle. It didn't matter what she was building; the act of putting things together was the thrill.

The competition wasn't so bad, either. Dr. Grimsby had three teams working to make all the hardware he'd envisioned, and there were other doctors in the building with their own teams attempting similar projects. Dora had already informed Fenella how every new breakthrough, every new functioning mechanism, brought accolades to both the team and the individual engineer.

Fenella found the right room and knocked, then remembered the subjects were locked in. Blushing, she fumbled her way inside with the key she'd been given. The room looked similar to her room upstairs: bed, table, two chairs, bureau. Her own table was cluttered with tools and projects, but this one was empty.

A man stood in the middle of the room, tall and broad-shouldered with dark hair and a bushy beard. His eyes were fixed on her.

"Hello," she said. "I'm Miss O'Callaghan, here to do your intake assessment."

"Intake assessment?" His voice had a bit of rust to it.

"Just some questions," she said. "You answer them, and I write down the answers, Mr. Medvedi."

He frowned. "It's Marek. I'm not a mister. Wouldn't it be easier for me to write them down myself? You may all think that folks from the Territories are idiots, but I'm literate."

"Dr. Grimsby wants it done this way. And I'm from the Territories myself, so I know you're not an idiot."

The man's thick eyebrows rose. "Are you? Where from?"

She sat down, opening the copybook. "Cascade."

"Huh," he said, sitting down opposite her. "I've never been that far west. I'm from Gallatin myself."

That was one of the questions she was supposed to ask, so she wrote it down and then started at the beginning. "Your birthdate, Mis—Marek?"

"April 29, 1847."

She'd thought him older than twenty, but maybe that was just the beard and that gruff, old-man voice. She returned to the questions. "Why did you join the army?"

"Nothing else to do. My parents died. My four older brothers had the farm under control. Had no use for me."

"Couldn't you have got other work?" Once the question slipped out, she bit her lip. It wasn't on the list.

"I was only half grown. Hard to find a job that paid much of anything. My brothers wanted to indenture me out, so they could keep the fee, but I wasn't keen on that. Then the army came recruiting. They'd take anyone, long as you had a heartbeat."

"How old were you when you joined?" she asked, returning to the list.

"Fourteen." When he saw her surprise, he grinned. "Told them I was seventeen. No one checked."

"Did you enjoy your time in the army?"

It was a stupid question. Who would enjoy fighting a war? She hoped he realized she hadn't come up with these questions herself.

"Well enough," he said shortly.

She pressed on with the list. "And after the war? What did you do then?"

"Went home, but my brothers didn't want me there."

"So you came here?"

He nodded. "No one in the Territories was hiring, and this place offered a hundred dollars upfront, and more money than I made in all my years in the army once I'm done."

She'd reached the end of the list. "Thank you. I'll be back next week."

"Are you the secretary?"

She laughed. "I'm a bio-mechanic."

His eyes widened. "Will you be doing the procedures?"

"No, that's one of my colleagues." The fancy words kept rolling off her tongue. Putting on airs, her mother would have called it, but she didn't care. "I built the device they'll be inserting, though." She didn't mention that it wasn't her design, and that it was very simple to assemble.

"Huh. Who would've thought, a little girl from the Territories doing all that."

She almost took offense, but he was grinning, and she couldn't help smiling back. After all, he was from the Territories, too. He understood.

Fenella had plenty to do that week. She was working on a new c-pump, a way to smooth out the process of connecting the subject to the helmet. Althea had invented the original pump, and each of them—Althea, Dora, and Fenella—were working separately to try to improve it. Dr. Grimsby said sometimes innovation came best in solitude.

Still, they had many meetings, collaborating on other things and talking through the latest phase of the Bestia trial. Marek's name was never mentioned, even as they discussed the first procedure in great detail, both before and after Dr. Grimsby and Dora performed it.

Marek had a bandage around his neck when Fenella went in on Monday. "How are you feeling?" she asked.

"All right. Didn't hurt much. 'Course, it's only the first procedure. Do they get increasingly painful?"

"No," she said, because she didn't want to say she didn't know.

Marek had been pacing when she'd come in, and he continued to do so even as she sat down and opened the copybook. "Shall we begin?" she asked, hoping he'd sit.

"Sure," he said, still pacing.

She let him be and frowned at the questions. She should have previewed them ahead of time, but she'd been caught up with a tricky bit of wiring and had nearly forgotten her session with Marek altogether. Now she felt foolish; the questions were nearly identical to last week's, clearly an error.

Except Dr. Grimsby didn't make errors, did he? If these were the questions in the copybook, then these were the correct questions. She pasted on a smile and said, "I'm afraid it'll be a bit boring. They're similar questions."

Marek frowned. "Why?"

"To check your cognitive function," she guessed. When Marek just stared, she added, "To make sure your brain's working all right."

He stopped pacing. She waited for him to ask why such checks were necessary, but instead he finally sat down. "Can I ask you questions, too? So it's fair?"

She didn't much like that idea, but he had a point. If she had to keep asking him questions, why shouldn't he be allowed to reciprocate? Dr. Grimsby had said it was her job to befriend him, and friends should know something about you.

"Sure," she said, and he grinned.

"Now, why did you join the army?"

"The money."

"What did you need the money for?" she asked. Extra questions might ease the monotony.

"No, my turn. How old were you when you came to the States?"

"Thirteen. What did you want the money for?"

"What does anyone want money for?"

"You can't answer a question with a question!"

"Is that a rule?"

"Yes," she decided.

"Fine. I wanted money so I could get away from my brothers. Did you win a scholarship?"

"To the Mechanical Institute. What's so awful about your brothers?" she asked, enjoying the rhythm of their questions.

"They always think they know best. See me and Gaba as nuisances. Treat us poorly. Shouldn't you be writing this down?"

"Is that your question?" she asked, hoping it would deflect from her embarrassment as she finally picked up her pen.

"No answering questions with questions," he chided. "Are you ever going back to the Territories?"

"I don't know."

"That's not an answer."

She looked up. "Of course it is. Who's Gaba?"

"Gabriel. My younger brother. He's sixteen now, but he was born with his back all twisted up. Our older brothers don't treat him well. I want to take him with me when I make a home for myself. Why don't you know if you're going back?"

"Well, it would be nice," she said, even though she wasn't sure she meant it. She hadn't been home since her first summer at the Institute. "But there are more opportunities here. Besides, I can't leave yet."

"Why can't—"

"My turn. Are you worried about Gaba, without you there?"

"Nah. We've got a sister, too. Hannie. She makes sure the others behave, more or less. She's got clout, because she does all the cooking and washing. Why can't you leave?"

"There was a contract during the war. Students had to sign it or be expelled. We owe the States five years of service after graduation."

Marek frowned. "But the war's over."

"Doesn't matter. Will you rescue Hannie, too, when you go back?" She'd got far from the original questions, but she didn't care.

"Of course," he said. "But it's not rescuing. Just a plan we made long ago. A story we'd tell each other to get through the hard times."

It was her turn to frown. "Calling it a story makes it sound like something you don't think will come true."

"Who says stories can't be true? Wait, don't answer. That wasn't my question."

She wished she could think of a glib reply before he kept talking, but she couldn't.

"What's your name?" he asked. "Your first name?"

"Nell." It slipped from her mouth automatically, despite not having used it in five years, and she was so surprised by its sudden reappearance, of the girl it turned her into again, that she mumbled an excuse and left even though she hadn't finished asking the stupid questions.

Fenella tried not to think about Marek all week, or the fool she'd made of herself scurrying out of his room. She fudged answers in the copybook, returned it to the Records Room, and put her mind to more important tasks.

Of course she had to go back the following week. Marek was pacing again. "Hello, Nell."

"It's Fenella, actually," she said.

"Fenella," he said slowly. "I dunno, you seem more like a Nell."

What did that mean? Nell was insignificant, a backwoods tinker. She had erased all traces of Nell at the Institute.

"Fenella," she repeated tightly.

"Sorry," he said. "Fenella it is."

She sat down. He kept pacing. "Would you please sit?"

"Do I have to? I'm in here most of the day. It helps to walk."

She shrugged and asked the questions. He didn't ask her anything in return until she was done and closing the copybook.

"What made you want to work here?"

"I was assigned."

"No choice whatsoever?"

"We filled in preference forms. There were interviews and aptitude tests. They made you feel that wherever you were placed was exactly where you were best suited."

"And were they right?"

She tried to pretend she'd never asked herself the same question. "I had the highest marks in biomechanics as a senior. Fitted out a squirrel with all sorts of devices."

Marek's eyes widened. "A...squirrel?"

"Yes."

"What did your squirrel do by the time you were done with it?"

She laughed. "Nothing extraordinary. The point was just to see if we could replace some of its parts with mechanisms."

He finally stopped pacing. "It survived all that?"

"Of course. I knew what I was doing." She didn't mention that the squirrel had been euthanized in the end anyway, so that the junior students could dissect it and examine her process.

"Well, aren't you a marvel, Fenella?"

She couldn't tell if he was being serious or not.

As the weeks passed, Fenella grew accustomed to Forestview. She earned praise from Dr. Grimsby, finished a project with Althea, finally managed to write a letter home. But it was Monday afternoons that she found herself looking forward to. Talking with Marek was a nice break to the workday, a reminder that there was a world beyond Forestview. He told her about growing up in Gallatin, of the place he'd buy someday with his money, how Gaba wanted to grow roses and Hannie would have a whole hutch of rabbits.

Marek's next procedure was the last Sunday in May. Dora bragged about how well it went the following morning, so it was a shock when Fenella found Marek curled up in his bed that afternoon. "What's wrong?' she asked.

"I'm going to puke," he mumbled, and she pulled the chamber pot out just in time.

"How long have you felt poorly? Hasn't the nurse been in?"

"I don't know. She was here before. Gave me something chalky to swallow. Said she'd be back later."

"Do you want me to get her now?"

"Nah. Your friend Dora said this was to be expected."

"She's not my friend. Is it just your stomach?"

"My head, too. The whole room's spinning."

"All right. Lie back." She poured him a glass of water, held his head while he drank, tried not to think how terrible she was at the biological side of biomechanics. If he'd been a machine, he'd be easy enough for her to set right.

"Maybe you should get some sleep," she suggested.

"Can't. Every time I shut my eyes, it feels like the walls might smother me." He grabbed her hand. "Is that normal?"

"Yes," she said, hoping it was. "You'll be right as rain soon."

"Right as rain," he repeated, and she knew he was clinging to the words the same way he clung to her hand. "Did any of them drop out at this phase? The other subjects?"

"I haven't been here that long," she admitted, but when his grip tightened she added, "but I don't think so."

His hand loosened slightly. "Good. If I get past phase three, I'm guaranteed seventy percent of the money. Can you make sure? If I die, I mean? The contract promised… I wrote down Hannie as my beneficiary… you'll make sure she gets it?"

She wanted to reassure him he wasn't dying, but somehow she didn't think he'd listen. "Of course," she said, even though she had nothing to do with payments.

"Thanks." He let go of her hand. "Would you stay awhile? Tell me a story, to keep my mind off things?"

"A story?' she said dubiously, even as she dragged a chair over.

"Anything. Tell me about Cascade."

Cascade felt impossibly far away, faded like an old book, but she told him about the little workshop she'd made in the attic, how she'd fixed her mother's sewing machine and made wind-up toys for her cousins. As she talked it all seemed real again, closer, more vibrant. She kept talking longer than she'd meant to, and when she finally stopped, Marek was asleep.

She crept out of the room, then went upstairs and found Althea. "What happened to the previous Bestia subjects?"

"All the previous trials failed. You know that."

"The trials failed, yes, but what about the subjects?"

Althea kept her eyes on her worktable. "You should read the reports."

"I have. They never give any detail on the subjects." Just on and on about how the mechanisms had failed, hypotheses on why this or that hadn't worked.

"Those were the mechanical reports. The medical reports are in the Records Room."

"Could you just tell me?" When Althea didn't answer, she tried again. "Does anyone die in phase three? With the nausea and the dizziness?"

"No, not for years. It usually passes quickly."

"Not for years? It used to kill them?"

Althea nodded. "We came up with a valve that slowed the integration process, stopped putting such a shock to their systems."

"What happened the time you were in charge of the data?" Fenella asked. "What happened to that subject?"

"His name was Daniel," Althea said quietly.

"What happened to Daniel?"

"It's all in the Records Room. You should really read the reports yourself. You haven't got attached to your subject, have you?"

Fenella didn't answer. She left Althea's room, but didn't go to the Records Room. She told herself she had other, better things to do.

\#

Fenella didn't return to the basement until the following Monday. After all, she had many important tasks to focus on, and Dora had reported the subject was feeling better during Thursday's meeting.

Sure enough, Marek was pacing the room again, though he looked pale, a bit thinner, his beard a little wilder.

"You're better," she said, part statement, part question.

"I still feel a little funny, but nothing like before." He paused. "Thank you."

"For what?"

"The stories. I don't think I would have fallen asleep without them. And I started to feel better once I woke up."

She shrugged. "Just doing my job," she said, sitting down and opening the copybook. "Why did you join the army?"

She didn't look up, but she still knew she'd hurt him. It didn't matter. He was just a job.

Marek answered the question tersely.

"Did you enjoy your time in the army?"

He never answered that one in detail, but today he said, "Do you know what I miss about the army?"

She looked up. "What?"

"It was the one place I felt like I belonged. I didn't like what we were doing. I didn't like why I was there. The marches were terrible, and so was the food. But the boys in my squad? They became family. We looked out for one another. We understood each other. The hardest part about going home wasn't my older brothers telling me I wasn't welcome. It was not being able to talk to Hannie and Gaba like before. Because we used to tell each other everything, but I didn't want to talk about the war. I didn't want to taint them with that."

"You feel tainted?"

"Of course! The things I saw. The things I did. We all were. So we understood each other."

"Do you think it'll ever go away?" she asked. "The taint?"

"I don't know. In here, on my own, there's too much time to think about it, and it feels like it never will. But maybe someday, back in the Territories, all that wide-open sky..." He paused. "Do you ever miss the sky?"

She went outside every morning for a constitutional, and Forestview was far from any cities, but she knew what he meant. The sky in the States just wasn't the same. "All the time."

He nodded. "I reckon that sky might take away just about anything, given enough time."

She nodded back, because she wanted to believe that was true, that somewhere something could wash her time at Forestview away.

She kept working. Days losing herself in her mechanical projects. Monday afternoons with Marek. It was her job to listen to him, after all. Just because she enjoyed his company didn't mean she'd become attached to him.

Then one Monday there was a note from Dr. Grimsby clipped into the copybook. *Going forward, you may notice lapses in the subject's ability to answer questions. This is an expected side effect. You should not assist the subject in any way, but you should be calm and reassuring. Should the subject become overly agitated or have difficulties forming intelligible speech, get me immediately.*

She read it through a second time. They had discussed phase four the other day, a series of serum injections to help Marek's brain adjust to what was coming next. No one had mentioned side effects.

She entered the room. Marek sat on the bed, said hello listlessly.

"Are you all right?" she asked.

"Yes."

She turned to the questions, and was surprised to find they'd changed. The first one asked, *Do you have family?*

"Tell me about your family," she said instead.

Marek frowned. At first she thought that he was unsettled by the change, too, but then she realized he was struggling to think.

"Hannie and Gaba?" she prompted. To hell with the note. "Can you tell me about them?"

"My mind's foggy today." He said it the way one might complain about a headache or some other minor annoyance.

"Do you want me to tell you?" she asked

"Sure."

She repeated every story he'd ever told her about his childhood, about all the dreams he had for that future home with Hannie and Gaba, pouring information into him until he began to add a few details of his own, which she dutifully recorded in the copybook. By the time they finished, he was answering without assistance, though hesitantly, like he was afraid of getting something wrong.

As she left, he whispered, "Thank you."

"You're welcome," she said, smiling like she wasn't horrified.

The next morning Fenella went to the Records Room and pulled the medical reports of all the previous Bestia subjects. She read them carefully, deciphering what all the fancy words boiled down to. That Forestview had killed dozens of young men, their names printed at the tops of the files but then turned into 'the subject' everywhere else.

After awhile she focused only on the end of each report. How the subjects forgot how to talk or walk or breathe. How they became simple or raving or violent. Some keeled over dead. Some were sent to asylums. Some were 'stopped by injection.' She stared at those three words, so innocuous looking.

She went upstairs, found Althea. She couldn't think straight, couldn't speak.

"You've read the medical reports," Althea said.

"'Stopped by injection.' That's what happened to your Daniel."

Althea looked away. "His mind started to break down… he got violent. But he still knew me. I was the one who did it, because I was the only one who could get near him at the end." She paused, looked right into Fenella's eyes. "It stops the heart. That's what they'll have you do to your subject, if it comes to that."

Fenella could only stare at her. "Why are we even doing this?" she asked. "Surely you can't think it's worth it?"

"Of course it's worth it," Althea said, sounding more like herself. "In the end, we'll succeed."

"Succeed at what? Creating an army of men ready to run to their deaths?"

"Not their deaths. Ours isn't the only project, you know. Dr. Scabere's team is working to weaponize soldiers' bodies. Guns built right into their arms, deadlier than any we have now and able to shoot endless rounds in rhythm to their heartbeats."

"That's terrible!"

"That's our job. Best accept it, or you'll fall to pieces. Have a breakdown like that engineer on Dr. Scabere's team last year."

"What became of him?"

"Nothing good," Althea said quietly. "They don't pat you on the head and send you home, you know."

Fenella didn't want to go home. She was tainted, like Marek said. But she couldn't stay here, either.

She went back to her room, sat at her worktable, but it felt like the walls were closing in on her. Tinkering had always felt as natural as breathing, the one thing in her life she was unfailingly confident about, but today…

She shook her head, tried to shake the doubt away. She was good at what she did. It was her job to succeed, to save Marek, and when had she ever shirked a job?

She picked up her tweezers and got to work.

#

The following week Marek was fuzzy-brained again, and this time it took him longer to join in as Fenella prompted him along. "It's getting bad, isn't it?" he said after they'd finished.

She nodded, took a deep breath. "You should leave. It's not worth the money, no matter how much it is." She kept her eyes on him, much as she wanted to look away. "It doesn't end well for the test subjects."

He huffed a laugh. "You think I don't know that? Didn't we establish that I'm not an idiot?"

She wanted to tell him she'd been the idiot, so slow to realize. That she wanted to leave, but she didn't know how unless they figured it out together. Instead she said, "How long have you known?"

He shrugged. "Awhile."

She wanted to shake him. "We could—"

"In the army, if you deserted and got caught, it was a public whipping the first time, but the second time it was a public execution."

"But we wouldn't—"

"I had to watch countless whippings. A few executions, too. No one ever thinks they'll get caught. And I doubt Forestview bothers with whippings."

She thought of those endless files, all those final pages. "It's still worth trying."

"I'm locked in, Fenella."

"I can sneak you out in the night, or—"

"No. That's not for you to risk."

"I can't just sit here and watch you..." "Die?" he offered. "And if I get caught and die anyway? They might kill you, too, for helping me."

Would they? She didn't know, and at the moment she found she didn't much care. "Better you die quick than lose your mind, your memory..."

"I killed someone," he said. "When I was in the army."

Could he just stick to the topic? "You were a soldier," she snapped. "It was your job."

"No, not like that. I killed a civilian. A woman." He looked at her as though expecting her to recoil, but she just stared back, waiting for him to go on.

"We were foraging, me and my friend Tom. Taking a little corn from someone's field because we were hungry. And then the shot came, and Tom fell. I didn't even hesitate, just shot right back." He winced. "It was a young woman. All she was doing was defending her food."

"She could have yelled first," Fenella pointed out. "She chose to shoot. She had it coming."

He looked at her like she'd just shot someone. "You're brutal."

"You shoot at someone who also has a gun, you're asking for trouble. Did Tom die?"

"No. Turned out she barely grazed him. Maybe she just wanted to scare us."

"And maybe she didn't and just had poor aim."

Marek shrugged.

"Why are you telling me this, anyway? Are you hoping to forget that? Killing her?"

"No. I wish I didn't have to carry that guilt around, but I don't want to forget it. Like it didn't matter. Like it's not part of me."

"Well, you're going to forget everything pretty soon," she said.

"Not if you keep reminding me."

"Marek…" Didn't he realize that wouldn't work forever? That one of these weeks, all the stories in the world weren't going to bring him back to himself? She looked at him, saw in his eyes that he did know. "Do you think dying here makes up for killing her?" she asked. "Because that's idiotic. The world doesn't work that way."

"Doesn't it?"

"No," she said firmly, because she wanted it to be true.

The next week when she walked into Marek's room, Dr. Grimsby was sitting at the table. "Sir?" Fenella said, mouth suddenly dry.

"We're having some unexpected anomalies with the subject. I'm trying to pin down their origin."

"Anomalies?" She tried to collect herself. "What do you think is going wrong?"

"I haven't quite formed my hypothesis. I just thought I'd observe."

Fenella sat and opened the copybook. Marek was sitting on the bed, his gaze distant.

"Do you have family?" she asked.

"No," he answered dully.

She clamped her lips between her teeth. Writing down those two letters took every ounce of her self-control.

"Why did you join the army?"

"I wanted to kill the enemy."

His voice had more life to it now, which made it all the worse. *You don't mean that!* she screamed at him in her head. *That's not the answer!*

She went through the rest of the questions mechanically, recorded his terrible responses, kept her voice steady. Dr. Grimsby didn't say a word until afterwards, in the hallway. "He's coming along splendidly, isn't he?"

"Splendidly," she echoed, and bared her teeth in a smile.

Fenella went back to her room, stared at the specs of the Bestia helmet again. Phase five would begin soon. Once she'd thought that if she did a good enough job, it might save Marek's life. Now she knew that whatever she was saving, it wouldn't be Marek for much longer.

She waited until late in the evening to go back downstairs. She could talk to him alone, try to talk him back to himself again. She could convince him to run.

But when she unlocked the door, she stopped short. Dora was there, hovering over Marek with a tube of liquid in her hand that was hooked up to his neck.

"What are you doing here, Fenella?"

"I'm missing my micro-wrench," she said quickly. "I had it in my pocket earlier, and I thought I might've dropped it here."

"Well, you didn't." When Fenella didn't move from the doorway, she added, "Go on. If you leave quickly, I won't report you to Dr. Grimsby."

She should keep up the charade, ask Dora why looking for a wrench was worth bothering Dr. Grimsby about. Instead she turned and fled, every footfall a reminder that she had failed Marek, that she hadn't done her job.

She went back to her room. Her mind was a million panicked pieces, but she took a deep breath and found paper, the way she used to do at the Institute during that terrible, overwhelming week before exams. A small voice in her head screamed that this was infinitely worse than exams, but she ignored it.

She just needed a plan.

It took her multiple pieces of paper and most of the night, but in the end she had one. She ignored the myriad ways it might go wrong, and set about putting it in order—what she needed to do when, how long it might take, how best to take precautions. Doubts clawed at her, but she shoved them aside and kept figuring out the next step.

She didn't have any meetings the next day, thankfully. She was supposed to build the c-pump for Marek's helmet. Dr. Grimsby had chosen Dora's design, but tasked Fenella with making it. She did so, following the specs exactly. Then she made another one, identical on the outside but missing some key parts within. And then she worked on a different contraption, this one of her own design and much tinier.

That night she woke at three, creeping around with whisper-soft steps. Her key no longer fit Marek's door, but she knew how to pick a lock. She slipped into the room, shook him awake.

He stared at her, but didn't respond when she talked to him. Still, he obeyed when she asked him to lay on his belly, and stayed still as she hunched over his neck, working on the valve. She spoke to him the entire time so he wouldn't be scared, so she wouldn't lose her nerve. It was difficult, fussy work, but in the end she managed to insert the little trap she'd built, so that the dreadful serum Dora was feeding into him each evening wouldn't go any deeper.

She went back every night that week. She emptied the trap, and then she talked to him, pouring in all the words she could, everything he'd ever told her about himself. When she ran out of his stories, she told him her own, about Cascade, back when she was Nell, just a little girl who delighted in tinkering.

He never said a word.

During the day she ignored her heavy eyes and did what she had to. She drew specs for Dr. Grimsby that she hoped she'd never build, showed them to him with practiced smiles. During her morning constitutionals she explored the nearby forest, smuggling things out in her pockets and leaving them tucked away there. One day she walked all the way to town—something that was not encouraged, though never expressly forbidden—and procured a map.

At Sunday's meeting, Dr. Grimsby told her, "There's no need to visit the subject tomorrow."

"Oh?" Fenella said, a cold trickle in her belly.

"He's past speech now. Can't answer any questions. He's quite docile, though. I think the new c-pump is going to be a real breakthrough, but we won't know until we start phase five. Can't have him docile after we put the helmet on, can we?"

"No, sir," Fenella murmured.

"We'll begin tomorrow," Dr. Grimsby said. "It will be thrilling for you to observe, but try not to expect too much. Mostly I'm hoping to gather some information we can user to further team one's work. Their current subject might be the success we've been waiting for."

Fenella watched Dora pout, knowing she was only thinking about how their team wasn't on top. She tried to imagine what Dora's face might look like tomorrow, when she and Marek weren't there.

She went over the plan in her head all day. At half past midnight, she got dressed, crept downstairs, picked the lock.

Marek's room was empty.

Her mind sped like a badly wound clock. Where had they—what if he—Should she...wait? No, he couldn't have left on his own. Even if he returned, which seemed unlikely, he wouldn't be alone.

She backed out of the room, went upstairs quiet as a shadow while fingering the back-up plan in her pocket. But when she picked her way into the office, the helmet was gone, too, so her decoy c-pump was useless.

She went back to her room. This was the kind of nightmare she used to have at the Institute, everything going wrong, closing in around her.

She could leave. Maybe she couldn't save Marek, but she could save herself, never have to play a hand in another man's death.

She stayed where she was. That wasn't the right ending. That wasn't a story she wanted to tell.

She didn't sleep. In the morning she went outside to the fenced-in yard where Dr. Grimsby had told them to meet. He was already there with Marek, whose eyes were downcast.

Where had he been stashed last night? If she had picked enough locks, opened enough doors, could she have found him before she got caught?

Dr. Grimsby had the helmet in his hand, gleaming and terrible, and gave it to Dora. "You should do the honors."

Dora beamed, fitting the helmet over Marek's head, then reaching to connect the c-pump to the port in his neck.

Marek began to twitch. First his head, and then all of him, arms flailing, neck twisting, shaking like he might shatter. Fenella stared, unsure if he was doing it on purpose or if something had gone horribly wrong, even though the helmet wasn't connected yet.

Either way, sometimes opportunity was the next best thing to a plan.

Fenella palmed her tiniest screwdriver from her pocket and stepped forward. "Can I try? I can calm him down."

Dora scowled, but Dr. Grimsby agreed.

The helmet had already fallen and Fenella picked it up, hoping no one noticed her hand inside it. She unscrewed furiously, while keeping her expression calm, her voice soothing. "This isn't going to hurt, Marek." Under her breath, just loud enough for him to hear, she added, "Don't stop."

Whether he heard her or it really was involuntary, he kept twitching, and when she moved to put the helmet on his head she let him collide with it, let it go flying, keeping a good grip on the c-pump she'd just removed and tossing the decoy from her pocket as the others watched the helmet fall.

"So much for your calming influence," Dora sneered.

"The c-pump dislodged," Althea said.

"Is it damaged?" Dr. Grimsby asked.

Althea picked up the decoy. "No. I can put it back in."

While she did, Fenella put her arms around Marek from behind, held him tight and close. "You can stop now," she whispered. "The helmet won't hurt you." She wished she could tell him everything would be fine, that they'd get through this and run away tonight, but she didn't know that, so she just kept holding him, even as he went still, even as Dora finally connected the helmet to his neck. She let go after that, but she hoped he could still feel her arms around him.

"All right, let's get behind the fence," Dr. Grimsby said.

She watched as he left Marek in the fenced-in section of the yard, and closed the gate behind him. There was an enormous shed inside the yard, too, and Dr. Grimsby reached over the fence and pulled its door open.

Fenella wasn't sure what she'd been expecting. The reports had referred to it only as "the fear stimulus," detailing the subject's reactions rather than the thing itself.

She hadn't expected an enormous bear to lumber out of the shed toward Marek.

She blinked. It was completely mechanical, of course. She'd seen such beasts at the Institute, had even worked on a few during second year. They were like big wind-up toys, popular at carnivals.

This one didn't look like a toy, though. It was fierce and menacing, with shiny teeth and sharp claws. The closer it got to Marek, the faster it moved.

Marek stood still at first, but then he began to back away.

"What's he doing?" Dr. Grimsby muttered. "He's supposed to be devoid of fear. He's supposed to charge it. Did you attach the helmet properly, Dora?"

"Yes, sir!"

"Well, something's gone wrong."

Marek backed away till he reached the fence, then edged along it. The bear, who had been programmed to a specific course, kept going straight, stopping when it hit the fence.

"What a waste," Dr. Grimsby said, opening the gate. He strode toward Marek, but Marek backed away from him, too, while pulling at the helmet.

"Boy!" Dr. Grimsby yelled. "Stop that! You'll damage the mechanisms. Stay where you are, I'll remove it."

Marek paused for a moment, then continued to move away, backing up against the mechanical bear's rump.

"It's for your own good, boy!"

Marek wrenched one of the claws from the bear's foot, held it out like a knife.

Dr. Grimsby retreated. "Shame," he said. "Ah, well. I'll be interested to crack his skull open, see what went wrong." He turned to Fenella, pressed something into her hand. "Do you think you can get close enough to sedate him?"

Her hand closed around the needle. She knew what it was, knew what 'sedate' really meant.

She crossed the yard, half hoping Marek would stab her with the claw. He watched her approach, the weapon in one hand, the helmet, which he'd finally managed to wrench off, in the other.

"What should I do, Nell?" he whispered when she was close enough for only her to hear.

She wrapped her arms around him, hid the needle between their bodies. "Just fall."

He collapsed against her, and she sank to the grass with him. Dr. Grimsby strode toward them, and she waited, waited, seeing that thick stack of files, all those boys he'd killed in the name of science, for the betterment of war.

She could be fearless, too. She could do her job as well as any soldier.

When he was right beside them she sprang, stabbing the needle into his neck and releasing its poison. She saw the shock on his face as he fell to the ground in spasms, and she wanted to be sick because she had caused this, she had done this—

"Fenella! Good lord, what did you..." Dora was rushing across the grass, pouncing like a tiger, landing on top of Fenella, her hands around her neck, a string of incomprehensible words and the world gone red and hazy—

There was a terrible thunk and Dora was beside her, Althea hovering over both of them, the heavy helmet bloodied in her hand and Dora still.

Fenella stared, struggling to sit up. "Is she..."

"Never mind that. Go! You'll have a few minutes at least before I find someone to report this to. I'm going to be hysterical and incoherent for as long as I can, but you need to take your boy and run!"

Marek was sitting beside her, wide-eyed. Her boy. She grabbed his hand and pulled him with her, ran out of the yard and into the forest, over streams and through brambles, hurrying and stumbling and making their way to places that hadn't seen a human in a long, long time. The map she'd studied made it look like they could get all the way to Mishigama Territory this way, if they kept going long enough. She didn't let herself think about anything but that.

When they couldn't run anymore, they walked, and when it got dark, they rested. She sat close to Marek, and didn't know what to say except, "I'm sorry."

"What for? You saved me."

She remembered Dr. Grimsby's vacant eyes, Dora's bloody head. She didn't want to think about them, or whoever might come after them. "Would you tell me a story?" she asked. "To take my mind off things?"

"I think we're in the middle of one right now," Marek said quietly. "Shall I tell you what happens next?"

"Please."

So he spun her a tale where they made it back to the Territories, fetched Hannie and Gaba and made a life for themselves somewhere with roses and rabbits and a little attic workshop, a place where the sky was wide and forgiving and her name was Nell. And even though she knew it was just a story, that none of it would ever be that easy, she fell asleep against him feeling like it was the truest thing she'd ever heard.

*Valerie Hunter teaches high school English and has an MFA in writing for children and young adults from Vermont College of Fine Arts. Her stories and poems have appeared in publications including Edison Literary Review, Storyteller, Room, Other Voices, and Cicada.*

# Juliet Silver & the Realm of Impossibility

## *Wendy Nikel*

In the burgundy-tinged light of the tea house, the airpilots didn't look so different than anyone else. They gathered there with their mustaches neatly trimmed and their collars buttoned tightly, sipping their oolong and Pu-erh and muttering in soft undertones, pretending they were merchants or bankers or clockwork tinkerers taking a mid-morning break from their shops.

Juliet knew better.

She knew who they were from the moment the first one sauntered in, setting the golden door-baubles jingling. He raised a hand to tip his hat with an automatic motion like a wind-up doll, and in that act, his sleeve slipped down his forearm, momentarily exposing a tiny tattoo in the shape of an airship's propeller. The pilot must have seen Juliet's curious change of expression, for he tugged his sleeve and glanced away, suddenly very interested in the brassy light fixtures dangling above the tables.

Perhaps it was because he didn't seem much older than herself or because his face gave the impression of innocence (or at least good intentions), but Juliet let him keep his secret... for the time being. After all, what business of hers was it if this stranger wanted to risk his life by breaking the embargo on sky ships?

"Peace and prosperity to you." She welcomed him with the traditional greeting of Ms. Chari's tea house as if he really were a merchant or banker or clockwork tinkerer and showed him to a table near the front window. His mouth turned up ever so slightly, as though he knew she was only playing along. "What would you like to drink?"

"Black tea, please."

Juliet gestured subtly to his napkin before nosy old Jarvis Marken in the corner could take note of the man's mistake. With an "Oh!" of sudden realization, he tucked it onto his knee and mouthed, "Thank you."

She felt his gaze following her to the back room. His eyes were as blue as the sky.

Slowly, others arrived. They filed in one at a time, always with the same, jerky salute at the door. Juliet smiled and nodded and balanced their drinks in precarious towers of brass trays. She'd have liked to pry them for stories about their lives onboard their sky ships. She'd have liked to see if the tales she'd heard were true — if there really were dark beings of wisp and smoke that hid among the clouds, and if that was the true reason for the long embargo.

But the most Juliet could do was weave through the tables, her glass kettle poised, straining her ears to catch even the slightest bits of their conversation. She felt like the mongrel that hung about the tea house's back entrance, which begged for any scrap of stale biscuit she might toss its way (which she did, whenever Ms. Chari wasn't looking).

"— he ought to have known better, steering the *Skydancer* into those clouds." The speaker possessed a glimmering monocle that he only seemed to need whenever Juliet approached his table.

"He couldn't help it, Stenson," muttered a man beside him whose suit fitted too tightly over his broad shoulders. Of them all, his disguise was the least convincing. "Clouds like that are where the devils dwell."

"Devils?"

"The Wispers, of course."

"Gasoline greaseboxes!" The old man called Stenson slammed a hand on the table, drawing the attention of the tea shop's other guests. He wiped his monocle on his vest and muttered a half-hearted apology. When the other tea-drinkers looked away, he grumbled more softly, "No such thing as Wispers, I tell you. Scientifically impossible creatures. Fairy tales!"

"Of course they're real." This time it was the young pilot, the first to arrive. Juliet left her washrag half-wrung out in the rollers of her wringer belt-attachment as she stopped to listen.

"How would you know, Brenton?" another man asked.

"I've seen 'em myself," Brenton said. "Back on old Matthews' *Perdition*."

The men hung their heads as one, and Juliet tried to recall where she'd heard the name before.

"He was a good man," the broad-shouldered man muttered.

"But you couldn't have been more than a tyke then," Stenson argued.

"True and true." Brenton blew on his tea. "He was a gentleman and an expert pilot, excepting the day he got it into his head to pursue that pair of cloud creatures. Those Wispers worked their way into his head and those of the other crewmen. I was there on the bridge to see it all."

"But you didn't jump, too?" Stenson rubbed his monocle again, as if clearing the lens would help him understand the situation better.

"Would I still be here if I did?"

"How'd you survive, then?"

"You said it yourself: I was just a tyke."

"Juliet!" Ms. Chari's face appeared over the tea-counter, though the rest of her remained hidden behind haphazard piles of tea boxes. "Stop your dawdling and get back here at once!"

The men all looked up at her and realized their error: she'd heard every word they'd spoken. The broad-shouldered man caught her wrist, pinning it to the table none too gently.

"I trust you won't be saying nothing to any authorities, miss?"

Juliet smiled serenely, trying to still the pounding of hot blood through her veins. "What's there to tell, sir? All's I've heard here are fairy tales."

\#

That evening, Juliet wiped the tables until they gleamed, washed the dishes, and counted the copper coins in the rusted old register. She threw her coat over her shoulders, snatched up her cycle goggles, she stepped out the backdoor. The mongrel was there, waiting for his evening meal with sad eyes. Juliet tossed him the remains of a crumbly tea biscuit that she'd rescued from beneath a table.

Her cycle was still leaning against the alleyway lamppost where she'd left it, but someone tall was standing beside it, his face hidden in shadows.

"You ought to know, I have a blaster in my jacket," she said loudly, with more confidence than she felt.

"Well, I sincerely hope you find no reason to use it." The voice was familiar, though it took her a moment to place it.

"You're the airpilot, the young one, from the tea house today."

"Tyler Brenton, at your service." He bowed low with a cordial sweep of his arm. "Though I'd prefer you'd use a lower voice if you'll be speaking so candidly of my occupation."

"At my service? Indeed?" Wouldn't that be a change, for someone to serve *her* for once?

"I'm here to offer you a proposition."

Juliet reached into her jacket for the purely theoretical blaster.

"A business proposition," Brenton clarified. "It would pay quite well, I assure you."

Juliet narrowed her eyes, but pulled her hand out of her jacket, which Brenton obviously interpreted as an invitation to continue.

"You see," he said. "The authorities have come down hard on airpilots as of late, and we're getting a mite anxious to get back in our ships. Life on land doesn't suit us so well. We'd arranged our meeting today to discuss plans to put an end to this embargo. See, the chancellor believes he is protecting the citizens and their goods by putting a ban on all air flight."

"Protecting them from what?"

"Why, from the Wispers, of course. We were losing at least a ship a week, sometimes more before they closed down the ports. Bad weather, poor piloting... all terrible excuses, but the people believed them. The chancellor has been covering up the true threat for years. You didn't really believe they were fairy tales, did you?"

"Of course not."

"Exactly. That's why you'll do quite well, indeed."

"Do what?"

"Why, fly, of course."

"That's preposterous. Now if you'll excuse me—" Juliet reached for the handlebar of her cycle, but Brenton placed his hand on hers.

"I know how to stop the Wispers."

"Oh, do you?" Juliet raised her eyebrow and slapped his hand away.

"I do. Like I said in there, I watched what happened, and I've been studying them, trying to work it out ever since."

Juliet pulled her cycle upright and started walking, but she couldn't bring herself to fire up the engine and drive away. "So? What did you find?"

Brenton jogged to catch up. "Well, for one thing, the Wispers haven't been around long — only the past few decades. Before the creation of the Gerald Hoffenstein flying particle disrupter, folks flew these skies for generations without ever spotting them. They're nowhere in history, myth, or legend."

"So you think that they have something to do with the particle disrupter?"

"I think they have everything to do with the particle disrupter. A friend of mine is a scientist, and I've asked him to study the disrupters' effect on cloud masses. He succeeded in creating a very small Wisper under isolated conditions in his laboratory, solely from the fumes of the disruptor."

"Why can't the pilots just stop using the particle disruptors in their ships then?"

"That's the plan. Most of us have already outfitted our ships to run without them. The problem is that the chancellor still won't lift the ban until all the Wispers are gone. They're still too big of a threat, traveling out there in that massive formation and driving men to insanity."

"What makes them so hostile?"

"We do."

Juliet drew back. "Pardon?"

"Well, not you, of course. But men. They only began wreaking havoc when men started hunting them, trying to find ways to blast them out of the sky. A useless pursuit; up until a few weeks ago no one could find anything that would harm them, but they still try, nonetheless. Sir Leon Bartholomew was the first to do so, about twenty years back, with an electrical current that only seemed to infuriate the creatures. Since then, it's as though they've gone on the attack, and they target those who they believe will harm them: men."

"And just how do you plan to stop these destructive, vengeful creatures that are impervious to harm?" Juliet asked. They were approaching the little, run-down apartment where she lived, and she suddenly felt rather ashamed of its rusted wrought-iron handrail and the door with the locking mechanisms that you had to strike just right to get them to work. "You've discovered how to stop them?"

"Oh, no, not me." Brenton shook his head. They stopped at the bottom of the apartment steps. "But my friend has. It's a reverse particle disruptor. He tested it on the Wispers he created in his lab. The problem is, we can't use it so long as the ships are grounded. If I could only get close enough to the creatures, I could try it on them, and it ought to reduce their size, if not eliminate them entirely."

"Sounds like you have it all figured out. What do you want me for?"

"The Wispers hate men. Not women. Not children. They left me and my mother both alive on the *Perdition*, though they killed off the rest of the crew. I have a ship. I have the device. I even have a way past the blockade. All I need now is someone by my side up there — someone who isn't a man — to help me keep a steady head and ensure that the job gets done."

"Well! Good luck with that then." Juliet leaned her cycle against the rusting handrail and pressed the button on its handlebar. A spring uncoiled. Gears shifted and strained as the mechanical padlock wound itself around the metal bars. As soon as the cycle was secure, Juliet started up the steps. It was late, she was tired, and although the airpilot's story was fascinating, if they kept talking like this, right outside Mrs. Perogi's window, the grouchy old landlady would surely ream her out in the morning. Besides, try as she might, Juliet couldn't imagine herself doing what Brenton described, being that person for him. It sounded daring... brave, too much so for a simple tea house girl like her.

"Wait!" Brenton pleaded. "Hear me out. The other airpilots have made a pact. Whoever can get rid of the Wispers and lift the embargo gets 10% of the other airpilots' earnings for the rest of their lives. That's 10% of twenty other airpilot's income. I'll split it with you. Fifty-fifty. It's still plenty for either of us to live on."

Juliet paused and stared at the exposed mechanisms of the door frame. From this close, she could see clearly the problem: one small gear had got bent out of shape, causing a whole series to loop around the same track over and over. Only a hard *thunk* would knock it out of its rut. Maybe this young pilot with eyes as blue as the sky was just what she needed to knock her out of hers.

"All right." She clenched her fists. "Tell me what I need to do."

The sky was bright and cloudless as the *Realm of Impossibility* launched skyward. Persuading the blockade guards to look the other way must have come at a rather great cost. Juliet tried not to think on the price of that or anything else, not now that she'd turned in her serving belt to Ms. Chari and moved her meager belongings out of Mrs. Perogi's small, second-floor apartment.

The berth Brenton offered her was twice the size of her old room, and the bed was so large that Juliet worried she'd become lost deep in the thick, fluffy blankets and mountains of pillows. But when she tried to protest, reminding him that she had no money for fare, he shook his head and refused to hear it.

"You're part of the crew," he said. "Your room and board is part of your pay."

"The crew sleep in bunks downstairs, not in fine state rooms like these."

"I certainly can't have a woman sleeping in the crew quarters. It wouldn't be proper. Besides, it's not as though we have passengers for this trip; it'd be a shame for these rooms to remain empty. Wasteful, in fact."

Juliet liked how he made it sound as though she were doing him a favor, so she shrugged and set down her bag.

"I'll let you settle in," he said. "If you need anything, I'll be just down the hall; my cabin is nearest the bridge."

"I thought captain's cabin was traditionally in the back of a ship."

"Of a sea-ship, perhaps. Things tend to go wrong more slowly at sea. An air captain must be prepared for trouble at any moment, even while he slumbers." With another of his jerky salutes, he left Juliet alone wondering what sort of trouble he expected to befall them.

A large, bowed window took up most the side wall, and when Juliet drew back the curtains, she felt like a bird. She was flying through white clouds as thick and plush as her pillows, with small snatches of blue bursting through. The sun shone more brightly than she'd ever seen, and way, way down beneath her buckled boots, was the solid ground she'd left behind.

"It only just occurred to me," Brenton said, leaning back into the doorway, "I don't believe I know your full name."

Juliet focused on a silver scribble of river far below, glimmering as it made its way to the sea. "Silver," she said, "Juliet Silver."

For the briefest of moments, Brenton looked puzzled, almost as though he somehow knew it was a lie. Then he nodded. "Good. In that case, welcome aboard, Ms. Silver."

\#

The following morning, Juliet was woken from a beautiful dream of white-feathered swans by the dinging of a bell. It took her a moment to discover its source: a pneumatic delivery chute beside the door.

She pulled herself from bed with a stretch and a yawn, wondering how she'd ever again go back to sleeping on a lesser mattress. The delivery chute's latch popped open at the slightest touch of her finger, and out dropped a brass ball. She turned it over in her hand, and it snapped open, revealing a paper folded in fourths.

"Juliet," it read. "I hope you had a restful sleep. When you've woken and breakfasted, please come find me. We have much to discuss. Sincerely, Ty Brenton."

Since the note didn't seem terribly urgent, Juliet took her time in bathing in the deep tub whose metal surface and plethora of knobs and spigots made her feel like she was in a submarine. She ate her breakfast at the window seat — along with a cup of bitter black tea, the crew's favorite — before making her way down the corridor to find Brenton.

He wasn't among the uniformed men calling out to one another in the bridge, but his cabin door was ajar, so she knocked politely and waited for an answer. Silence.

She hesitated, but her curiosity compelled her to press gently on the door until it swung open, revealing a state room not terribly unlike her own, though with the personal effects of someone far more at home on this ship than she was. Beside the door stood a round, wooden table whose single leg, bolted to the floor, reminded her a bit of the peg-leg of pirates in the stories of old. The table was cluttered with correspondence and telegraphs, but among them, Juliet spotted a tintype image of Brenton's smiling face. She glanced about her, then snuck the picture out from underneath the other letters.

Ty Brenton crouched beside a group of small children, who clung to him like rust on old iron. Their faces, though smudged and messy, all shone with bright smiles, and above their heads was the archway of an old building with a crooked sign whose letters Juliet had to squint to read.

"Portmouth Children's Home?"

Juliet flipped the tintype over but only had time to decipher a few words — *Thank you again for your generosity...* — before the jingling of the washroom handle startled her. She slid the photograph back under the other papers and called aloud. "Mr. Brenton?"

Brenton didn't seem surprised to see her there, though his hair was still wet and rumpled from bathing. "Good morning, Ms. Silver. I hope you're well rested. We've a lot to do today."

"Is that so?"

"Of course. Many of my men spent years learning to pilot a ship such as *The Realm of Impossibility* and fend off pirate attacks in the process. You've a matter of days or weeks, depending upon how quickly we can find the Wispers. Or rather, how quickly they find us."

"Pilot the ship? Fend off pirate attacks?" Juliet's voice wavered, betraying her sudden, crippling apprehensions. It was one thing to linger over customers' tables as they spoke of such terrible, exciting things, but the thought of taking part in them herself was, to say the least, unnerving.

"If Wispers drive all the men insane, and you're forced to tie us below decks to keep us from leaping to our deaths, you'd better be able to steer us out of harm's way." Brenton must have read her surprise, for he turned to her with a crease worrying his brow. "You didn't imagine that you'd be spending the voyage sitting in your cabin, sipping tea and reading penny novels, did you? You're here because I need your assistance."

Juliet pursed her lips shut, for that was precisely what she'd been imagining. When he'd spoken of her keeping the Wispers from driving him mad, she'd imagined herself directing him where to maneuver if the creatures somehow altered his perceptions, making him tea and wiping the perspiration from his brow, or perhaps even so much as slapping the sense back into him, if it came down to that. He'd never said anything about piloting the ship or defending it from marauding pirates.

"One moment." Brenton opened a trunk at the foot of his bed and sorted through the contents, pulling one particular item free. It was made of leather and brass plates, with nets of chains hanging over the top like the glimmering of diamonds in the sun. Juliet drew nearer, trying to discern its purpose.

"Here." Brenton held it up. "You'll feel much braver with this on, I assure you."

Juliet took it from him and examined it. It was armor, but with a delicacy and lightness that surprised her. "I'm to wear this?"

"It's designed to slip on quickly over your clothing." He lifted the armor piece and slid it over her head in one smooth, deft motion. It fit snugly around her torso and arms and down past her hips, with a hood in the back that could cover her entire face, save for a long eye slit. The layer of leather nearest her skin was soft, yet allowed air to pass through it. The individual links of chain clattered in and out of their rows and columns as she shifted and moved, so that the armor never bunched up nor pulled too tight. Between the layers were thin plates of brass.

"This is incredible."

"Each of the crew has armor to don if the alarm goes out that there is danger nearby. The pirates have many tricky ways of boarding an airship from nearly any direction, so once they've been spotted, there's no time for muddling about with tricky clothing."

A ding of the delivery chute interrupted, and Brenton read the message to himself. "It seems that your first lesson will have to wait. Will you meet me again after dinner? Good. Keep that armor with you. I doubt we shall need it before reaching the Mage Sea, but better to be safe."

As he turned to leave, his eyes still on the note in his hand, Juliet spoke up. "How is it that you happened to have a set of women's armor lying about?"

Brenton looked up and gave her a melancholy smile. "It was my mother's."

From then on, Juliet trained with Brenton in every free moment that he wasn't eating, sleeping, or flying the *Realm of Impossibility*. She attacked each lesson as a challenge, a test of her might and daring. Brenton was a tough instructor, giving her the same firm commands that he would any other member of his crew, but every once in awhile, Juliet's keen eyes would catch a poorly-concealed look of pride — and perhaps something else — and she took secret pleasure in these small glances.

By the end of the first week, she knew all of the parts of the ship, from the sharp bowsprit protruding from the front all the way to the powerful rudder on the stern; from the crow's nest high over their heads to the holds that carried their cargo far below.

The second week, she learned how to tell when bad weather was coming, the speed of the wind, and what rain smelled like from above the clouds. She learned navigational skills in the third week: how to read a compass and the stars.

By the fourth, Brenton determined that she was finally ready to learn the crewmen's duties. The two of them dangled high off the ground in leather harnesses and goggles, with nothing to hold them but a pulley and rope as he demonstrated how to repair minor tears to the ship's giant bladder.

After that, she learned to pilot the ship, to single-handedly man the bridge, to maneuver the ship to fend off pirate attacks, and all the ways they'd try to stop her.

Throughout these weeks, Brenton taught her swordplay as well — something for which she had a natural aptitude — so that as the sun set on the fourth week, and they finally reached the notorious Mage Sea, Juliet finally, for the very first time, found herself poised over Brenton's body with her blade pressed against his throat, instead of the other way around. Her eyes met his sky blue ones, and for a moment, the two simply remained there, breathing shared air.

Juliet lowered the blade.

"Well," Brenton said, pulling himself up from the floor. "If I didn't know you quite so well, I'd be concerned that you'd try to seize my ship out from under my nose. You'd make a fearsome pirate, Juliet Silver. I dare say you could beat half the lugs on this crew. Have you ever considered a life in the clouds?"

Juliet blushed and replaced her sword in its scabbard, which had been skillfully affixed to her armor. "With 5% of twenty men's wages, I shouldn't need to work again at all. Isn't that the idea?"

Brenton gazed out the window as the dusk-pink clouds floated by. "I'd rather be poor in the air than rich on land."

It struck Juliet as a curious sentiment, until she remembered the tintype she'd found among his letters so many weeks before. "You'd give it all away," she suggested boldly.

"Ah, so you did see the photograph that day. I'd thought my mail was a bit out of order."

"Who are they?" she asked.

"Children."

"The world has many poor children," Juliet challenged. "Why them? Why the Portmouth Children's Home?"

"They saved my life," he said simply. "I only wish to return the favor."


Juliet knew that the day would come eventually, that somewhere in this vast and peaceful sky, the Wispers would find them. She'd only hoped it wouldn't come so soon.

The alarm sounded in the middle of the night, and Juliet rose and donned her armor, praying that it was merely pirates. Weeks before, she'd have laughed at the thought of preferring pirates over anything else, but pirates were mere people, and Brenton had taught her of their strategies, their ways, and how they fought. Pirates would certainly be cause for alarm, but Wispers... Wispers still terrified her, for she hardly knew what to expect.

She passed Brenton in the corridor. He, too, was armored and ready, though it wasn't a sword in his hand as she had hoped, but the small black box that contained the reverse particle disruptor.

"Wispers, then?"

He nodded, his face looking paler and more tired than she'd ever seen it. "The crew are already locked up in their cabins. The time has come to test your mettle."

Through the massive windows of the bridge, Juliet saw the dark cloud and immediately knew that this surreal, unnatural formation was indeed, where the Wispers dwelt. It looked as though instead of water, the foreboding cloud could rain down pure malevolence and death. It grew larger and larger in the window as the *Realm of Impossibility* drew nearer.

Then, suddenly, it was upon them.

"Quick!" Brenton shouted, squeezing his eyes shut as if in pain. "Give me the blindfold and the earpiece. They're already at work. I can hear them beckoning."

Juliet brought him the items he needed and helped him set them in place, just as they'd practiced.

"The device!" he shouted, louder than he needed to. Was it due to his own impaired hearing, or to be heard over the Wispers in his head?

Juliet placed the reverse particle disrupter in his hands and closed his fingers around it. She kept her hands on his for longer than necessary. Just as she was about to pull away, he reached up to her face and leaned in toward it, planting a single, soft kiss on her lips.

"I've never had the courage to do that before," he shouted. "Now it's your turn. Be courageous for me."

Brenton attached one end of his life line to the base of the ship's wheel and the other to his harness. Though blindfolded and deaf, he maneuvered the ship gracefully, expertly, and was gone, out the port side hatch, before Juliet could gather her thoughts or stop the spinning in her head.

The slamming of the hatch, however, acted like a jolt of electricity. Juliet recalled where she was and what she was to do. She planted her feet before the ship's wheel and — with a breathless prayer — steered the *Realm of Impossibility* directly into the center of the terrifying, stormy cloud of Wispers.

Brenton's voice came through clearly in her earpiece, with the same clipped, steady tone that he'd used when they'd gone over their plan. They passed into the cloud, and it closed around them, casting a shroud about the ship and obscuring Brenton from view.

"I'm powering it on," he said. "Hold her steady!"

Juliet braced herself against the wheel. Across the bridge, alarms blared and red lights blinked of danger, but Juliet didn't waver, pushing the warnings to the back of her mind.

The reverse particle disrupter sprung to life with a click and a whir, and Juliet's heart leapt as the thick clouds surrounding Brenton swirled and thinned. His figure slowly came into view, a ghost in sparkling armor, balanced on the edge of the ship. One hand clutched a handhold and the other grasped the spinning device. His teeth were clenched tightly, and his head thrown back as if in pain. "I won't do it... I can't..."

"You can do this, Ty Brenton," Juliet shouted, hoping against hope that he'd hear her through his earpiece over the voices filling his head. "It's working. Just hold on. Just a few seconds more. Don't give up. Don't you dare let go."

The cloud swirled about, and now even Juliet could hear the howls and roars of the Wispers. They pressed their ghastly, half-formed bodies against the window glass, their faces distorted and ever-morphing. They'd discovered her deceit. They saw her purpose there, and with that realization, they called to her, too.

*Let go... Join us... Come and fly with us... Leave that silly ship behind and join us... Join us... Join us...in the air.*

Juliet squeezed her eyes shut and shouted nonsense words, listed flavors of tea from the menu of Ms. Chari's, recited her times tables and poetry she'd memorized in grammar school. Anything to keep them from her head. Anything to keep them away.

Over the chaos, she heard a familiar voice, one she'd grown to love.

"Juliet!"

At the sound of her name, her eyes sprang open, for she knew somehow, deep down, that it wasn't just a cry for help. She knew, somehow, it was goodbye.

Clear blue sky nearly blinded her. The Wispers, barely visible now, floated away, high up in the atmosphere, to gather with harmless cirrus clouds. Their voices were silenced, the hostility that had thickened the air gone, as if it'd never existed.

And hanging out of the port side hatch, a severed life line whipped in the breeze.

Even after Juliet landed the *Realm of Impossibility*, the world seemed to spin around her with dizzying speed. At the airdocks, she left the ship and the crew, not daring to look behind her for fear that she'd crumble to bits. Without Brenton, she couldn't seem to get her bearings. The world seemed so different now that she'd seen it from above.

Mrs. Perogi's apartment seemed even less welcoming than before, even staler and danker and — above all — too still. Sometimes the air seemed unbreathable. Ms. Chari accepted her return to the tea house with a curt nod and the bellowing order, "And hurry up! There's dishes to be washed!"

Every jangle of the golden baubles above the door reminded her of that day he'd first walked in. In the end, she took a broom handle and smashed them, calling it an accident. She saved one piece of the shimmering metal for herself.

With the baubles broken and nothing in place to announce the customers' arrival, Juliet was taken aback when, one morning, someone spoke her name.

"Juliet Silver?"

"Who are they asking for?" Ms. Chari bellowed from the back room.

"I've got it," Juliet hollered, then dropped her voice. "Who are you, and what do you want?"

The man wore the dark suit of a lawyer, and Juliet wondered if her little adventure had finally caught up to her. The blockade had been lifted, so she couldn't imagine that they'd be after her for that, but still... She reached for the sharp sliver of bauble-bit in her pocket.

"My name is Uric Lindenheim, and I've come to ensure that you receive that which is due you."

"I don't know what you mean."

Lindenheim turned the dials on his briefcase, and from a slot in the top popped a stiff document. "You have inherited an airship, Ms. Silver, one by the name of *The Realm of Impossibility*."

The ship dove and weaved, bobbed and cut in, until it was close enough to the *Bearer of Bad News* that they could haul it in. The crew laid planks between the two so that their captain could board the opposing ship. Heavy boots fell on the planks, and when the hatch burst open, the crew of the *Bearer* looked up from where they were cowering with expressions of shock and surprise.

"Who are you?" the *Bearer's* captain asked, sheathing his sword. If he'd had his monocle, he might have recognized the airpilot standing before him as a tea house girl who'd once served him a cup of Earl Grey.

"My name is Juliet Silver, the captain of *The Realm of Impossibility*, and I've come to collect what I'm due."

Stenson turned to his crew with a chuckle. "Stand down, boys. She's just a girl. I'm afraid, though, young lady, that I don't know what you mean."

"10% of your earnings to the pilot who rid the skies of the Wispers. That pilot, old man, is me."

"I'm afraid you weren't part of the deal." Stenson's face suddenly turned stony.

"Perhaps not, but Ty Brenton was, and he's left me in charge. I won't be put off by a technicality."

"I don't want to harm you, girl." Stenson narrowed his eyes and drew his sword.

"Oh, I assure you. You won't."

Ten minutes later, Juliet Silver released the *Bearer of Bad News* back into the skies, a few hundred golden coins lighter.

"Do you think that he'll do it?" her first mate asked. "That he'll tell the others that you're calling them out on their refusal to hold up the bargain?"

"He does pilot *The Bearer of Bad News*, does he not?"

"You do know that we'll be considered pirates now, ma'am?"

"Someone once told me that I'd make a good pirate. I suppose now we'll see if he was right."

The first mate nodded thoughtfully. "Where to now, Ms. Silver?"

Juliet's hand strayed to the belt in her pouch, to the tintype that she kept within it. "Next stop, Portmouth Children's Home. We've a delivery to make there."

*Wendy Nikel is a speculative fiction author with a degree in elementary education, a fondness for road trips, and a terrible habit of forgetting where she's left her cup of tea. Her short fiction has been published by Analog, Beneath Ceaseless Skies, Nature, and elsewhere. Her time travel novella series, beginning with The Continuum, is available from World Weaver Press. For more info, visit wendynikel.com*

# Pirates of the Tomes

*Riv Rains*

"… passed today. All literature of a non-council legislated variety is to be surrendered to the state in an unprecedented initiative to curb social disorder. Any material not surrendered voluntarily within the month shall be seized and destroyed on sight. Authorities warn that charges will be laid for noncompliance. From today, authorities will be out in force..."

Lassa snapped off the wireless and wedged soft, pale, academic's fingers into arduously coiffed, earthy curls.

A literature prohibition.

Curse the lot of them.

Pushing up from her desk with an agitated growl, she kicked savagely at pretentious aubergine skirts all the way to her ridiculously opulent, antique brass webbed window.

Such a society! Useless!

Beyond the glass lay trash strewn waters, smoke-stained stone, billowing steam, raging fires, and the incessant clanging of warning bells. Since the ice caps had finally melted, it was a place gone mad.

Rain slicked down the panes, forlorn in its attempt to wash the city clean. Over the last seven years, she'd watched from the library as the waters rose. The coast and fields had drowned first, then the industrious suburbs—sprouting with all manner of adapted floating villages—then, finally, in an inching, muddy creep culminating three months ago, the city proper.

That's when the 'important' people's panic built. When the high society and Council noticed. When things started changing for worse rather than better.

Lassa's sigh steamed the window.

From the onset, there'd been rioting. Eventually, the incensed populace had been pushed out of these higher areas, and the streets had been lifted as piers to bob on the filthy water. For a good few months, the high society folks had strolled in peace, parasols fluttering, brass gleaming. Lately though, it had come full circle.

Shortages had begun eating the stitching from the richest pockets.

She slumped against the glass, watching a child below. He'd turned skipping charred deck boards into a game on his way home. At least, she hoped he had a home. Many didn't.

Lassa herself had secretly moved into the library.

Her solitary office now housed her meagre possessions. No one ever came to the second floor anyway. If they did, they'd find the librarian washing in her sink and reading while eating cold beans from an outdated can. Except for the books, it wasn't comfortable, and the boy on the pier seemed far happier than Lassa had been in a very long time.

Brooding, she stalked away from the window, out of her mezzanine office and down the wrought-iron stairs to the main stacks. Tiny brass lamps, warmed by lazy filaments, yawned as she passed.

At random, Lassa took down a volume and let her fingers flick through its comforts. The shadow and fall of each soft sheet soothed her soul. Palm laid flat on a page, the author seeped into her bones.

'—*the dazzling brass spiral stair seemed to welcome her. A glittering coil, leaping above on the far side of the expanse, its crest catching at a darkened landing and perhaps, a way up and out.*'

Ashen, she sank, her skirts mushroomed upon the aged carpet, sorrow sweeping out in hollow wails.

The waste of it all!

Was she supposed to go home to... what? Sweep docks? Weld? Oh, she'd happily do the work, but such wasted years! Folding over her knees—book clutched to corset—Lassa pressed into her grief.

"You alright, Miss?" Mister Stoney, the door guardsman, hovered at her hip.

Lassa sucked in her heart and pushed up. "Oh! No, I'm not." She sniffed—alright, snorted. "I just heard the announcement that they'll be destroying all this." The tremble of her hand waving about her sanctuary tightened into a fist. "I hate it. I hate them all!"

Stoney, acting the gentleman, tried to avert his eyes from her dishevelled form. Rocking on restless boot heels, hands gripped behind his jacketed, vested back, he flattened blunt lips and shook a head of mousy hair. "I heard it too. Thought maybe I should call on you, check you weren't..." He flushed.

His efforts were almost enough to make her smile, if only she wasn't at despair's door.

Her inhale fluttered the ribbon-tails upon the shelf, before bursting forth in a tsunami of drowned etiquette. "I'll have to go home!" The wail howled through the antique rafters, disturbing spiders and lifting dust from the iron bracing.

Grasping at propriety, he hovered about her. "Miss Lassa! There, there! It'll be alright!"

Poor Stoney, casting about for help that wasn't there. The library was closed. Had been for a week since the country had fallen into unrest. The desks all sat in darkness, their echoes muttering to themselves more each day.

Eventually, the air began to find its way about her ribs again, and Stoney ventured into verbal waters.

"I'm so sorry Miss Lassa." He shook his head at the stacks. "Makes you wish there was some way of smuggling them all out, doesn't it?" He chuckled awkwardly, like it was the silliest notion in the half sunken world.

Which it was.

If you weren't married to the bloody things like she was.

Smuggle them?

Could they do that?

"How?" She blurted it, clutching at the shelves, her fingers sliding down the many lives kept there.

Stoney's gaze landed squarely on her tear-stained face. "I beg your pardon?" He offered her his hand.

"How?" The word leapt out of her again as he deposited her exuberantly on her feet. Goodness, he was strong. Just the thing for smuggling books.

"I'm sure I don't know what you mean, Miss."

"Mister Stoney." Lassa brushed at her skirts, buying time to collect her scattered wits. "Would I be right to assume your livelihood is also in jeopardy—as well as mine—if all of these shelves are burned?" She fixed him with a sharp stare not even water could outrun.

"If they burn it all?" He glanced about. "I can only assume my services here will stumble upon hard times, yes." He narrowed a patina-green gaze at her sudden mischievous grin. One eyebrow lifted. "Miss Lassa, I do believe you are going to get me in trouble."

Lassa beamed. "Call me Lass, please." She gave him a crooked smile. "And Mister Stoney? I do propose a partnership!"

The next dawn, Stoney found himself still awake, fortified by sweet black tea, pouring over hastily detailed plans in Lassa's office.

"How big could the crates be?" Lassa tapped at a page of calculations and crumpled her brow into considering the complexities.

"To carry them down there, around one and a half feet square, if we can find them that size. Need to be sealed and nailed too, and marked as some incongruous sundry, like soap cake." He leaned on the table across from her, attempting to keep his mind on the job.

She wasn't making that easy.

Lassa shook her head at him, scribbling over her sums. The hair he'd longed to weave through his fingers for years danced morning light across the backs of his hands. Distracted, Stoney made tired, mollifying sounds, until her words dawned on him.

"I beg your pardon? That was surely the number of books, not crates?" He couldn't have heard her right.

"Six hundred crates, Mister Stoney." Her velvet brown gaze hooked onto his. "Eighteen thousand books. Approximately thirty in each, including protection."

He felt the lump in his throat stick. Disbelief lodged there like a turned sheep in the drafting race. "Let me get this straight." He jerked a thumb over his shoulder at the stacks. "Exactly how many of these are you expecting to take?"

A wickedness unfurled on her face. There was no other way to describe the change. It wasn't light so much as colour. A rose in her cheeks, the white of her teeth as they clicked together behind her devilish smile, and not to be outdone, those velvety brown eyes of hers, flashing like that sun across his hands. Oh mercy, he was done for.

"All of them."

"*All* of them?"

"All of them."

Oh, dear god. He was going to hang.

A week had passed. The first six dozen crates had been delivered, ripe for packing, and that evening, the master craftsman himself would arrive by boat at the side portico to secure his initial payment.

The flutter of excitement preyed on her lip all day.

Following the announcement, they'd been placed under a restricted order. Lassa was to find and catalogue all the volumes the Council sanctioned. Naturally, Lassa wasn't surprised when the council's own members began visiting, then sneaking off with unlisted books under the pretence of 'legal insight'.

She was almost certain there was little common law within the pages of Eve's Giant Peach.

In silent retaliation, her own favourites had been hidden in her office for days. She was stowing several more beneath the foot of her desk—clutching the first to be sacrificed to the craftsman against her chest—when the library's front door banged open.

Lassa's head thumped up under the desk.

With a panic, she swept to the second-floor banister, one hand grasping its brass rail, her skirt hoops knocking the decorative iron panels with a twang. Someone had come into the library, and by the sound of Stoney's overly loud commentary, they weren't there for the best of reasons.

Clattering down the stairs, she flicked her eyes to the clock. Its black and brass majesty dangled two stories up, each of the five identical faces now showing ten-minutes-to-six with antique Victorian certainty.

Bloody hell! The craftsman came at exactly six o'clock!

Stomach churning, Lassa skidded to a halt just beyond the foyer, her free hand doing a brief composure check in a polished copper panel. Skirts, breasts, hair. Good.

She plastered a charming smile on her face and swanned around the corner.

Her *free* hand.

Her heart skipped a cog.

She still held the volume promised to the craftsman.

The mistake chipped her smile, just as the intruder turned from removing his gaudy saffron bowler hat and matching coat—ego in hand.

A Councilman. A founding member, no less.

Councilman Menthor's portly belly waltzed over to Lassa, introducing itself with a flash of polished adornments. "The Librarian herself! How wonderful! I'm *so* glad I got to meet you before all this delicate business claimed you, my dear!" His smile was gold and lurid. "Councilman Hubart J. Menthor Senior, at your service." His hand swept up hers, clasping it within a clammy, pudgy embrace, seemingly chopped into sausages by a variety of heavy rings.

Lassa grimaced, teeth audibly clicking together beneath her painted smile.

Council members like him, stood in offices like hers—with less backbone than her corset—making architectural plans to shore up their favourite boutiques, and little else.

Delightful.

As the man salivated kisses upon her imprisoned fingers, her gaze flicked to Stoney. A struggle of frustration and apology appeared to be taking war with her guardsman's face. She shook her head once, pointedly dragging his gaze to the magnificent clock.

Eight-minutes-to-six.

Lassa cleared her throat. "The pleasure is all mine, Councilman, though a true pity under such circumstances." She spoke to his balding head, while attempting to smoothly tuck the booked hand behind her back. No such luck.

A pudgy hand snaked out to snatch at her other wrist.

"But what's this? Such a law-abiding lady as yourself, surely not reading in a time of prohibition?"

To her dismay, his fingers attached to the book with an alligator's strength. She watched hopelessly as hers went white in resistance, the book's leather squeaking in protest.

Heart in mouth, she licked her teeth.

Seven-minutes-to-six.

No help from Stoney, he seemed mired in a sort of ashen-sweaty hell.

How could she keep that book? It was the only thing the craftsman wanted for his silence!

Lassa righted her smile.

Her fingers firmed on the volume, her smile deepening into the socially acceptable version of purring acid. "Oh, come now, Councilman! Don't you entertain such a notion!" She tugged on the book, while tipping at the hip, bringing her eyes level with his. "I merely catalogue, of course."

His eyes flicked from the book to her breasts, and finally—thankfully—up to her face.

A moment of tension followed. A pendulum in the Councilman's eyes, deciding if it should swing left to freedom, or right upon their necks.

Lord help her, she winked.

It swung left.

"Marvellous! Of course you do." Mercifully, he released the book, both of his hands instead patting at the one of hers still captured.

Behind him, Stoney deflated, the tense line of his shoulders folding in a silent exhale. He glanced at the clock.

Would it read five-minutes-to-six?

Lassa flattened her lips and straightened. "So, what can you and I, the last of the literates, do for a man such as yourself on such a late hour?" She fluttered her lashes, hating herself for every bat.

Finally, he released her hand. It took a will not to wipe it off in the folds of her skirts.

"I rather thought I'd check you were in order here. Obviously, we know where these books are, so there's no great hurry in that regard—all destroyed in due time don't fret, got to keep the people from straying—but I do want to implore you to think of safety!" He leaned in conspiratorially. "There have been some worrisome reports that certain… *items*… may have been removed from these premises." He cast his eyes back at Stoney. "Do you perhaps need more… *reliable* security?"

It took a moment for her strained mind to catch the meaning. Stoney? They suspected Stoney? The gears in her head stuttered and hauled. No, something else… someone had seen the council members 'borrowing'. He wasn't going to say who—he'd never implicate his own— but instead, he'd pay such a visit, not accompanied by law enforcement, and because he was now endeared with her, he'd err on the side that Stoney was the problem.

"Mister Stoney?" She wet her lips. To lie? To admit? To bluff? Finally, she circled on the only option that would keep them intact. "Why he's an absolute doll!" Sheer, dim wittedness. "I don't know what I'd do without his burly shoulders to lean on!"

Two-minutes-to-six.

Please don't let him be early!

Her thoughts clattered. Could Stoney head the craftsman off? Keep him from using the damned side-door bell? No, he couldn't leave his post without condemning himself. So, it was all about timing. Namely, getting the Councilman across the threshold as swiftly as possible.

Time to go!

She twirled herself around the Councilman's girth, slid the book to Stoney in a skirt covered sleight of hand, collected the saffron hat and coat, then somehow shoehorned the man into both while ushering him to the door.

Lassa shot Stoney a covert apology before she drew the Councilman in for her own spot of confiding. "Truly, I'm not certain how bright he is—I swear I've never seen him read a word—but he is ever so sweet, always doting on me, and really, how can we disparage him for that?!" She laughed gaily, tipping her head back like a limpet, hating the way he stroked her throat with his eyes.

One-minute-to-six.

He stepped through the open door in her hand.

"Ah. Well, helping those who know no better is what we at the Council are all about! We'll be in touch before this is all done and dusted." He leaned back in, assaulting her senses with his sticky breath. "And don't you worry, for a charm such as yours, I think perhaps we can find some *other* suitable employment when that time comes."

He winked.

She shuddered.

Lumbering down the tiled steps, the Councilman turned back at the bottom, a line of lamp-lit sausages winking farewell as he dipped his hat.

The majestic clock rang six.

Lassa breathed out, her adrenaline leaking down the stairs after him. She sagged against the frame as he disappeared down the sluggish street-pier, hopefully for the final time.

As she turned, the faint tinkle of the side-doorbell rang through the library.

Lassa smiled.

He was doing it for her.

Stoney grunted as he lowered the crate carefully beside the trapdoor. His laboured breathing showed just how damned heavy they were, even for a man built like him. Glancing at the pocket watch hitched to his vest, he dropped upon the crate for a few minutes of peace until their first loading was set to begin.

It wasn't to be a swift process. The 'borrowed' barge would arrive below, then be loaded by Stoney throughout the day, until the clock struck eleven each evening.

Upon that hour, Lassa's contacts would supposedly reappear at a side portico and spirit the books out through tunnel and night.

He reached up with both hands, stretching the kinks from his punished shoulders. God, he was sore, and it was only day one! Stoney swatted the hanging gantry system out his way, barely ducking before it made its comeback to clout him.

He glared up at the wicked hook slung around a series of large, geared cogs and pulleys, all designed to lower the crates easy as a feather. Most would assume an engineer or docky had rigged the gears, but they'd be plum wrong.

Lassa was more than the circumference of her skirts.

In fact, Lassa was incomprehensibly clever.

"Are they here yet?" The lady in question swept in, raising an eyebrow at the sight of him loitering about.

With a bemused groan, like those you utter after Christmas dinner, he hoisted himself up with two fingers in the crook of that hook. Stoney glanced at his watch, just as a ringing thrum sounded from chains below.

"You're sure you want to do this?"

Lassa implored the ceiling. "For the hundredth time, yes."

"And this is family?"

"Certainly is."

"You're sure we should include them in this?"

"Certainly am."

The cloying stench of old sewage assaulted his nose as he threw back the timber hatch. She set her toes to the edge and peered down into the gloom. "Hello, Dad! We'll be down in a pinch!"

Stoney stood still, looking between her and the dark in disbelief. "Your father? He's the one in on this?"

"Yes. Do stop being obvious." She huffed about, pacing the edges of the trap door while undoing corset laces. "Now, the real question is, how are you with women on ladders, in their underwear?"

He wasn't sure what she was expecting, but the full rolling laugh she won from him felt better than all his days gone by. He couldn't help it. She was sensational.

Twenty-two days to move a library.

What could possibly go wrong?


Lassa was woken by yelling in the streets.

The last few weeks, she had been falling asleep at her desk. As she groped her way through the dark office, orange flashes of light danced across both skin and ceiling.

Flames.

To be more specific, bonfires on barges. Rows of them. Soldiers marching in and out of buildings, arms loaded with books. Precious, innocent books.

Lassa's heart wept.

While she watched, their regimented boots drummed upon winding stairs, rickety landings, and bobbing piers to the floating, burning piles. Some folk stood back, hugging, cowled by the show of force, others yelled from their knees; their hands cuffed behind their heads to the pier railings.

No matter which group, they all witnessed knowledge's extinction.

Below it all, like a wailing mourning, she heard the authors crying.

Her knees buckled. She fell, skin squealing down the glass in her near faint.

Stoney's hands wrapped around her corset.

He lifted her, steadied her knees, not flinching when her fingers flattened over his, gripping his strength to her heaving ribs.

Beneath his grasp, the first wail ripped out of her, book flames shining in her eyes. Without a word, Stoney turned her away, his arms wrapping her soundly. She let her face fall into the safety of his chest; let the soft scent of him fill her burning lungs. He was soap, he was comfort, and a faint musty note from far below the streets; a reminder of all they were trying to achieve.

It wasn't enough—not when the streets were burning—but at least to her for a moment, he was hope.

Lassa cried.

She woke on the chaise lounge, the folds of Stoney's overcoat sliding from her shoulder.

The library door crashed open.

A gust of cool, smoky air swept through the stacks, climbed her stairs, and toyed with the golden lace on her indigo hems.

Lassa leapt to her feet, breath already hurried. Who was that? She heard male voices. Too many male voices. Sweeping to the rail, she plunged down the staircase as fast as her boots and hems would allow, glancing at the few remaining packed crates hidden away in the stacks.

Tonight's load was the last.

The clock presiding over the library chimed eight.

Still loading time. That meant Stoney was down below.

No one would keep them from entering.

Lassa hiked up her skirts and bolted for the foyer, hoping it wasn't too late. She skidded around the final corner to face the heavy double doors, keenly aware she stood within the empty bones of her institution. Once she opened those, the only thing between her and misconduct was one visible stack, prefaced with the Council's sanctioned tomes. They were useless things not worth their bark, but right then, she sent them a prayer. They would have to be enough.

She jerked her silken corset low, flipped her hair, heaved back the timber, and sashayed into the foyer.

To find soldiers.

Forming up on her vintage tiles.

At their side, stuffed like a turnip into a plum velvet sack, was Councilman Menthor. The wind left Lassa's chest in a whoosh. He was speaking to a commander in his self-important way. The commander and his men—all pressed in black and brass—stood like soldier dolls, their weapons and buttons glinting in the lamps. Lassa caught at a door, nails biting the grain.

Nothing for it.

She had to get rid of them.

With or without her father, the barge had to finish the load and be gone.

Her tongue caught sharp between her teeth, dissecting options. She eyed their holsters. Dark leather at their hips, more hanging over their shoulders. Rifle barrels bristled like a forest over their heads. Indeed, it looked ominous, yet she was nearly certain they wouldn't harm her, even if they did know what the game was.

"Gentlemen." She swept as far into the room as she could, while still using her hoops to block the doors. "So many of you! And so well appointed! To what do I owe this pleasure?" Lassa tried to purr; to ingratiate as many as she could before they dismissed her as a ruse and shoved past.

She shifted her weight, each weapon concealed about her person feeling unusually heavy. Who ever heard of an armed librarian? Books were her weapons. Knowledge was supposed to be her power.

"Ah, the Librarian!" The Councilman abandoned the commander's sleeve, waving back the soldiers as he waddled to catch up Lassa's limp, outstretched hand.

Lassa half curtsied. "Back so soon? Surely we aren't due to be… cleaned… for another few days yet?" While he was salivating over her wrist, she eyed her foyer's temperament and rehashed her calculations.

They weren't going to be dissuaded easily.

Loaded or not, their exit was now scheduled.

Lassa cursed the Council. They'd been banking on that extra time to ensure the trail was cold before anyone came knocking.

Would her father be safe? Would her family?

The Councilman's pungent breath wafted over her. "It's the council, you see. They simply cannot abide this dangerous resource standing while there's such foolery in the streets."

A hollow pain emptied her of any response. Foolery? People were suffering out there! And the burning? All that knowledge… her jaw worked, mute of sound. Disgust began filling her from the boots up. Was she supposed to agree with such dross? As her heartbeat raced, all she could feel was the destruction she'd stood witness to hours before, and the willing, steady comfort of Stoney's arms.

Would Stoney stay hidden?

Her neck muscle twitched with the desire to glance back for him. She thought she covered it well, plastering on a smile to shame the lamps, but the slow lift of Councilman's chin told her otherwise.

"Dear lady. Where is your guardsman tonight?"

Lassa felt her smile ratchet too tight.

"My Guardsman?" Her gaze flicked over the various fingers, only a syllable away from so many triggers. "Would you believe he didn't show today? Just left me in the lurch! Defenceless!" She cast an aptly trembling hand over her bodice, seeming to flutter at her heart. "And with all that... mess in the streets!"

Lassa stepped forward, clutching at the Councilman's wrist and lapel, crushing his ostentatious velvet in truly desperate hands. Her watery doe eyes gazed into his, beseeching him to feel her plight.

She felt the confusion set him off balance.

Perhaps a man built such as he, should have been more prudent of such a thing.

She spun him on his heel, his wrist jerked up tight between her breasts and his back, stuck her tiny brass cleavage pistol in his ear, and smiled sweetly for the foyer full of barrels, now expertly trained over his shoulder.

"Now then. Let's not ruin his revolting velvet, agreed?"

All the way to the far end of the Library, the Councilman spat profanities. While some were colourful, none were as repulsive as the growing stench of exertion and frustration wafting up from his overstuffed collar.

"Unhand me, you waxen wench! Pitiless prude! Pockmarked pariah!" The purple of his complexion nearly matched his suit.

Alliteration? She longed to roll her eyes, but they were firmly trained on the heavy foyer doors, hastily barred behind their shambling retreat.

As she hoisted him along, Lassa spared a forlorn glance for the railing of her office and the parts of her that would remain there. Never again would she stand on that landing, at that window, or perch on her desk. The only place that felt like home in the whole blasted city, gone from her reach.

"Treacherous tramp! Dissident dogue! Filthy whore!"

Absurdly, a laugh bubbled out of her. Finally! Straight out cussing!

While his free hand waved wildly, grasping pointlessly, she glanced over her shoulder. Nearly. Not far to go. She edged as quickly as she could around the final stack, aiming for the shadowy door in its far reaches. Halfway down, three crates still waited.

Books; her friends for so very long, left behind to die.

It carved a piece of her heart out to abandon them, but there was nothing to be done. The Councilman ranted tunelessly in her ears as a wad of sadness filled her throat. A waste! Worse, while they had packed and stowed a good deal of their gear in case such a thing happened, every abandoned clue would lead the Council that much faster to her family.

Blinking back tears, Lassa fought her first flush of regret.

The scream of shattering glass rang on every side.

She was surrounded?!

She was panicking!

Lurching backwards, gasping for courage, the door handle struck her hard in the shoulder blade. A short rush of relief was swiftly swamped as the Councilman began throwing himself about, bellowing their location. She clapped a hand over his golden teeth with a curse. How was she going to get out? She had no intention of taking him with them, but the thought of actually shooting him…

Chaos and the heavy thud of large boots pressed her heart to the door.

Gunfire smoked across the remaining shelves, bursting through the timber in a shower of antique splinters.

Lassa shrank against her exit. She had one move left.

Her pale academic's finger slid, sweaty upon her brass trigger. One after the other, the pistol gears began twisting—

The handle turned in her back.

Through a crack, the sweet, calming voice of Stoney slipped by her ear.

"My lady, your chariot awaits."


There was no other way. Both on their backs, legs in the air, panting.

"I think I'm getting the hang of it, either that or I can no longer feel my feet. What about you?" Lassa's whisper echoed through the tunnel, a breath dancing around dripping stone and plunking... other things.

"Perhaps," —his chuckle turned his whisper hoarse around the edges— "Maybe we've found the rhythm, but I'll have it noted this was not my idea of stealthy transport." He wheezed a little as the current beneath them shifted, the long narrow barge pressing their knees into their sockets against the walls.

Lassa couldn't blame him. Canal Legging—on your back upon a barge outrigger, walking the tunnel curve as propulsion—wasn't the funnest way to travel. In order of preference, there was most likely airship, steam ferry, steam buggy, steam train, horse, cycle, foot and probably rowboat, *then* Canal Legging.

It was so distasteful in fact, that it hadn't been done for hundreds of years. Her father used the steam engine and a docky on either side to pole the walls, but Lassa didn't have two experienced assistants, nor a way of hushing the engine while being hunted.

Which made Legging perfect for the duo's silent escape beneath the city, despite the fact it was murderously slow, exceedingly difficult, and utterly exhausting.

"How much further?" Stoney's growl issued from the dark.

Lassa consulted the compass and clock on the leather bracer she'd strapped to her left arm—from previously stowed items—complete with miniature finger dynamo to illuminate them. "Ten more minutes, one more lift gate and it's engine time." It came out grateful. In truth, her adrenaline had ebbed out to exhaustion. Had she nearly pulled the trigger? Surely not. Discomfort of every sort abounded. She might be free of the hoops, but her thin undergarments were soaked, grit and slime kept falling in her mouth, and an abominable cramp may never leave her left hip.

Thank goodness she knew where she was going.

When the floods were coming, the city had sealed the effluent water tunnels off and hoped for the best. Some had held, others hadn't. No wonder, since some basement access like Lassa's still remained undetected. She'd travelled the undercity passages with her father's work boats as a girl. Lassa could still navigate the flaking paint markers and rusting lift mechanisms from all those years ago.

Afterall, one should never underestimate the Shipwright's daughter.

"Lass?"

"Stoney?"

A pause in the dank dark, laced with the steady rhythm of their timed steps and breathing.

"I'm sorry I didn't come for you straight away."

He hadn't come bounding to her rescue, no. He'd loaded a final crate, hidden their traces using pre-prepared dust buckets, and readied the barge for a hasty departure even though she was above, fielding the Councilman.

"No apologies. You did what I would have; what needed to be done."

In the following silence, she listened to the swirls of his breath dancing along the tunnel, wondering what he was thinking. Could he tell she nearly killed a man?

"Just, thank you for trusting me." Stoney's voice rose softly in the shadows.

Lassa exhaled slowly. When was the last time someone had thanked her? She blinked back the sudden blur from her eyes. "Thank you for not running scared."

That seemed enough for then.


Stoney ran a forearm over his brow for the hundredth time. Damn fog. Surely they both looked a sight. Gone were the suits and skirts of finery made for society row. Before emerging from the tunnels, they'd changed entirely to typical docky garb—complete with leather vests, stained greaser caps, and a clinking assortment of brass trappings.

Lassa blinked up at him, hands on the wheel bitten pink by cold. The damp night glittered on her lashes in the wash of golden console lights.

She was gorgeous.

"Two more miles and we'll see the Yard lights." Lassa had to raise on tip toes to yell it, still only coming to his chin. Now they were in more open, everyday channels, the engines were in full choir, a billow of steam thickening the fog behind them.

"Good! I could use a drink!" He tucked the words in the back of her collar over the splash of the hungry rear paddle wheel.

Stoney leaned on the pitted brass sheeting of the engine cover and let it steadily strip heat from his arse. At least it lessened the ache in his legs, if not his head. His sharp eyes never stopped moving. While it was normal for dockies to be armed, their regalia was perhaps a little more than standard.

Holstered at both hips, then draped with cartridge belts, they'd agreed to overlook the discrepancy in authenticity, purely to enforce the idea that they in fact, meant business.

True to her word, the haunting amber burn of her father's Yard lights soon swam into view. Stoney'd heard the industrial waters were unique, but he wasn't prepared.

Like ghosts from the gloom, all around them floating livelihoods emerged. Warehouses, forges, market gardens, workshops—all watching from the dark—a hodgepodge of salvaged metals sheeting each roof and wall.

Home was amongst all of that?

He was just cracking his jaw to ask, when a recognizable ahoy set them on a flurry of readying ropes, venting boilers, and back paddling.

"Aye! Here be pirates!" Lassa's father's jovial smile swung into focus, bending a salt and pepper beard around the lamp in his hand. "Get in here before we all get scurvy." He belly-laughed and swept their line around an overhead mechanical monstrosity in expert loops.

"Dad! You made it! I was so worried! The soldiers, then the fog—I was wondering if you'd be here to haul us in at all!" Lassa skipped across the gap, throwing her arms around her father's neck.

Whether Stoney was ready or not, the barge began to whine in sullen protest against the secured line. It appeared he and it were being towed along the work dock towards cavernous, pontooned doors by a geared arm, greased and blackened within an inch of its life.

Cursing, he clamoured across on his knees before they both disappeared.

The damp seeped through his wet shins with a sarcastic laugh.

Boats. Why did it all have to be boats?

"Stoney, no trouble I trust?" Mister Harper—or Harp as he preferred—was watching him fumble about on the dock with an amused glint in his eye.

"No trouble, Sir. Just the usual, and the fact I can't seem to walk on water like your girl, here." They both smiled down at her affectionately.

"You might want to work on that, sonny. Seeing as what you've signed up for." He squeezed Lassa. "You filled him in?"

"No, I was waiting to show him! If we go to the Yard…"

Harp laughed. "Why don't we get him warm, then dry, then drunk, and *then* fill him in."

Her father's gnarled hands clapped them both on the shoulder, even as Lassa began to protest.

Stoney let out a relieved sigh. "Harp, I like you more all the time."


"That's the last of it."

Lassa pushed her hair back with the cleanish section of forearm, catching her vented brass welding mask with the other hand. She blinked, squinting at Stoney's silhouette approaching down the work-barge, cut against the bright rectangle of the Yard's open door.

He rolled to a cautious stop beside her, his water legs getting better every day—though not if you asked him. He handed her a battered tin mug, curls of steam still drifting from the contents. Yard tea was restorative stuff. Even Stoney had got behind it.

Before she could intervene, he leaned one hip on the hull she'd been welding, raising his mug to his mouth. Of course, the two barges parted at his pressure. He squawked, leaping away in a flurry of arms and legs. A slosh of tea hitting the water in a cascade of sorry steam.

Unable to stop herself, Lassa tipped her head back and laughed uproariously.

Hands to knees, Stoney bent, panting, his mug hanging empty from one finger.

Coughing up guilt, Lassa swooped in and tugged the mug from his grip.

"Am I ever going to get used to this?" His face tilted up to her, tired and worn. He might not be a natural at the craft or the water, but he was working hard as any other. Stoney had proved tough as good leather, warm as a blanket, and strong as the steel she'd just welded.

With a deft flourish, she poured a half portion of her tea into his mug. "That depends how long you do it for." Resolutely, she pulled him up and pushed the mug into his hand. Lassa wrapped her scarred, dirty fingers around his. "Give it time, Stoney."

"You make it look easy."

His downtrodden tone took little chips off her heart.

She squeezed at his fingers. "For me, it is. I was born to this. For you, it'll come. Just need to be patient." Her voice fell gently between them, brushing the curls of steam up into his face. She had the sudden urge to nuzzle his jaw.

Stoney's gaze searched hers. "Why do you want me here?"

Unbalanced, Lassa stumbled back, her mouth opening and shutting like a guppy. "I… umm, well, you were there!" Lassa grimaced. That was an unfortunate choice of phrase. "No! I mean…" She trailed off, knowing she was already defeated.

His gaze had cooled. The shutters rattling down over anything that had just played between them. "That makes sense. Sure." Stooping, he poured the re-gifted tea back in her mug with a slosh. "You earned that more than me." He turned, heading for the gangway. "I'll let you get back."

The ways in which to undo his hurt scattered like ball bearings. "Thanks for the tea!"

It hung hollow as his mug.


Stoney hadn't left.

He'd thought about it. He was running out of time to throw his part in, but as yet, he hadn't the conviction.

They were loading, the sinuous line of the five copper-clad ferry barges—each eighty feet long and twenty wide, hulls rusted as the water was brown—swaying eagerly against the lines and dock bumpers.

Harp's most trusted workers scrambled over every rivet of the vessels like work-stained crabs. The Yard was alive with the virgin splashing of testing paddle wheels, the yells and clanging of adjusting rudder linkages, and a soft fog of steam as they tempered the boiler.

And Stoney? He hauled crates, then held heavy things in place, while everyone else did the real work.

Useless.

He didn't belong. Maybe that's why she'd never asked him to come on the next leg of her venture.

Broody steps carried him to the quiet end of the dock. Buried back in the Yard shadows, the piles of rope and parts usually gave him somewhere to sit and think.

"Jus' you get down here a minute and hold this for an old timer."

It took Stoney a moment to find Harp. Ludicrously, the man was hanging on a roped board slung over the stern — lantern in hand — boots inches from the water.

Bemused, Stoney wove his way through the crate lined carriage, got belly down on the deck and peered over the edge at the crazy Shipwright.

Harp's nod indicated a paint pot by Stoney's shoulder. "Hold that down 'ere where I can get at it better, will ya?" After a few moments of careful, meticulous brush strokes on the hull, Harp broke the silence. "What's troubling ya, sonny?"

"Why did Lassa leave?" Stoney creased his brow at his own unexpected question, then hurried on. "It's just, she seems so happy here. She's a natural at all of this. It's perfect for her. The books, the work — it lights her up." Stoney shrugged, sloshing paint dangerously. "I just don't see why she ever chose differently."

Harp considered, while turning the tail of his painted letter out with a flourish. "Well, truth be told, she didn't want to leave. Matter of fact she damn near disowned the lot of us for making her." He shot a look up at Stoney. "There was nothing here for her but settling down. That didn't suit. Besides, we weren't as well off then," — he chuckled — "less books!" His cheeks hitched in a smile, then turned to a weary sigh. "All we had for her was a future of mud and heartache." He shook his head as if remembering. One white-painted finger scratched in his beard. "Was mad as a cut eel for a good many moons, but she came round once she found her library. Gave her something to hold on to. The great pursuit of knowledge! Reckon that's the only reason she stayed put in the end. Otherwise, she'd have washed up on my dock the minute she finished studying like a bad buoy."

Stoney blinked. "She never wanted to go?" Why hadn't she mentioned that? He frowned. She'd stayed for the books? The memory of her pistol buried in the Councilman's ear flashed down his spine. A cold realisation caught at his gut. "She'd do anything for those books, wouldn't she?"

Harp poked the brim of his hat higher with the back of the brush, surveying his work. "I might be old, but I still see the truth before I fall over it."

Stoney blinked. Harp might, but apparently, *he* didn't.

Shoving to his feet, Stoney marched square shouldered back to the dock.

'Anything' included *him*.


"Go on. Ask me. I'll wait." Lassa watched Stoney's arms fold over his chest, the borrowed work-shirt straining at the seams.

Her tongue stuck to the roof of her mouth.

Stoney rolled his eyes. "Were you ever going to invite me on this next part, or just tow me along, assuming I wanted to be a pirate lackey for life?" His face was a cross between anger and hurt, which forced it into shapes that cut at his brow, and her insides.

Carefully, she wiped sweaty palms down her work pants.

If only she could read humans like books.

"Lass? Don't try to choose your words!" He threw his hand along the line of waiting barges, for all the world looking like he'd bite a hole in every hull. "If I keep trailing along, I'm *in* this! Preserving knowledge isn't enough for everyone ya'know! What about my future? Or the cost? What's in it for me? I'll sink for this, fast as you or your family."

Lassa knew that. It kept her awake at night. Her voice stuttered to a start. "Can... you please bring that?" She indicated the box of perishables on the dock. Lassa turned away from his angry jaw.to pick up her own, and motioned him with her shoulder. "Come on. I'll try to find you some answers."

The space between them lengthened. A vice around Lassa's heart squeezed. Finally, just as she was going to call back, he fell into step behind her.

Hope. It gave her hope.

His presence on the whole venture gave her hope *and* peace, but that guilty truth wasn't going to solve anything, was it?

Their talk waited while they traversed the gang plank, stepped across the deck, and ducked through the hatch into the lead barge. It was the quarters—a series of narrow bunk rooms off a long dark companionway, opening out into a commons and kitchen—beyond that, the pilot house reined, all now equipped with boxes of essentials. Lassa set her addition on one of the benches between original emerald-green booths and pressed her hands to the timber either side of it.

She heard the disillusioned thud of Stoney's, then nothing but his silence.

Lassa began. "I'm not good with people. Not really. I... did this all wrong. There was such a rush! I should have explained, told you what it might cost you... I certainly should have given you a chance to leave after they stormed the library." She chewed at her tongue. "I've been so focused, I haven't discussed what this all means for you. I'm sorry."

Lassa cringed. She hated admitting failure.

"You're... I don't want an apology." Behind her, Stoney spoke slow, haltingly.

Yet, she bristled.

He didn't want… didn't he realise how hard that was to get out? Bloody hell! The strain of the last few weeks bubbled up.

Lassa cracked.

She rounded on him. "No? Then what do you want? A paycheck? A ticket into my skirts?"

Stoney recoiled like she'd shoved him. "I…!" He stared at her a heartbeat, then stepped forward with a roar she'd never heard before. "How dare you! I'm here, aren't I? Helping? But we're leaving!" He jabbed his finger into the space between them. "No, *you're* leaving! With or without me! This whole time working? No invitation. Not once! After all we've been through, all I've thrown in, the least you could do is actually *ask* me on the next damned part with you!"

Incensed, she watched him suck his outrage back behind his teeth.

Her turn! "I've been busy!" She peppered the ceiling with the syllables, then turned to insipid sarcasm as they dripped back down. "Oh, Stoney! Won't you please help little old me with this big old train?" Lassa batted her lashes, angling for damsel.

She saw his teeth grind.

Good. Lassa forged on savagely. "Those books are the only friends I've had in twenty-eight years! Everyone else runs hard and fast into the mist! I need your help, but I won't ask you, because you've got nothing for me besides strong shoulders, and I'm nothing to you but trouble!" She stabbed her finger towards the cabin door, viciousness biting. "Now it's on you! Don't let the gangplank slip on your way out!"

She spun back to the bench, fingers running across the worn grain repeatedly. She sniffed, the blur of regret already thick in her lashes.

Curse emotions!

He stood behind her, quiet as a mountain.

What could she say? She risked a glance into the porthole to her left. Its old bubbly glass reflecting him back to her—not the expression—but the stoop of his shoulders, the way he cradled his hands in defeat...

"Stoney! Get down!"

He saw it, the second she brought his attention up.

Council guards on the dock.

Stoney hit the deck. He rolled to one side, desperately trying to unholster his revolver while the porthole burst apart in a shower of minty-green glass.

"Bastards!" His bellow was buried under the deafening drum of gunfire against the river train's walls. They wouldn't get through. Harp had seen to that. These weren't average passenger cars. Built for the ice caps, it might look like simple copper, but between those two skins was wadded flocking for insulation.

Lucky, that.

He brushed glass from his hair and found Lassa, already ten feet away, boots disappearing into the pilot house. "Lassa! There's too much glass up there!" What was she doing? She'd get herself killed!

With a grunt of frustration, he scrambled after her. There weren't many portholes in each carriage—three down each side—but he reminded himself just how many bullets it took to kill a man.

One.

Lassa slid to a crouch and disappeared over the hatch edge. He made a mental note to remind her of that calculation, too.

Stoney made it to the door before the firing stopped. An eerie silence drifted in the carriage, coloured by the gentle brush of the water, bright against the metal hulls below, and the odd tinkle of settling glass. It seemed at odds with the bellowing commands of soldiers up on the Yard docks.

The floor began to vibrate beneath Stoney's hands.

Lassa was feverishly bobbing up to shift and check controls on the console. To his astonishment, she began to ease the rotary steam turbine from tempering idle, to a full roar.

Was she… no. She was *leaving*?

Stoney's incredulous stare held back his blink. Was she mad? Her family were back there! Her father! He'd be arrested, at best! Stoney eased up enough to glimpse from the forward-most porthole, its jagged lower half riddled with cracks. Seemingly unconcerned about the wreck of a shot-up river train, the soldiers were securing the premises. They marched about, lining up Harp's dockies, until a whole row of them rested on their fronts—hands on heads—waiting to be cuffed.

On the closest end lay Harp himself. Not yet restrained, his chin jabbing into the dock beside his hat, eyes trained on the lead carriage.

Harp knew.

Maybe he knew the ship vibrations, maybe he could see the steam building, or maybe he just knew his daughter, either way, he was ready. Harp's eyes slid down to lock with Stoney's. He might not be able to see the man's intention from twenty feet away, but he could guess.

"Lass?" Stoney's hoarse whisper came as foot-beats hit one of the rear gang planks. "Time to go!"

"What? We can't yet! The haul-arm's still attached! Those lines can't be reached from here!" Lassa was panting. There was no time to decide if it was from exertion or panic. Either would need to do.

"I think that's not gonna be a problem! I'll be right back! Just go!" He roared the last, springing to his feet and powering through the cabin, ducking and leaping through hatch doors.

Lassa watched him vanish with fear held firmly between her teeth.

Idiot! It would only take one bullet!

Not daring to peek through the blown-out pilot house windows, she blinked back tears and wriggled over to tap the turbine gauges, urgency in the flick of her fingers.

She heard revolver gunfire. Two heavy shots.

The glance over her shoulder told her nothing.

A splash and answering gunfire stilled her chest.

No! Please not him!

*Focus!* Just a few more minutes and they'd have steam up. Still, even then, the ropes had to be cast off, the gangplanks unhooked… and to gain enough initial speed, someone had to engage the pressure transfer system. It was an ingenious system; a network of brass overhead pipes with flexible leather collars that fed smaller paddle wheels on every following carriage. Manoeuvrability, propulsion, precision. Perfect.

Without all those things, the soldiers could simply walk beside them, firing.

She tapped the gauge again.

A resounding crash and splash, followed by yells and gunfire reverberated through the Yard. Lassa ducked, waiting to be peppered with bullets, but unfolded when they seemed further away. More gunfire, a second splash. The river train gave a lazy lurch sideways, like she'd been shoved from the dock.

What in the world?

Lassa crawled through the glass and pressed herself to the lower wall of the pilot house, half concealed beneath the original timber console. With unsteady fingers, she cast about, coming up with a piece of shattered window the size of her hand. Gingerly, like holding a match to a flame, she stuck the glass up and twisted, until she could see—well—anything.

Boots. Many running feet. All soldiers. All headed further into the Yard, where the commotion was coming from. She tried to angle her glass, but the shadows were too thick, distance too great.

The river train gave another caterpillar shudder, its floating lengths weaving away and back to the docks. A third clang and splash issued closer, eliciting roars and firing from the other end of the dock.

A soldier's voice rang around the pilot house. "There he is! He's doing them out of order! Get barrels trained on every line and plank!"

Who did they mean? Stoney?

Lines—planks—he was throwing off the gangplanks!

A nervous surge of hope rattled through Lassa, ending in a smile.

But there was no time for smiles.

Her glass went up again.

Where was her father?

Naturally, she cared about all their dockies, but most had been working on what they thought was a cargo of regular old black-market soaps for across the border. No one, not even those her father had used for the sewer barge, knew officially what lay in those crates.

*Clang, splash!* That was four.

Would the council spare them for that?

Her father had no such protection.

About to give up hope, a flash crossed her glass. Grey hair. Sprinting for all he was worth past the pilot house.

*No.*

"Stop!" A new shout rang out. "Get back here! He's running for the door!"

But he wasn't. Lassa's throat choked on a sob. She scrambled to her knees, hurling her chest against the front splintered frame, heedless of being seen, inwardly begging him to *stop, stop, stop!*

He ran for the haul-arm line, just as fast as his bandy old legs would carry him. She watched, horror in her gut, as he snatched up a hatchet—left along the docks for just such a reason—and with an almighty heft, raised it high above the final inch-thick line.

The hatchet struck.

Lassa screamed.

The last gangplank crashed into the water.

The rope sheared away in slow motion, the river train parting from the bumpers, already drawn by the natural currents as her father fell to his knees, one hand surrendered above his head, the other pressed over his heart as his daughter drifted away.

She saw him fall as the bullets hit.

His body teetered sideways, in slow motion, plunging from the dock, dropping the six feet to the river, a smile on his face.

Lassa wailed into the murky depths, shoving herself over the frame to reach for him, even as strong arms pulled her back.

"Lass! Lass! I'm sorry! Tell me what to do! Tell me!" Stoney was shaking her.

She knew he was shaking her, but she couldn't care. Huddled on the pilot house boards, clutching at the drifts of snowy glass with bloodied fingers, as broken as it was.

Her father was dead.

It was all for nothing.

"Lassa, if you don't get us moving, he died for nothing."

The callous echo stopped her breath.

A dead laugh bounced in her chest where her heart should have been. She sucked air through her teeth, the gunpowder tang mixing with his words to form a bitter burn.

The tears poured down her cheeks, but she lifted her head and slapped Stoney as hard as she could across the face regardless.

How dare he?!

Six weeks loading crates didn't give him the right to brandish her father's memory! Lassa kicked him off, not caring if he got hurt in the process, and sobbed her way through the commons and companionway, gaining ground on the engine room hatch each time she scrubbed her eyes clear enough to check.

She knew why he'd said it.

Curse the man!

Although, she still needed to hate him for a while.

Far too soon, Lassa had a new problem. With a moan, she gazed up at the hull hatch gantry, tucked patiently—uselessly—out of the way in the roof. Bullets still drummed the carriage shell, some skipping through shattered portholes.

Exactly how many did these guys have? She choked back a useless sob.

Little choice but to haul it by hand.

Straddled around the solid steel hull-hatch—fighting for leverage—she found it even heavier than anticipated. Lassa clenched her teeth and heaved, scrambling to wedge her knee in the gap while she regrouped. The weight bit at her skin and bone, sending her bite through her tongue.

Blood flavoured her mouth.

Curse it!

But it had to be lifted.

Another hacked off sob.

Lassa screwed her eyes shut, inched her fingers in beside her bruised flesh, and hauled up as hard as she could.

The hatch leapt up from her hands.

"I lift the heavy things, remember?" Stoney grinned at her from flat on his back, shoulders braced against the floor, head hanging into the engine bay, arms bulging in a bench press of the hatch.

A grateful, wretched hiccup broke out of her.

His grin turned lopsided and shy, before he furrowed his brow and growled like an uncomfortable bear, shifting the hatch weight. "But let's not take all day about it, alright?"

Not trusting herself to speak, Lassa slid around him, thankful for no hoops, and dropped into the four-foot-high hull recess that housed the turbine, gearing, and master paddle wheel couplings.

Her confidence frayed.

She tightened her grip on her heritage. More than ever, Lassa Harper needed to be her father's daughter.

A true Shipwright was all about the method.

She got to work.

The rotary steam turbine. Such an efficient engine. Her father's design. One of a kind…

Her throat constricted. *Focus!*

Coal for the turbine.

Check.

Engage the pressure transfer system.

Check.

Ensure the rudder linkages had been completed.

Check.

Open the valves to the paddle wheel couplings — apprehensively — for the first time.

Lassa sucked at the blood of her tongue and lingered. Amid the thunder of outside and thud of her own heart —

she fretted over each whistle and groan as the wheel couplings took the pressure. She urged them to please, *please* convert it into slow, methodical, spherical movement for the three-foot flywheels—without destroying her.

Slowly, like mixing batter, they picked up enough speed to tear the whole boat apart.

She listened—heart hammering—to the off-beat of the mechanicals.

Not right.

Please don't explode! Lassa closed her eyes, praying to her father, and by some miracle, perhaps under his guidance, the comforting harmonic rhythm finally— mercifully—settled.

Check!

Her hand clutched at her heart. "Thank you, Dad."

Right.

Time to make him proud.

She flew back past Stoney, pausing to plant an impulsive kiss on his cheek, which adorably, he lifted his jaw to follow, and dashed for the pilot house.

Steeling herself, Lassa hauled up to grasp the five-foot brass wheel—ignoring the shouts of Stoney, and the ferocious cascade of bullets striking water and metal on all sides. She selected her gearing.

Her target; the fast-closing Yard doors.

She could do it.

She gritted her teeth.

Lassa had always wanted a new life—a new dream. Beyond those doors, was a renegade run for the state border. It came with a country drowned in shallow water, a Council beating its people to dust, and folks soon so starved for knowledge, they couldn't fix any of it alone.

Behind her, braced on the commons hatch, Stoney fired up at the Yard docks with a will.

No. *They* could do it.

"Stoney?! Wanna come with me and all my friends?"

She kicked over the wheel-brake lever.

The deck jumped violently.

So did her heart, because he was laughing.

"You always gonna ask after we've already left?" His shout was thick and wry with amusement.

"Probably!"

Their river train shuddered into motion, churning so much spray from ten-foot paddle wheels that it doused the docks in waves, washing soldiers out at the ankles.

Yells and curses followed them out of the too-slow Yard doors.

Delightful!

"Then I'd better just say yes to everything right now!" He fired several more shots down the deck, but the shadows hid any soldiers still firing back.

That was it. They were gone. On the run. Together.

"Did he show you?!" Stoney hollered over the lessening din. "What he painted on the stern earlier?"

Her throat caught as they passed out into the open channel. "No! What did he paint?"

"The name, Lass. He painted her name."

Lassa snatched a look over her shoulder, sharing damp eyes with Stoney's sad smile.

She blinked, heart fluttering. "And?" It was the only word that would choke out as the water fell still as glass.

"*Pirates of the Tomes.*"

Tears glistening in the sunshine, Lassa laughed.

*Riv Rains is a collection of rusting gears lubricated exclusively by chocolate. Bookgeek, author, and conjurer of creative daemons, she'd have a lot more time if she wasn't also captain and chief to two kids, four boats, and one husband. Born amid the sticks of rural Australia, she finds words in the magick of sunsets and river swells, chassis and unsuspecting rib cages. Riv welcomes you to seek out the spawn of her tumultuous mind at rivrains.com or @rivrains, and hopes to reach for you through the gaps of many more heartfelt pages.*

# The Kraken Heist

*Jennifer Lee Rossman*

I hate boats.

I hate the way they smell like rotten fish, I hate how they bob about and make me all queasy, and I especially hate the fact that you need a whole other vocabulary the instant you step off land. Kitchens become galleys, right becomes starboard... Haven't figured out what the land equivalent of "bilge" is yet, but from context, it's nothing good.

I basically hate everything about boats. Except my outfit. I quite like a high-waisted trouser. And the suspenders! Hoo boy, do I enjoy casually hooking my thumbs in them while hanging out on this here boat-porch.

Okay, so I'm not exactly a natural at being a man yet. So sue me; I've only been one for a few days, and a lifetime of etiquette lessons and froofy dresses don't exactly lend themselves to this kind of life.

At least I'm a *gentleman* thief, not one of those blue-collar criminals who thwap people over the head and steal their aether-phones. Not that that doesn't sound fun, but I would never fit into that world and I'm hardly in shape for thwapping.

Hell, I'm hardly in shape for walking on this boat. Even now that I have my sea legs -- nifty new prosthetics with gyroscopic pneumatics that automatically adjust my stance as the boat shifts underneath me -- I keep finding a way to trip.

At least this time, it's in the direction of Sandrine.

She catches me with a laugh and helps set me upright, her weathered hand lingering on my shoulder.

"Are you alright?" she asks, glancing at my cheeks. "You look flushed."

"Cold air," I lie, willing my blush to recede, but no chance of that with her hand still on my arm.

Sandrine is the polar opposite of the lady I used to be. Short and stocky, muscles built from manual labor as a ship's mechanic. Always greasy, her true skin tone likely darker than mine but hidden under smears of black. She swears like a man and dresses like one, too, but not the way I do, not to hide anything. She's all woman, even if she isn't anyone's idea of a lady.

Am I still gay, if I'm a man who likes women now, instead of a woman who likes them? It doesn't sound like it, but I'm definitely *something*.

"I'm fine, really," I insist, clearing my throat when I hear how high my voice got there. "How's the boat-luggage?"

"Cargo," Sandrine corrects with a grin.

I cross my arms. "Nope. Not going to learn your nonsense boaty words. Once we're parked in the boat driveway, I'm never stepping foot on a boat ever again."

"Boat driveway? You mean port?"

I make a dismissive sound. "You also use that word to mean left. We dry folks had the good sense to invent entirely different words for those things."

She grins, and I can't keep up the haughty facade any longer, bursting into laughter.

"So, you wanna meet 'im?" Sandrine asks, pointing with her chin to the door that leads to the boat-downstairs or below-deck or whatever they call it.

My smile freezes in place. It's happening. *Finally.*

The aether bulbs cast an eerie blue glow on Timothy's tank. Rather ordinary name, Timothy, but the creature is anything but.

At first glance, he looks like a mass of red-brown eels writhing around each other, but when he senses us coming, Timothy unfurls himself to reveal his true form. Sharp beak. Giant, unblinking eyes. Tentacles lined with suckers that will latch onto your skin and never let go. This is the mighty kraken, scourge of the deep and nightmare of all sailors who dare traverse his seas.

And he's *absolutely adorable.*

Timothy may well drag ships to the bottom of the ocean and snack on their crews one day, but he's just a baby right now, his bulbous head about the size of my fist. He bobs excitedly on the other side of the glass, so energetic that he accidentally flips over and just kind of hangs there for a bit, wondering why the world got so upside down all of a sudden.

I am not being hyperbolic when I say that I have never wanted anything more than I want to cuddle this kraken right now.

But I'm a man. I'm tough and don't get all gooey in the emotions. I can't just--

"Eeeee!" says my mouth, accompanied by a sideways tilt of my head. Immediately, I pretend to stumble. "Oh, the boat," I say weakly. "Eee. So tippy."

I glance at Sandrine, who smiles and pretends that didn't just happen. It seems my body still runs on the feminine oils. I'll have to fix that somehow, if I'm going to make a habit of being a gentleman. Or maybe I'll just be a girly man. That sounds fun.

"Timothy," Sandrine says, gesturing to me, "this is Dax."

It sounded like a cool name when I thought of it. Like a badass thief name. Which was... maybe not the best idea for someone trying to blend in and not look like a thief. But I'm stuck with it now, so at least I like the way Sandrine says it.

"Pleased to meet you, sir," I say to Timothy, tearing my eyes away from his cute blooping motion to case the tank.

Thick glass sides, undoubtedly thick enough not to break if struck by a kraken's hard beak. Metal of some sort along the corners. Steel? I know less about metallurgy than I know about boats, so let's say steel. That sounds like a good metal. There's a locked hatch at the top of the seven-foot-high tank.

"For feeding?" I ask, pointing.

Sandrine nods. "I'll show you." She goes to get something, coming back with a fish and a stepladder. "They caught him up north, near Iceland," she says, climbing up. "You can still see the sucker marks on the hull where his mum attacked them."

Them? I was under the impression that she'd been with them when they found Timothy. She comports herself like she's been on this ship for years.

But, fascinating as she may be, Sandrine is not my reason for being here. I watch as she unlocks the hatch with a gold key on a chain around her neck and tosses the fish in.

Adorable Timothy turns vicious the instant the food enters the water, turning it cloudy and chummy. I wince at the carnage. So... gloves. I'll need a good pair of gloves if I don't want to lose a finger. Or possibly my entire forearm.

I spend the next few days studying the schedules of the crew. I don't think they appreciate a passenger interfering with their work -- probably think I'm from corporate, here to improve efficiency or something. Do boats have a corporate? I assume it's structured like my fathers' clockwork factories, but I must admit, I've never seen anyone walking around with a clipboard and talking about coffee breaks, so this may be one more perplexing way life at sea is different than on land.

I try to make myself useful. I was never allowed to work, not proper work, the kind that leads to sweat and calluses and whatnot, but I used to sneak pocket watches into my bedroom and tinker. The ship doesn't have much in the way of clockwork, as the salty spray corrodes too quickly and renders automata more trouble to repair than they're worth, but the captain keeps a collection of clockwork miniatures. He lets me tune them up, and from his boat-office, I can monitor the door to the downstairs cargo hold.

Once I'm certain I've figured out a time of day when no one will be around, I can get to work on the rest of the heist.

I couldn't steal the key too early before the theft. Sandrine would probably notice. I also couldn't steal Timothy long before the boat parks in America. Sandrine would definitely notice me walking around with a kraken stuffed down my shirt.

Although my shirt is already pretty stuffed and she hasn't said anything; she might just see it and think, "Hmm. Dax is looking *particularly* bosom'ed today." I don't know how it works at sea, but on land, the size of your gentleman friend's chesticular area seems as though it would fall under the umbrella of things you don't mention out of politeness, like your hat being adorned with fake phoenix feathers or why the baby looks like the mechanic who takes care of the horses.

Still, I don't really fancy the idea of having suckers and a sharp beak that close to my threepenny bits, so I best stick to the original plan.

On the day before we expect to see land, I go down to Sandrine's room. Supposedly it's a cabin, but I don't see it.

More of a servant's quarters dipped in the vague stench of low tide.

She looks up from a pile of loose papers at the sound of my sea legs tapping on the floor, her kinky brown hair falling over her face. She quickly shoves the papers aside, looking flustered. "Dax."

"Sandrine." There, we've established that we know each other's names. Now what? And why are my hands so sweaty? Am I that anxious about tonight? I wipe my hands on my man-pants. "Can I come in?"

A second too late, I realize the impropriety of what I've just asked. I may not have been raised as a boy, with all the implications such an upbringing might have on how I act around women, but I'm not a lady. I can't just assume women will be comfortable being alone in a room with me.

But things are different on boats. Or maybe just Sandrine is different than the ladies I grew up with. I think she sees me for who I really am; not that she thinks I'm feigning gender or anything, just that she gets me. She knows I'm harmless, at least as far as her honor is concerned.

So she doesn't show any indication that I've made a faux pas. She just pats the bed, having no other seating in the room. I go in and sink down beside her, grateful to give my legs a break. The room still sways with the boat, but with no visual movement cues, it feels more like all the liquid in my body is in constant motion.

"Mind if I take these off for a minute?" I ask, indicating my legs.

"Your trousers?" she asks with a wicked grin.

I know she's only teasing, but all of my blood rushes to my cheeks all the same. "Legs!"

"Ah. Good. Not that I wasn't interested in the trousers, but..."

She says it so casually that I can't tell whether its a joke or not. There is *no* possible way I can respond.

I roll up my pant legs and unclip my sea legs from my bronze garter belts, letting them fall to the ground with a clatter as I rub at the sore skin of my stumps. I think I need a better cushioning.

Sandrine doesn't stare, but she can't hide her curiosity, either. Suddenly I wonder if taking off my pants might have been the less intimate option.

"My legs were crushed by a mech pony when I was little," I say quietly. I don't mention that it was my pony, or that my father turned his clockwork toy factory into a prosthetics factory to make me the best legs possible. It was a big to-do in the news and I'm afraid she might recognize the details.

I watch her reaction closely. This is the first person I've ever really talked about the accident with. The first real person anyway; high society is nice, but you can't always trust that people are being themselves. Sometimes we forget who we are in all the dances and froofy dresses.

There's no pity in Sandrine's eyes, no repulsion. She's curious, and I bet she wants to touch the scars, see what they feel like, but despite all her brusqueness around the sailors, she shows restraint and just smiles that sweet smile of hers.

There's a funny tingle in my chest.

...Oh *no*.

Do I... do I fancy her? No, this is *terrible*. I only wanted the key!

And there it dangles from her neck, the one bit of shine on an otherwise grubby but gorgeous woman.

It isn't fair. All this time I've spent befriending her because she was the one with access to Timothy, and I have to go and ruin my first ever heist by falling for my mark. I'm a terrible thief.

And it isn't fair to Sandrine. She looks at me and she sees a good man, one who isn't scheming and who can be trusted in her room without a chaperone. Even if she doesn't *like me* like me, she still *likes* me.

"Something wrong?" she asks gently.

I shake my head. Then I reconsider and nod. "I don't want to talk about it." There, that's not a lie. I really *don't* want to talk about how I have absolutely zero options and even less money when we land in America, not if I don't finish this job.

But that's the truth, and as much as it hurts me, I can't just abandon the plan because I like Sandrine.

"Could I hang out here for a little while?" I ask.

Pretending to fall asleep next to Sandrine is a more pleasant experience than I deserve to have.

She snores. Cute little snorts like the steam-powered bulldog I had when I was a kid. And she mumbles to herself in her sleep. What's the boat word for adorable? Probably something like scurvylicious.

Sandrine is scurvylicious.

And then there's me. I'm a liar and a creep who watches ladies sleep.

I guess I *am* good at being a man after all.

When all this is over, I'll have to write to her and apologize. Although I'm not entirely sure how to send mail to a steamer ship, so... that'll be a trip to the research library.

With the practiced hands of a tinkerer, I unclasp the necklace and slip it into my pocket. She barely stirs.

"I'm sorry," I mouth, strapping my legs back on. Every tiny sound makes me wince, but I make it out of the room without waking her.

It's peaceful out here on the boat-porch at night, the sky splashed with diamonds and the sea all glassy and black. Almost looks like we're on an airship, the sky stretching for miles in every direction. For a moment, just a moment, I forget how much I hate boats.

Everything is fine on board the Wayward Daughter. I'm a fashionable man named Dax, there's a girl who makes my heart go all fluttery, and until I get back on land I don't have to worry about anything but seasickness and dodging seagull poo. But that's all over now.

I stick to the shadows cast by the aether-lights on the masts as I slink to the cargo door. The captain's light peeks through his window, but at this time of night he'll be reading or playing with his backgammon automaton; no risk of him coming out here to see what I'm up to.

I go down the stairs, realizing too late that I should have practiced to see where the creakiest parts are. Not that anyone should be around to hear.

Timothy bobs to the front of his tank when he sees me.

"Hello, Mister Adorable Face," I whisper. "Who's a squishy little squish face? You are. Yes, you are."

His tentacles flap up and down.

"Yes," I say, fetching the stepladder, "and you're a little squish face who's going to live in a nice, big aquarium in a magical land called Florida."

I pull on a heavy pair of gloves and grab a fish from a bucket in the corner, gagging at the smell. At least I don't have to touch it with my fingers, I reason, climbing the stepladder. I'm just unlocking the hatch when I hear the stairs creak.

Dropping the fish, I scramble for cover behind the tank, watching through the burbling water as a figure enters the room, dressed all in black and stepping carefully. Another thief?

The wavy shape resolves itself as the person nears the tank.

Sandrine.

We lock eyes through the glass. "What are you doing here?" we ask at the same time.

I decide to go first, and step out from behind the tank, my gaze on the floor. "I'm stealing the kraken."

"No, you aren't," Sandrine says. "*I'm* stealing the kraken."

I frown. "Why?"

"Because he deserves to be free," she says, like it's obvious. "The captain is just going to sell him to the highest bidder. Probably someone who wants to turn him into a delicacy."

That's... a good reason. That's a *much* better reason than my reason. Wow, she's a way better person than I am.

"Your turn."

For a second I wonder if maybe I could pretend that's why I'm here, too. But I'm not cut out for lying, and the truth spills out the instant I open my mouth.

"I'm stealing Timothy to sell him to someone my parents know because that's the only way I know of to make enough money to start a new life as a man."

The boat still pitches wildly, but the sick feeling in my stomach lessens somewhat. Is it possible it hasn't all been from seasickness, but the stress of keeping this secret? Only one way to test that theory.

"When I was born, people thought I was a girl. So did I, for a while. Sometimes I still do, but most of the time, I feel like I'm a man. My parents own Crowley Clockwork, and they're very nice people but they don't want the public scandal of having their daughter become their son. So I ran away to start a new life, but that's expensive. So when I heard about a baby kraken, I thought maybe I could steal him and sell him for new life money, and I became a gentleman thief."

My head spins a little. Next time I give a big confession, remind me not to talk so fast that I hyperventilate.

Sandrine just kind of stares at me for a moment. "Okay, I have questions."

"I have breasts," I say. "But they're... manly ones. I don't super hate them, but they do limit my ability to wear an open pirate vest."

"Not what I was going to ask. Did you befriend me because I was the one taking care of Timothy?"

"Yes."

She touches her neck. "Did you pretend to fall asleep in my bed just so you could steal my key?"

My ears burn in shame. "Yes."

"What kind of people do you like to kiss?"

The abrupt change in subject throws me. "Wait, what?"

She ticks off my options on her fingers. "Men? Women? Both? Other? None of the above?"

"Oh, um. Women. Women and, uh, other not-men people."

She steps closer to me, smiling. "Do you want to kiss me?"

I have never nodded so hard in my life. I can feel the heat coming off her skin, our faces nearly touching. Just when I think my heart can't beat any faster, Sandrine pulls away, whipping her head to look at the tank.

The *empty* tank.

The hatch at the top is open, the fish missing and a trail of water dripping down the sides. The stairs creak; the door at the top opens just wide enough to let a baby kraken through.

A second later, there's a shriek. Sandrine and I take off running.

"Is this how your heists normally go?" I joke.

"You'd be surprised how often."

"Wait, is this not your first heist?"

She just grins.

The door to the captain's office is open. We rush in to find Timothy trying to make a new friend. I'm not sure the captain particularly appreciates having a baby kraken on his head, but it gives me a chance to learn some new curses and I think I might have finally figured out what "bilge" is.

"Timothy!" Sandrine scolds. She takes the gloves from me and peels the kraken away with a series of wet *pops* as the suckers come unstuck from the captain's skin. At a loss for where to put him, she just holds him awkwardly away from her body.

"I'll get the bucket."

But as I go outside, I see the oblong shape of an airship overhead. My contacts.

Oh, bilge. I forgot they were coming tonight. I duck back into the office. "Hi, me again. Slight problem. The people I was going to sell Timothy to are here."

The captain starts yelling but Sandrine cuts him off. "This isn't about you." She turns back to me. "Do you still want to sell him?"

I kind of do, because money is nice, but I shake my head. "You're right; he should be free."

She smiles. "I had a feeling you were a good man. Did you sign anything for them? A contract?"

I shake my head.

"Then you can't be held liable if the kraken was stolen by another thief before you got to him." She gives the captain a warning look when he starts to protest. "Still not about you. You stole him from his natural habitat; we're just putting him back." She looks to me. "What do you say, Dax? Want me to let this little guy slip overboard to my friends waiting off the starboard bow?"

I do. I *so* do. But what happens to me? Doing the right thing is great and all, but it doesn't exactly pay.

Sandrine senses my reluctance. If she wasn't holding a squirming kraken at arms' length, I think she'd hug me. "Hey, it might not be the life you wanted, but there's a space for you on my crew, if you want it. Travel the world, help cryptids in danger... *actually* fall asleep in my bed..."

That sounds so nice, I almost burst into tears. Very manly tears.

Sandrine presses a kiss to my cheek before going to release Timothy. "You're going to love our boat!" she calls over her shoulder.

Well. It's a good thing I love boats so much.

*Jennifer Lee Rossman is a queer, autistic, and disabled author from Binghamton, New York*

# East Wind in Carrall Street
## *Holly Schofield*

Wong Shin pulled down on a lever, scraping his elbow against the metal framework within the clockwork lion. The lion obediently approached Margie where she stood in Shin's family courtyard. Over and over, he made the lion step forward, then retreat, keeping a light hand on the crucial levers. When Margie shot a guilty look over her shoulder at the brothel behind her, Shin copied her glance, awkwardly peering upwards through the screening above the lion's broad nose. Margie's aunt was not at the second story window. He let out his breath. Fully four years older, he felt responsible that they not be seen together. Practice time was short so he gave all his attention back to the controls, completing the sequence of dance steps, as focused as if he were performing a traditional Chinese lion dance in front of his father's business associates rather than for the amusement of a ten-year-old White girl.

From his cramped spot behind the lion's eyes, he twisted a bamboo rod, snapping the lion's mouth open and closed, imagining the traditional drum beats. As cables tightened, a pulley triggered another line attached to the puffy silk balls mounted on the lion's paper-mâché face. He let the silk decorations waggle a bit then he pressed a ceramic spring-loaded button next to his knees, sending the clockwork lion's gears ratcheting noisily. As he pumped his legs in the iron stirrups, the lion's front feet followed suit, dancing a complex jig. Dust billowed up between the gaps in the stirrups, making him cough.

He pranced again toward Margie, his knees reaching up around his ears. "Go away, Mah-jee, go away!" he called out, laughing.

Margie giggled and twirled out of his way. "You mean run away! Or flee!" she called back, eager to improve his English, as always.

He chased her across the unkempt courtyard, picturing the layers of colorful cotton swaying behind him. This morning's improvements meant the lion's iron framework was now the length of a large horse – fully a dozen *chek* long. There was nothing like the clockwork lion in the city of Vancouver's Chinatown, nor in British Columbia, nor perhaps in all of the Dominion of Canada – despite it being a complete sham.

Tomorrow, across Carrall Street at Teck Woo's new bakery, the drummers would play: at first, slow beats, then becoming gradually faster and faster. The crowds would yell encouragement and, as the excitement grew and the lion danced, Shin would snatch the all-important red envelope of money through the massive lion jaws. And no one would know that it wasn't a true clockwork lion.

Shadows crept up the brick wall of his father's grocery store as the afternoon wore on. A dial on the lion's interior panel indicated that the clockwork's energy coil was almost spent. Shin's arms and legs began to ache from the repeated motions in the confined space.

As he sashayed one more time across the yard toward Margie, making the ears wiggle and the beard shimmy, she looked past him toward the grocery and her eyes grew wide with fear. He stopped, in confusion, just as his father's voice rang out.

*"Shin-Shin, neh jow mat yeh, wah?"* Shin-Shin, what are you doing?

Shin laboriously turned the lion fully around to face his father, hoping the cotton-clad framework would shield Margie's escape. She would need time to climb the fence and his father blocked the only front exit that led between brick buildings out to Carrall Street.

*"Doy em jee, Baba."* I'm sorry, Father.

"Why are you practicing out here? The neighbors must not see!" His father's village-accented Cantonese harshened in displeasure.

"Sorry, Baba, the workshop floor is not big enough anymore for the full routine." Shin let the lion's knees sag, relieved that Baba hadn't caught sight of Margie; his father was simply worried that the clockwork lion would be seen by the neighbors. No one in Chinatown, aside from Shin and his father, knew that the boy steered the lion from within. In the two years since the lion had been completed, Shin's father had convinced the Chinatown businessmen's association that the lion was truly clockwork-run. The scale and complexity of such clockwork had been attempted without success since the start of the Qing Dynasty and his father had quickly grown famous. If the businessmen knew that this lion was controlled by a boy pulling levers, they would not pay the ten-dollar fee for an opening good-fortune ceremony; instead they would hire Lee Chan and his brawny son to provide the two-dollar, man-powered version.

"Since you are already out here, practice the lettuce-retrieval ceremony. Grab that maple leaf up there." Shin's father pointed at the woodshed roof, cluttered with twigs and debris. "Balance your front legs on the old chicken coop."

"Yes, Baba." Shin steered the lion to the dilapidated wooden structure that hugged the woodshed. They hadn't had chickens since Mama had died during childbirth seven years ago. Now, thistles filled the coop, spilling out the top and sides through wire mesh. Shin pressed a lever to raise the lion's left foot onto the top corner of the rickety structure, praying to the earth god *Dabo Gong* that the chicken coop could withstand both the lion's and his weight. He knew he'd grown taller since Baba had designed the lion head when he was twelve – he was now up to Margie's shoulder – and he must have put on a few *catties* of weight too. He almost blurted out that this stunt would be more difficult than placing the lion's front legs on two pre-positioned barrels as he would tomorrow, but he bit the words back. Baba would know all that and have factored the risk, like men did. If it was fated to collapse, it would. Shin clamped his mouth shut, even as the huge lion foot made the top board creak. If he didn't attempt difficult things, Baba would never call him Ah Shin and treat him like the adult he was.

He eased his weight forward, the energy coil unwinding with a squeal. An indicator on the left panel said he had about ten *fan* of energy left – just enough to make the lion grab the large green leaf and drop down to kneel in front of Baba.

The chicken coop creaked again. Thistles rustled. Shin looked down between his leg stirrups. A wisp of blonde hair was caught among the thistles. More rustling and blue eyes peered up at him.

"Hurry up!" Baba's voice came from behind, near the grocery's rear door. His father must have stepped back, most likely expecting Shin to fail and fall. He hadn't seen Margie.

In the chicken coop, Margie's eyes filled with tears. The lion weighed as much as three men. If the chicken coop couldn't support its weight, it would surely crush her just as being born had crushed his little sister. The baby that was to be Shin's little sister had only lived a few days, not long enough to name.

Should he tell Baba that Margie was in the coop and save her life? She could run home. He glanced upward at the building behind. A woman with a mound of hair on her head stood at the brothel window, scanning the alleyway. His father would thrash him with a bamboo stick if he knew about Shin's friendship with Margie, but that was nothing compared to the beating Margie's aunt would give her for associating with filthy heathens such as himself.

Perhaps he could pretend to roll to one side, as if he wasn't in control? Surely the lion, made with his father's sturdy workmanship, could handle such a fall? But Shin would bring shame to his ancestors if the controls got smashed and were unable to function for tomorrow's ceremony.

Shin balanced on the left leg for so long, his thigh muscle trembled.

He heard his father hawk and spit on the ground in disgust at Shin's delay.

He couldn't crush Margie, he couldn't. Perhaps he could fall to the left, very slowly and gently, controlling the lion's iron spine. He raised the lion's right foot and placed it close, deliberately too close, to the left foot. He slowly eased the main lever upwards, arching the lion's spine, placing the centre of gravity slightly over the paws. Too much! The lion overbalanced and crashed forward. Shin quickly threw his body leftward. His head hit iron bars and the lion hit the ground. He closed his eyes until the dozens of sewn-on bells stopped jingling.

It was almost a relief when Baba, still swearing, opened the neck hinges so he could scramble out onto the dirt of the courtyard. The left side of the chicken coop was smashed to bits, loose boards dangling at all angles. Snapped cables littered the ground near the lion. The giant head was crushed and broken in several places. The far end of the chicken coop appeared undamaged but it was hard to tell.

He listened for the rustle of thistles as he helped Baba carry the broken pieces into the grocery-cum-workshop but heard only the inauspicious caw of a crow. He gave a final look back, the lion's bright horsehair tail dragging in the dust behind him, but there was nothing to be seen.

After a meal of rice, dried salmon, and unsellable black-edged greens, Shin crouched on the floor of the workroom. The lion head lay on a workbench and his father hunched over it, cursing loudly and slamming various hand tools around. The bakery opening would happen at first light. The almanac had been consulted and it was an auspicious day. The ceremony could not be delayed.

Shin's offers to help were ignored so he did his evening shop chores, including winding the springs on the little shop heaters needed to ward off the springtime chill. Shin's failure to do his duty to the family drummed through his head even as he took pride that his fingers no longer bled during the endless turning of the tiny keys. Small gadgets like the heaters could be human-wound, unlike larger coils that required teams of men trotting in circles, or oxen like the White Men used. The lion's clockworks were powered by a mid-sized coil and Baba had arranged delivery of a new pre-wound one at sunrise. The fee – a fifty-cent coin – gleamed under the oil lantern by the door.

Shin tinkered for a while with a clockwork monkey he had been working on for Margie. Over a period of months, he had taken apart an old tofu-maker and reassembled the sprockets and gears. He had shaped the framework from cedar, rather than the more traditional, and more expensive, bamboo. Daringly, he had travelled six blocks, his first foray outside Chinatown, giving his Spring Festival money to a dark-skinned Indian down by the stockade in exchange for a raw beaver pelt. After soaking the skin in an oak stump, he had softened it to a felt-like material that he thought might resemble monkey fur. He had crafted robes and a headband from scraps of Mama's dress that Baba had been using as a window covering. The shade of yellow matched the cover of Shin's proudest possession, a book of tales about the Monkey King's many journeys.

The rebuilt clockwork mechanism functioned well enough to make the monkey wave its hand; however, Shin wanted to do better. He took a used wax cylinder – its grooves blurred by overuse – and began to cut new and intricate lines with his pocketknife.

The day that Margie had shown him the White Men's wax cylinders had changed his life. She had snuck him into the whorehouse's laundry room to show him the shoe-polishing machine, thinking he would be impressed. Shin had opened the machine's repair hatch and been appalled at the White Man's crude and clumsy clockworks. "Like a beast would expel," he had told her. But, he had been fascinated with what had conveyed the wondrously precise instructions to the poorly-engineered clockworks: wax cylinders, each grooved with a thousand tiny lines. Even the richest Chinese didn't have such marvels. When Margie had given him dozens of spent cylinders, he had clapped his hands in glee.

He put down the knife and opened a page in his second proudest possession, a programming manual that Margie had stolen for him last month. He had been explaining to her that the last new moon was the beginning of the Year of the Monkey and, later that day, she had brought him a slice of bread dripping with salt pork fat. She had some concept of birthing day anniversary gifts that made no sense to him. He had politely eaten the bread. Baba had told him many times that the diseases White Men got by drinking unboiled water and eating uncooked greens were many and complex, challenging even for Chinatown doctors and pharmacists. Shin had carefully watched his bowels for days but there appeared to be no ill effect from the treat.

He flipped a page in the book, looking for a certain coding sequence that would help the monkey move its tail in synchronization with its hands. Margie's aunt had boxed her ears soundly for the book theft but then covered for her, telling the irate customer it had been taken by one of the maids. Margie had spent hours teaching English numbers and coding symbols to Shin, as well as all the algebra and geometry she learned in the school for White children. In return, he had patiently drawn diagrams of simple clockworks on scraps of butcher paper, explaining them in his broken English, sitting cross-legged beside her in their favorite spot atop the greengrocery roof.

He tossed the monkey aside, not in the mood to work on it when all of his dreams were being dashed by his foolish actions. He watched Baba grapple with the broken lion as fresh waves of shame washed over him. Over the past few months, the yin and yang synergy of elegant Chinese clockworks and White Men's wax cylinders had filled his thoughts. Ideas had poured out of him faster than he could form the English words to tell Margie: how wax cylinders could perhaps someday be used to guide abacus beads, making giant calculating machines. When he was old enough to run Baba's greengrocery, he would investigate such things in the evenings, like men did, much as Baba tinkered nowadays with clockworks.

"Come." Baba pointed at the bicycle in the corner. Shin squeezed between crates of carrots and gear parts and mounted the bike. The length from the seat to the pedals had become too short for him. With a strong push, he started the pedals turning, then settled into a fast, even pace. In front of him, the lengthy bike chain spun and the friction welder started up. His father grasped an iron rod with bamboo tongs and pressed it in the collar of the welder. He touched the lower end of the rod to an interior brace of the lion head which lay wedged in a vise below.

As Shin kept up a furious pace, the rod began turning fast enough to blur. It would take a long while to heat enough to form a proper weld. He let his thoughts drift. There was no point in buying Margie *bao* or other pastries for her birth celebration, whenever it might occur; her calendar was too strange to have much meaning. Plus, she had smilingly refused every piece of food he had ever offered her. The thought of food made his stomach growl, empty again. As acrid smoke swirled around him, he imagined the wonderful contents of Teck Woo's market cart, soon to be a full-fledged bakery in a new finely-styled brick building across the street. Businesses were springing up every day. White Men might refuse to hire Chinese for even the worst jobs at Roger's Sugar Mill, but that would not break the businessmen's spirits; the community would build their own new China here in the Dominion of Canada.

"Steady, Shin-Shin," Baba said, as the end of the rod began to glow a cheery red. By the time the sun had set and the automated oil lanterns clicked on, the many necessary welds were completed. Shin stepped down and dried his sweat on his too-short jacket sleeve. His stomach rumbled again. The store's income was not enough to live on; without the lion ceremony earnings they would be hungry next winter, like they had been before Baba had built the wonderful mechanism.

Coming to the "golden mountain" was to be a new start for the Wong family. Baba had come first, earning money laboring in the fields on the mainland to the east, paying off his head tax and landing fees. Years later, Mama had left her small village and travelled in what she had called "in fear and boredom" along with several other women in a large stinking ship. Both had worked hard at the greengrocer business as baby Shin played on the store's splintery wood floor amid clucking chickens and broccoli stems. His first toy had been a broken abacus. His second was a broken automated wok-stirrer he had first turned into a toy warrior, then a stick-like doll for Margie.

Margie's story was similar. Her mother had come from a mountainous place over the ocean to the east, where people slid on snow with boards tied on their feet. Margie wanted to be an architect, designing buildings like the new brick Driard Hotel where fine ladies drank tea. Meanwhile, she did kitchen duty at the brothel, saving up customers' tips for an architecture mail order course from the Simpsons catalogue. Once she had shown Shin a paint set a customer had given her. She had swirled powders together, yellow and blue. "That's like you and me, together we can make the Dominion of Canada better than either of the two alone." Shin had answered in his stumbling English that Canada was more like the many colors of vegetable fried noodles – a mixture of everything but a blend of nothing.

"Come. Try this." Baba's wiry body swung the lion head to the floor, not bothering with the hoist. Together they reattached the long body to the head in the cramped space, laying the drooping middle over some barrel staves at the rear of the shop and looping the legs and back feet towards the head by the big door at the front.

Shin swung his short queue over his shoulder to his front as he examined the rebuilt lion. It would be a tight fit. Baba had reinforced the head with more cross supports, threading iron rods past the leg braces to the back of the head. Shin hastily reattached the yellow cloth, sponging off the dirt from the yard, and brushing out the red and gold horsehair fringes while his father repositioned cable housings every which way. Baba was a competent craftsman, Shin suddenly realized, but his designs were less elegant than the sturdy oxen White Men used to wind coils.

"You, east wind, get in." His father gave an impatient gesture and Shin got down on his knees beside the head, a second insight flooding into his head. His father's continual reference to the famous battle in China that depended on a late-arriving east wind – a wind crucial to the success of the fire ships being sailed toward the enemy – was not a compliment to Shin. Instead, his father was ashamed of their deception to the community and ashamed of the necessity of using Shin to operate the lion. Shin studied the stern line of his father's mouth. There was no time to dwell on the matter.

Shin bent his head so that Baba could lift the lion head over him. Bowing his head had not been necessary even three months ago. He must have grown a full *tsun* – a handsbreadth – since then. His wrists jutted out from his jacket as he helped lower the lion head over his own.

A gasp, a grunt, and the head – now probably weighing as much as Baba himself – came down hard on his thighs, cutting off all light but for a faint glow though the nose screen. One of the new iron rods crushed down on Shin's knees. He shoved a leg out the side of the head and under the huge rear paw on the side away from his father. He tucked his other foot under his buttocks, where it was useless to power the leg controls.

"Good, it works." In relief, Baba waggled one of the lion's silk balls, the connected bamboo handle striking Shin on the ear. "Now, get out. A short sleep is still possible."

Shin quickly tried various other positions as he clambered out from beneath, Baba holding the lion head aloft. In the poor light, Baba hadn't noticed Shin's struggles, how his legs stuck out. How he had failed.

Shin's mouth tasted like raw bitter melon.

He no longer fit inside the lion.

A small part of him thrilled at the thought that Baba's shameful fraud could not continue. He pushed the thought away. The red envelope money would go unearned. He had let down Baba and all Wong ancestors. And Teck Woo's bakery would forever have bad luck.

As his father climbed the narrow stairs heading to the sleeping mats, Shin stayed huddled on the cold dirt floor. He didn't deserve to sleep tonight.


The lion weaved and dodged, as graceful as bamboo in the wind. It danced closer to the barrels, surrounded by smiling, dark jacketed men who nodded with delight. Lucky green onions tied to its horns waved merrily. The drummers intensified the beat, luring the lion closer and closer to the leafy green lettuce hanging over the bakery doorstep and the red envelope tied within. The lion approached, cocked its head at the lettuce, put a foot on a barrel, then stepped off again, turning its head to wink coquettishly at the crowd.

A toddler emerged from between a man's legs and headed for the lion, probably attracted by the glittering metal discs sewn to the red and yellow layers of cloth. The lion continued to dance, oblivious, stepping forward and back in a tradition as old as gunpowder.

From his perch atop the greengrocery roof, Shin wrapped his arms around his bruised knees, the clay tiles cold under his thin slippers.

Finally, a woman scuttled from between the men and grabbed the child's arm, dragging it back into the crowd.

Shin let out his breath. The monkey's cylinder programming was set to a specific pattern. There was no altering it, for toddlers or anything else. He pictured the energy coil unwinding in the body of the lion, powering the mechanism even as the monkey pushed and pulled levers and switches in an intricate pattern; its hands and feet, even its tail, manipulating the lion in a dance more complex than a Chinese acrobatic display, all seven cylinders spinning madly. With wooden blocks tied to its feet and a wire hook embedded in its tail, the monkey had fit inside the lion perfectly. He had used the yellow robes to tie it securely to the framework.

"That's charming, that is." Margie settled beside him on the roof, tucking her green skirts immodestly under her. Her right arm hung in a sling made from a paisley scarf and a long scratch ran down one cheek.

"Therefore no birth present for you," Shin answered tensely, keeping his eyes on the lion.

Margie giggled. "I never understand you even when I understand you. Here, I brought you a present because you saved me. Don't worry – I waited until dark yesterday then I told my aunt I fell from a tree." She shoved a pastry in his hand, ruby and gold in the morning sun. "It's called rhubarb pie."

"Rhu-bah pie," Shin repeated absently and bit into it. He hadn't had time for rice porridge this morning and working hard all night had made his stomach hollow. Baked wheat flour and tart juice filled his mouth, sliding down as pleasantly as Teck Woo's sweet red bean *jian dui.*

The clockwork lion grabbed the lettuce in the final dance sequence, as the drumbeats grew staccato. From his vantage point above, Shin saw the small brown hand flash out and draw the red envelope inside the jaws. The crowd cheered, Baba loudest of all. For the first time since he'd seen Margie hiding in the chicken coop, Shin began to relax.

Finished, the lion lumbered back across the street, the crowd parting way. A grinding noise drifted up as the grocery's large workroom door opened, its escapement mechanism perfectly timed. The lion marched steadily toward the grocery as the door rose higher and higher. Several *chek* before the workroom entrance, the lion turned sharply to the right, stepped up onto the wooden sidewalk and rammed face-first into the grocery's brick wall.

"Ah Shin! Ah Shin!" Baba rushed toward the lion as it made a horrid grinding noise and the front legs collapsed.

On the roof above, Shin bit down on his knuckles. Baba's use of "Ah Shin"--the adult form of his name-- shone through the awfulness of the crash.

Below, his father prodded the ruins of the lion. He gave a start then, just before the other men reached him, pulled off the yellow restraints and shoved the monkey beneath his jacket. He made calming gestures at the men and laughed with an open mouth. His words drifted upwards – assurances that the lion could be repaired. After all, he said, it was clockwork-run and the best technology in all the continents.

Shin licked blood off his knuckles, careful of the large blister on his hand – a result of winding the monkey's coil for many *fan* last night. He felt his chest swell with pride. Combining the White Man's cylinder technology with traditional clockwork meant that the shameful deception of the lion could stop. And, equally importantly, his father saw him as a man.

He looked out over the rooftops as a gentle rain started. In the distance, Chinatown's clay tiles blurred together with the White Man's cedar shingles.

He grinned at Margie and crammed the rest of the pastry in his mouth. "Two countries, both east wind," he said around oily crumbs and laughed when she shook her head in confusion.

*Holly Schofield's stories have appeared in Lightspeed, Analog, Escape Pod, and many other publications throughout the world. You can find her at hollyschofield.wordpress.com*

# Mech-Mage

## *Lisa Short*

*Baltimore, 1903*

Becks was used to making the lengthy trek from the Gallery, just a few levels below the city proper, all the way down to the bowels of the Labyrinth. It wasn't too bad, at the start—the upper part of the Labyrinth had doubled as living quarters for the miners who'd dug it out, and they'd prized their comfort. Becks's hand lantern swung unlit at her side as she hurried down the broad square corridors; most of the sconce lamps and ventilation fans wedged into the smooth-polished walls still worked, and while nobody could have called the air *fresh*, it was at least moving strongly enough to stir the ragged ends of her hair under her cap.

But soon enough, the cheerful golden glow of the sconces and the rackety roar of the fans faded behind her, swallowed up in the black silence of the narrower, deeper tunnels further down. The chromium veins had been mostly played out by the time the miners had gone that deep, and they hadn't been so particular anymore about their tunneling. Grumbling, Becks slowed her pace, running a hand along the crumbling rock wall to keep herself oriented. Familiar as she was with the tunnels, she still managed to stub a toe twice and catch a good crack on the shoulder from an overhang she hadn't remembered was even there until too late.

Her irritation didn't last long though, not once she finally reached the Mole. Its running lights were bright sparks of welcome in the darkness; Becks hurried to it and fondly patted its battered steel side. She'd never understood why the miners had abandoned them—to own such a powerful, beautiful (to Becks's partial eye) creation and then simply *leave* it was beyond her comprehension. Low to the ground as it was, the Mole was easily four times as long as Becks was tall and made twenty of her in girth; she crouched companionably down beneath its great cutterhead and began rummaging through her toolbag.

After some pondering, Becks decided to work on the Mole's tunneling teeth—she'd noticed they were getting dull. She pulled the sharpener out of the bag and settled into the task. The sharpener's rasp was soothing, and the ache settling between her shoulder blades almost comforting in its familiarity; she was half-asleep at her work before the realization gradually intruded that the tunnel was too quiet.

The vermin that shared the Labyrinth with the Mole crews were accustomed to Becks. Once she'd settled in to whatever work the Mole required on any given day, the rats, bats and roaches emerged from their various nests in the tunnels and hissed, crept and flew about just as if she weren't there. Becks never could achieve the same insouciance towards them—just the thought of one of the giant cave roaches dropping off the ceiling into her hair was enough to make her jam her cap down even tighter on her head. But they were silent now.

*Somebody's scared the vermin away.* She tried not to react visibly to the thought, but her back stiffened up anyway; the sharpener's worn grip slipped against her suddenly damp palms. She lowered it carefully to the ground and picked up the cutterhead spanner instead. With its reassuring weight in her hands, she edged around the Mole's bulky cylindrical body.

But Becks had figured out long ago that it was best to at least *seem* unafraid. "Whoever you are, you'd better come out," she said loudly. "Sal don't like *unauthorized personnel* hanging around his Mole." His very phrase, too—it had taken a much younger Becks quite a while to figure out it was two separate words, much less what they meant apart from each other. But whoever the intruder was apparently didn't know what it meant either, or was just unimpressed by it. "Right, that was your chance. I'm leaving now, and telling Sal the rats got too bad in here and we got to seal this tunnel up and fumigate it. You won't like that, friend." She paused for a split second, but nothing answered back. "Fine!" She turned on her heel and stalked toward the exit, mentally bracing herself for Sal's temper—fumigation was a last resort, as it left the Mole unusable for days after.

A small avalanche of rocks clattered down behind her. Becks whirled around, clutching the spanner tightly enough to hurt her fingers; a collection of stones ranging from pebble to fist-sized were rolling to a halt some feet away. A wild look around still didn't reveal anything out of the ordinary—but no, *something* was gleaming, waist-high, in the crevice behind the Mole's rear treads. Becks bared her teeth and raised the spanner; the intruder scuttled out, hands raised up in front of himself like a shield.

It was a kid, a *little* kid—words failed her, and she simply stared. He stared back, his eyes so wide open she could see the whites all around. "Holy hell," said Becks blankly. Was he one of the crew's kids? She couldn't remember anybody on Sal's crew having a *little* kid— "Are you lost?"

A shudder rippled through his frame, then he shook his head once, sharply. The Mole's running lights cast deep shadows under his eyes and little ones in the cracks on his lips. Becks inched backwards; his gaze clung to her as she squatted beside the Mole's cutterhead and came back up with her canteen in her hand. "You don't look like you've been drinking the water down here, which was smart of you. Here." She extended the canteen towards him. He looked at it with obvious longing; his hands twitched, then clenched back together at his waist. Inspired, she uncapped the canteen and took a quick swallow, recapped it, set it on its side and gave it a hard push with her foot. It clattered across the rough stone floor and the kid dove forward and snatched it up, clawing the cap off and gulping at it frantically.

Becks hadn't felt so sorry for someone in years. She waited until he had drained the canteen dry, then said kindly, "There's no shame in getting lost down here, you know. They don't call it the Labyrinth for nothing. I can probably walk you back to wherever it is you ought to be, after I finish up with the Mole."

The kid's eyes shimmered, then squeezed tightly shut and he shook his head again. "What?" said Becks, bewildered and starting to get annoyed. "You sure as hell can't want to stay *here*—"

A voice, suddenly raised, drifted into the tunnel. Becks fled back to the cutterhead, scooping the sharpener up and industriously applying it to the Mole's teeth. Faint scrabbling noises from the other side of the Mole led her to hope that her small intruder had hidden himself away as well.

"Oy!" Becks didn't look up. "Who's there?" It was Sal himself—Becks reluctantly unfolded herself from behind the cutterhead, keeping her head down. "Becks? How's the Mole?"

"Fine. Just finishing up the headwork."

"The Mole'll be ready first thing tomorrow, then, aye?"

"Sure," muttered Becks. She waited for the echoes of Sal's footsteps to fade away, then squeezed out from behind the Mole. The tunnel was silent around her now, the shadows unmoving. "You can't stay here," said Becks, low-voiced. "Sal and the rest of the crew'll be back at dawn tomorrow. You have to find another place to hide."

More silence answered her. Becks gathered up her tools and bag; her elbow bumped against her empty canteen pocket. She hesitated—but she had plenty of canteens. She cast one last look around, then hurried out of the tunnel.

The next day, the crew had a fine run; a celebration was in full swing that evening when Becks stuck her head into the Gallery. Past the jiggling shoulders of the dancing crew and a handful of others that Becks didn't recognize—likely whoever had hired Sal that week to transport their goods via the Labyrinth rather than the heavily taxed and regulated Port Authority—Becks could see several new crates and bundles stacked up against the Gallery's far wall. Good enough—and a good time to go down to the Mole, too; nobody was likely to trouble her at it.

Sal's crew had staked out, and impressively managed to keep, a fine bit of territory in the Labyrinth. The Gallery alone was likely coveted by many another crew, with its high-arched ceiling, ample air vents and plethora of cubbies, blind drops and even a few awnings big enough for private habitation. Becks knew she'd been lucky— lucky that Sal's Mole had picked just that time and place to break down all those years ago, only one tunnel over from where she'd been huddled miserably in the dark, already second- and third-guessing her decision to run away from the baby-minders—lucky that Sal's gang had been on the run from Port Authority and were desperate enough to trust a quick repair job to a nameless Labyrinth waif. That knowledge had her hesitating far longer than she might have otherwise, outside the nook off the Gallery that they used for a kitchen.

But memories, old and new, of small, hollow cheeks and frightened eyes decided her. She dashed inside and scooped up a fresh-baked loaf of bread and, more daringly, a tiny pot of honey. Becks stuffed the loaf under her jersey and the pot into one of her capacious trouser pockets, where it clinked against the extra canteen she'd already stashed there, and nimbly darted back out, past the Gallery and into the drop that led below.

Becks felt sweat start along her hairline and the nape of her neck as she entered the Mole's tunnel. At least the crew had left the Mole's running lights on, so she wouldn't walk smack into hot metal in the dark. She hadn't dared bring her hand lantern along; if she got caught at any of this, she didn't want to chance losing the lantern entirely or worse, inspiring anyone to wonder aloud how she'd got her hands on one in the first place. She cast a quick look around, then a more searching one. Was that a bulge of shadow where none should be, a little too close to the Mole for comfort?

"Hullo," said Becks, tentatively. "I brung you something. If you're still here, and I'll look like a fool if you aren't, aye?" She squatted down and placed the loaf on the gritty rock floor, then the little honeypot, then the extra canteen. "The Mole's too hot for me to work on yet. So I'm going to leave this here, and go away. I'll be gone for *hours*. Hours and hours."

She started to back away, towards the exit. A faint scrape on rock alerted her and she stopped in her tracks; a few seconds later, the kid emerged from the shadows behind the Mole, cheeks flushed and pale hair soaked dark and flat to his skull. When Becks didn't move, he edged out further, then tiptoed towards the small pile of provisions, stare glued to her face. Not wanting to terrify him back into hiding, she only cranked up the corners of her lips the barest amount; he stopped and gave her a twitch of his own lips in return.

Becks settled herself cross-legged on the tunnel floor, but once he got his hands and teeth into the bread, the kid didn't spare her any more of his attention. "There's honey in the pot," she said, after a few minutes of watching him devour the bread. He stopped long enough to pick the pot up, but the wax seal obviously confused him.

"Here, gimme." She stretched out a hand; he rolled the pot over to her, much as she had rolled the canteen to him the day before, and she picked it up and stripped off the seal. She couldn't roll it back, though, not without wasting its precious contents on the floor—she held it out to him instead. Bread briefly forgotten, he stared at her with eyes grown enormous once more—despairing eyes; was he so afraid of her approaching him any nearer? Well, it wasn't hard to think of why he might be—something of those thoughts must have shown in her face, because his eyes puddled in the yellow glare of the Mole's lights.

Then the little pot twitched in Becks's fingers. She tightened her grip on it involuntarily, but it only wrenched harder against her hold. With a stifled shriek she let go of it, but it didn't so much as slip an inch toward the floor; it hung in midair instead, entirely motionless. Becks gaped at it, then at the kid, who was staring fixedly at it, breathing in short hard pants. The pot began to wobble its way across the intervening empty space between them. The kid's eyes never left its progress, and when it was close enough he reached out and gripped it tightly, then sagged into a ball, shoulders shaking.

"You," Becks whispered. "You're a Flinger? Are you?" The kid looked up; the tears had broken and run down his cheeks, leaving muddy tracks behind. "I guess you are." She paused. "I didn't know Flingers could do it so young as you." And it had been hard for him, she could see that—if that was *all* he could do, it clearly wasn't much of a help to him now. But if anybody else found him—besides all the other uses a little kid might be put to, if anybody snatching him up found out he was a Flinger—"You really ought to let me take you back where you belong. You really—oh, why *not?*" as he determinedly shook his head.

His lips parted; he coughed, dryly, and after another few seconds tried again. "It's safer here," he whispered hoarsely. Becks glanced at his throat; a ring of dark mottled flesh was raised all around it.

"All right," she said finally. "You can stay. For a while. But if anybody finds you hiding out here, you *don't* know me. Got it?"

He nodded solemnly, pouring the honey atop the remains of the bread.

The Mole's idling engine sounded coarse—Becks had checked its power gauge first thing, but its ambergris was still comfortably charged, enough for months yet of operation. She listened to it for a few minutes more, then shut the Mole down and laboriously cranked the back cover open, exposing its mechanical innards.

"Mmph." Becks folded her arms across her chest and glowered down at the exposed engine. The kid leaned around her elbow to peer interestedly into its depths. "See that?" Becks's accusing finger pointed at the roughened plane atop the Mole's primary piston. "They ran the Mole too fast, is what they did, and they didn't top off the oil feed first. I tell them and *tell* them to do that and they forget and they don't."

The kid nodded vigorously up at her, furrowing his eyebrows down into a frown to match hers. Becks grinned reluctantly. "Do I really look like that? Well, I hope I do!

That's fierce. You know, if you won't tell me your name, I got to call you something. How about 'Fierce?'"

They had fallen into something of a routine, she and the newly-named Fierce, for a few weeks now. Becks had made a habit of filching extra provisions from the kitchen, and had got used to the constant low-grade anxiety about being caught at it. She made sure she got down to the tunnels at least once a day, too, even on the days when she had no particular Mole duties to fulfill. Fierce looked better now than he had when she had first laid eyes on him, there was no doubt about that.

His stubbornness about his real name didn't really trouble Becks—she doubted half the current residents of the Labyrinth went by the names they'd been born with. She was unhappier about his flat refusal to so much as hint at where his home might be. Besides the worry of looking out for him on a daily basis, she was starting to suspect that he didn't belong in the Labyrinth at all; he was just a little too jumpy around the vermin, a little too clumsy in the dark, to have grown up cheek and jowl with it. He'd likely wandered down either from the harbor or the Market...but how had he got all the way down to the Mole tunnels? They were nowhere near the dockside entrances or the Market, where street vendors and taverns habitually spilled down a level or two into the Labyrinth itself, catering to denizens of the Labyrinth and the city proper alike.

"Your name is Becks," said Fierce, in his familiar hoarse whisper. He wrinkled his nose. "That's not a girl's name."

"Well, it is, because I'm a girl," said Becks dryly. "But I do my best to help everyone else forget that, aye? It's short for *Rebecca*." She drew the syllables out, grimacing, and Fierce giggled soundlessly. "I don't think much of it either, do you? Becks is better." She squinted at the piston.

"So, I need—hey!" Her strap wrench floated up, only a little wobbly, to bump against her knuckles. "That's right! For a Flinger, you do got a bit of a knack for this too."

Becks buckled down to work on the engine, and Fierce really was a help—he was picking up her Mole lore at a smart pace for a kid who still had most of his baby teeth. Was it possible he had a Spark—a Spark *and* Flinging? But that wasn't too likely—the only folks who had more than one thing, and even having one was rare enough, had to have it from *both* their parents, everyone knew that. The Lords and Ladies of the city were the only ones who were many-magicked, and they mated amongst themselves like rats in a warren trying to spawn as many more as they could, shocking even to Becks's Labyrinth-inculcated lack of morals.

No, Fierce was likely just a result of the Lords carousing in the docks or the Market, heedlessly sowing their magick seed, which they did all the time. Not that the Ladies didn't get up to similar hijinks, but they took their wombs back home with them after—it was lucky those seeds and wombs were so barren, or the whole city would be knee-deep in magickal babies. She snorted at that mental image.

"Becks?"

"Hmm?"

"What's a Spark?"

Becks jerked backwards violently enough to bang her head on the engine cover. *"Ow!"* She clutched the back of her skull with her free hand. "What? Why?"

Fierce was squinting up at her warily. "I just wondered. Is it like Flinging?"

"No!"

Fierce flinched back, and Becks was immediately remorseful. It wasn't so strange, after all, that he would know what Flinging was, without knowing much about the Spark or any other flavor of magick. He might never have met, maybe never even seen anybody else besides himself with any magick at all his whole life.

"No," Becks said, more temperately. "It's not like Flinging—well, it *is* magick, like Flinging. But the Spark has to do with machines, especially mech-magickal ones, the ones powered by ambergris. I dunno if the ambergris is magickal when it comes out of the whales, or if the Mech-Mages make it magickal somehow, but I do know they can charge the ambergris up again after it runs dry. And they got, you know. *An affinity for machines.*" Somebody had told her that, years ago—she hadn't known what that meant, then. But now—she scowled down at the engine.

Fierce tugged on her trouser leg. She tried to look down at him, but a greasy lock of brown hair had escaped her cap and fallen over her eyes; she irritably shoved it back as Fierce pulled harder on her trousers. "What?"

"Becks? I thought I heard something, last night." His voice was even threadier than usual.

"You probably did. Us eating down here isn't the greatest idea, you know. Rats, bats, roaches—" She shuddered.

"Besides those. Something *else.*" His eyes were enormous in his dirt-streaked face.

"Like what?" Becks glanced around uneasily. The shadowy corners of the Mole's tunnel seemed even more impenetrably black than usual.

Fierce looked shifty. "Something big." He tightened his grip on her trousers. "I'm scared to stay down here by myself."

Becks's mouth compressed into a line. "I've said I'll take you home, any time you want, just say the word—"

"Why can't I come to *your* home?"

"Because I don't really have one. I have a hidey-hole, away from everyone else, and I don't take nobody there. Not even you. I told you that already." She blew out an exasperated breath. "Look, I don't want to try and make you go back to a bad place. I'd never do that. But this maybe isn't the best place for you eith—aw, *don't* cry, wait!"

But it was too late—Fierce had bolted out of the tunnel. She doubted he'd go far; the passages this far down were only irregularly lit and if a person didn't know his way around them like the back of his hand, he'd get hopelessly lost. Fierce was smarter than that—she hoped. No, he *was*, but he was also just a little kid and she almost gave in then, almost yelled out that she'd changed her mind, he could come with her when she left for the night—but her throat closed up and she just couldn't do it. Her hidey-hole was the only place in her whole life she'd ever been able to let her guard down, not tensed up waiting for the next blow to fall or something even worse. Her first six months in it, after she'd joined Sal's crew and claimed it for her own, had been just like the Heaven she'd heard the preachers in the Market going on about. To let someone, *anyone*—even just a little kid—into her own, *private* place—no.

But her eyes stung anyway; she swiped at them with her knuckles and went back to reassembling the Mole's engine cover with hands that were rougher than they had to be. He'd either come back, or he wouldn't; she'd done enough for him already, hadn't she?

Fierce hadn't come back after all, by the time she was ready to leave for the night. She lingered a bit longer, pretending to give the Mole's cockpit windows a last-minute polish they didn't need, but the passage outside remained utterly silent. She finally gave up and trudged the long way back to her hidey-hole. Once in it, though, she couldn't sleep at all; after tossing and turning on her pallet, she gave up and groped for her hand lantern.

She was still proud of that lantern—she had stolen one of the dead wall sconces that littered the Labyrinth to build it, though she didn't know if *stolen* was the right word, since nobody else had ever shown any signs of caring about them after they burnt out. The sconces, like the massive iron ventilation fans and the Moles themselves, were mech-magickal—and she had just wanted to *see* one up close.

Becks didn't know if anybody else ever *saw* machines the way she did—there wasn't anybody she dared ask. She stared down at the lantern and let her gaze unfocus as her fingers lightly stroked the curving steel of its outer cage. In her mind's eye, a picture of the insides of the lantern was forming—entirely fanciful, maybe, or maybe just her memory of assembling it, piece by piece, from bits of the sconce and various other odds and ends she'd collected over her years of fixing machines—she didn't know. But she could *see* them now, just as clearly as she could see the rest of her hidey-hole, *see* the tight-wound springs and gears in their intricate, functional patterns, and as she leaned forward on her knees, pressing both palms into the cold, smooth metal, she thought she could *feel* the shining heat of its ambergris core bleeding into her bare hands.

*Do* I *got a Spark?* That suspicion had awakened in her a few years back, and done nothing but grow ever since no matter how much she tried not to think about it. She thought the Spark, if she had one, might be growing, too. She was of an age for it—near to becoming a woman, she thought, though she was hazy on the exact number of years that had elapsed since her birth. But she didn't know what to do about it if she did.

Everyone knew the story of Billy Turner, magickal Splitter, Market-born a good half-century before—he'd manifested at twelve, murdered his whole family and gone on to rule the tunnels below the city with an iron fist. He'd finally made the fatal mistake of trying to expand his reach aboveground, though, and the Pinkertons had got him in the end. And now nobody, in *or* out of the Labyrinth, wanted to hear ever again about one of the Labyrinth's own maybe having a Spark or any other kind of magick.

She fell asleep at some point in her musings, curled up around her lantern; a formless time later she awoke with a start, nearly cracking her skull against the low ceiling. Her heart was pounding, her breath coming in short hard bursts she tried to stifle under her hand. The sound that had awoken her, that she hadn't even had a chance to convince herself had only been her imagination or a dream, came again—a tiny, choked sob.

*Fierce?* She started to reach for the ragged curtain that she'd fixed up across the crevice that led to her hidey-hole, then froze as a low, coughing growl echoed off the stone walls. *That* sure as hell wasn't Fierce— *"Becks!"* shrieked a voice, a child's high-pitched wail of terror, and Becks flung herself through the curtain, scrabbling for her precious hand lantern as she went.

She found the lantern's ignition switch just as her feet hit the floor; bilious light flared all around her. Fierce was cowering against the stone wall a few feet from her hidey-hole, and barely five feet further on was a *Thing* like Becks had never seen before in her life. It was clearly mech-magickal, just like the Mole and her hand lantern were, but the purposes the Mole and lantern alike were intended for were obvious, clean and lacking in malevolence.

Crouched on all fours, the Thing's head easily reached as high as Becks's shoulder; the shuddering light picked up coppery sparks from the overlapping scales covering its upper body and silvery ones from the rows of thick, stubby horns on its back. Each of its four feet ended in a huge single claw, matching the one that projected forward from its narrow triangular snout. If it had any eyes, she couldn't see them, but it did have teeth—a double row of serrated fangs lining its terrible maw.

The Thing let loose with another deep-pitched growl and lunged towards Fierce, then stopped, straining—at *nothing*. Fierce was panting, fists clenched so hard his knuckles shone white through the skin. The Thing jerked forward, three times in rapid succession, each time gaining a bare inch or two of rocky floor towards him. Fierce sobbed and thrust his fists out at it; it lurched backwards an entire half-foot, but then regained it as he sank to his knees, his face now as white as his knuckles.

Becks struggled free of her horrified paralysis and stumbled forward. The Thing ignored her, its entire attention focused on Fierce. She couldn't even begin to imagine how strong it was, or how Fierce was managing to restrain the weight of that much metal so determined to reach him, but it was clear he couldn't do it much longer. She thought of jumping atop it, but likely it would have her off in seconds and then pounce on Fierce, if it didn't take the time to roll over her and grind her to jelly first with those horns. Her lantern swung uselessly from her clenched fingers.

Her lantern—

Her *mech-magickal* lantern—

*Well, now's the time*—shock and terror had wiped all the emotion from the thought. *Now's the time to find out if I really got a Spark or not.*

It was easy enough to *look* at the Thing as she had looked at her hand lantern, as she looked at the Mole. She could still see it as it was—metal scales and horns and snapping jaws lined with glittering saw-edged teeth, rear claws gouging the stone floor for purchase—but she could also *see* it, see how it must work, how each of its parts fit seamlessly into the others and gave it motive force, leverage-driven strength and fine control. And within its heart, the snarl of pistons and valves and rings that substituted for that living organ, she could *feel* the ambergris that energized all its mechanical being.

But all she had ever done was *look* and *feel*. That was all she'd done to build her hand lantern with a scrap of stolen ambergris—she hadn't needed to do anything else, to make it work. She hadn't needed to do anything else to fix and cosset Sal's Mole all these years. She'd been too scared to ever try anything more—scared in roughly equal measures of success (images of the Mole shattered to pieces and herself shredded by its shrapnel) and failure (what a laugh, to imagine that she, Becks, was somehow *special!*—nothing but a Labyrinth whore's bastard, after all).

*Well, if I fail now, at least I won't be around afterward to feel bad about it, aye?*

Becks sprang forward and slapped her free hand down on the Thing's thick metal flank. It roared, head whipping about on a suddenly extensible neck, and then Becks *reached*.

It felt a lot like dunking her head into a bucket of boiling water might. She didn't know if it was always like this, or if the Thing's obvious awfulness made it somehow worse—she gritted her teeth and *reached* harder. There— *there* was its ambergris core, far bigger than the Mole's, held tight in a bracket of copper and chromium steel— both her fists clenched involuntarily along with every other muscle in her body as she drove into that core with single-minded desperation. *Crush! Break! DESTROY! DESTROY! DESTROY—*

The Thing bellowed, so loudly that needles of pain drove into Becks's ears and something broke deep in her sinuses. A bright flare blinded her and her legs collapsed as if her bones had turned to water, crumpling her into a heap. Through her streaming eyes she saw the Thing slowly topple sideways and hit the floor with an oddly muffled clang—*muffled,* she thought dimly, because something wasn't quite right with her hearing. Was it *dead?* Becks tried to *see* it, *feel* it, but all that happened was that her vision tilted alarmingly and her stomach lurched right along with it. And if it *wasn't* dead—

Becks managed somehow to stagger back up to her feet, though she couldn't have stayed there without Fierce's bony little shoulder wedged under her elbow. His fingers dug into her arm; she looked down at him, meaning to tell him that they had to go, *run*, but still couldn't quite catch her breath to speak. It wasn't necessary, though, because he had clearly figured that out already and was tugging her towards the bend at the end of the passage.

Becks let him lead her—she was in no shape to lead herself, and it wasn't likely he could wander anywhere in the Labyrinth that she couldn't eventually find their way out of. Gradually the ringing in her ears died away and her thundering, hitching pulse slowed and she was finally able to hear what Fierce was muttering up at her— "Nurse was gone, I think they *killed* her, Becks, and they put a bag over my head and then I woke up down here and they laughed at me when I peed my pants and they set one of those monster *Things* to watch me and when I tried to run away the first time it *choked* me—"

"Shh," Becks mumbled, rubbing at her nose with the hand that still thankfully clutched her lantern, then stared blankly down at the new dark smears across her knuckles. "Wait." They'd been moving for a while; Becks thought it was reasonably safe to stop now. She sat limply down, digging her back into the rough stone wall, and looked around. They'd got all the way to near the Labyrinth's dockside exits; there were patches of sea-moss growing where the walls met the uneven arch of the ceiling. "Good job," she said hoarsely, and gave Fierce's head a clumsy pat; her limbs still didn't feel quite right, strangely disconnected from the rest of her.

Fierce knelt beside her. "They were waiting for the *hand-off*," he whispered. "I saw them thinking about it. The men that took me from Nurse. And the lady with them. She wanted to hurt me." He shuddered, and Becks patted him again consolingly, then froze with her fingers tangled in his matted hair.

"You saw them *what?*"

"I'm a Thinker, too." Fierce eyed her nervously. "It's how I found your hidey-hole. Don't be mad, Becks."

"Of course you are," Becks said faintly, and shut her eyes.

But the dam had finally broken on all Fierce's reticence. "They told me that if I ever tried to go back home they'd kill Mama and Papa too, next time—" The words tumbled out, as if he'd been physically restraining them all the time they'd been together. "Not just Nurse. And they meant it, I could *see* they did. I did think that maybe they couldn't do that, especially not to Papa…but maybe they *could* have, maybe Mama and Papa might not have believed they could do it either and then they could take them by surprise and *kill* them and take me away again—" Becks pried her heavy eyelids open, sighed and held up an arm. Fierce dove down and pressed himself up tight against her side; she wrapped the arm comfortingly around his shoulders.

"But," Becks said as firmly as she could manage, a few minutes later after his shivering had abated, "I really *don't* think you're safer down here anymore—"

Fierce sucked in a shuddering breath. "I know. I knew when I, I heard the Thing—or I *saw* it—I'm not sure, I just knew it was near. Coming for me again. It isn't like people—it doesn't have thoughts like people, but I knew it was there. Close. That's why I didn't come back, even though I knew you were waiting for me. I didn't think it would want you, so you would be safe." He twisted his neck around to gaze solemnly up at her face. "It might want you now, though."

It was Becks's turn to shudder. "Of course it wouldn't want me. Why would it want *me?*" Fierce's lips parted, clearly intent on expounding as to *why*—Becks clapped a hand over his mouth and glared down at him until he subsided. "What did you mean by 'hand-off,' anyway? Why would anyone take you away from your parents?"

"The people who took me called it that, in their heads. They were going to get lots of money for it." There was an awful sort of knowledge in his eyes, clear and colorless as water in the lantern light. "Mama and Papa never let me go outside our house, or even walk around in our garden without at least Nurse. They said it was too dangerous. But I guess I wasn't really safe in our garden with Nurse either."

Kidnapped, and held for ransom...? By who? *Who'd dare?* The only obvious answer sent Becks even tighter back up against the wall. *Other Lords and Ladies*—Becks hadn't known they got up to such things as *kidnapping,* amongst themselves. She had always imagined them, when she'd thought of them at all, as some sort of massed, united, decadent front—

"So," Becks said, in what she hoped was a bracing tone, "Where *is* your house?"

Fierce rubbed his eyes. "I don't know—I'm not lying, Becks, I swear! I just don't *know*." His face was miserable. "I don't know where home *is*. I don't know any street names. We always took our carriage everywhere."

That was a conundrum. "Huh. I'd ask your parents' names, but honestly, it's not like I know where any particular Lord or Lady lives either." Becks frowned in thought. "Wait—tell me about *around* where you live. Maybe a train station, or a big park, or someplace I've ever heard of—"

"There's a big building!" Fierce said eagerly. "A *really* big building—it's all white, and it has arches at the bottom. It's just down the street from our house." His face fell. "But I don't remember what it's called."

But Becks knew it. It was one of the few places in the city aboveground that she did know—not that she'd ever dared go anywhere near it before, nor had any reason to. "Has to be the Continental Trust building—where the Pinkertons are," and her voice trailed off. The police were for the ordinary, magickless and law-abiding folks—well, she hadn't turned out to be any of those things, had she? The Pinkertons were for the Lords and Ladies when they needed the law's help. She certainly wasn't a Lord or Lady either...but Fierce was, or would be someday "Well. It's not like we have to actually go *inside* it..."

Fierce stared all around, mouth hanging open. "I guess you didn't come down to the Labyrinth by way of the docks," Becks remarked. "They're something, aye?"

The sun had risen while they were making their way out of the Labyrinth; now it shone dully down on the scene before them, a tarnished silver disk in the overcast sky. Row after boxy row of buildings spread out away from the ledge on which Becks and Fierce crouched, towards the heart of the city, with the occasional steeple upthrusting from the sea of chimneys. The huge wooden sign proclaiming *Port of Baltimore* swung, creaking, in the cool wet wind from the sea, reeking of fish even to Becks's hardened nose. Passenger ships hugged the harbor's crowded east end, nearly bouncing into each other with each gentle swell of the tide. Fierce pointed wordlessly at the west end of the dock, tugging on Becks's jersey with his other hand.

"Oh—that's a Carcharodon. Ambergris traders—see, there's one of the kobolds that crew it, down on the docks." The kobold stood at the end of the Carcharodon's gangplank, motionless except for its swiveling head, yellow eyes like beacons tirelessly sweeping the piers. The Carcharodon itself, in all its massive painted-steel glory, was secured to the dock with chains thicker around than Becks's thighs, making horrific screeching noises every time it rode up high on a wave. "They trawl for ambergris out on the open water—over at Rocky Point you can sometimes see a bunch of them out on the beach, raking the sand for it. I heard they hunt the whales too sometimes, the special ones that make the ambergris. I guess they don't always want to wait for it to come out on its own—" Becks grimaced. "Nevermind. Come on, let's climb down."

Once at street level, Becks kept them close to the walls, away from the rapidly increasing foot traffic of more legitimate citizens. Fierce didn't need any urging to stay plastered to Becks's side. The Continental Trust building loomed over its neighbors, a good sixteen stories high; Becks had only ever seen it from a distance before, never up close. She parked herself and Fierce in a convenient alley across the street from it and tried not to gape up at it like a rube—she had to crane her neck so far back her head was nearly parallel with the ground, just to glimpse the topmost floors. Fierce barely gave it a glance before squinting anxiously up and down the street, then grabbed Beck's hand and yanked her forward. *"There!* That one!"

Halfway down the block, he pulled her across the street, nearly into the path of a trolley—*"Fierce!"* *"I'm sorry, Becks!"* —then up to a pair of stone lions guarding a set of steps leading up to a massive wooden door. "This is my house," Fierce whispered, now clutching her hand with both of his.

There were a whole row of houses there, all squashed together—the rightward wall of one seemed tightly molded to the leftward wall of the next, all the way down the line. But they were *tall*—not anywhere near as tall as the Continental Trust, but a good four or five stories high apiece, much taller than Becks had ever imagined houses would be.

Fierce stepped forward; Becks very reluctantly followed him up the stairs. Standing on his tiptoes, he could just reach the door knocker with his fingertips; it was solid chromium steel, gleaming against the black wood of the door. After a few failed swipes, Fierce finally managed to give it a healthy bang against its backstop, making Becks flinch.

After several seconds the door swung silently back and a tall, slim young man with thick light-brown hair in a queue and livery grand enough to shame an emperor gazed down his nose at them. Speech was apparently more of an honor than he was willing to bestow upon them—nose wrinkling ostentatiously, he stepped backward and reached again for the door.

*"Mama!"* shrieked Fierce, as the door began to swing shut in their faces—it stuttered to a halt, and before Becks had time to react, Fierce had barreled forward, slamming so hard into the door that, in spite of its size and heft, it

bounced back a good three feet, spilling the silvery sunlight in a torrent into the shadowy hall beyond.

A woman stood in the hallway, frozen in midstep, head lifted high on a long, graceful neck. She wore a powder-blue skirt and matching silk jacket, and her snow-white blouse spilled a waterfall of lace from throat to waist. Her hair was a brighter, deeper gold than Fierce's, but of the same flyaway straw-straight texture, wisping out of its elaborate coiffure of loops and coils around her porcelain face. Becks had never in her life seen anybody so beautiful up close.

Then the woman fell to her knees and held her arms out just in time to catch Fierce in them. *"George!"* she screamed. "George, come here, come *now!"*

Boots pounded down the stairs at the far end of the hall and a man dashed into view, even before the last echoes of the woman's scream had died away. "My God, is that *Harry?* Harry, my God!" he shouted, and he caught both of them together in what looked like a bone-crushing embrace.

Becks, swallowing hard against the mysterious lump in her throat that had appeared out of nowhere, began to back away slowly—indulging herself long enough to linger and watch them for a minute more, and that was her mistake. She should have cut and run as soon as Fierce's mother started squeezing her son nearly to death; instead, her lagging steps gave Fierce enough time to wrestle his head out of his mother's neck and twist around in her arms, his own arm swinging up to point at Becks.

Warning bells went off in Becks's head—no matter how much gratitude Fierce himself might feel towards her, his parents' feelings were a lot less certain. She started to turn on her heel to bolt, and then found that she abruptly *couldn't.* It was like being enveloped by a huge, invisible pillow; her heart hammering frantically in her chest, and her lungs now pumping like bellows, were uncompressed by that terrible hold, but her arms and legs and head were utterly immobile no matter how hard she strained. Both the man and the woman were staring at her now, the woman with her mouth opened wide and the man with a face like stone.

She heard the woman's voice then, distantly— *"Stop, George, you're frightening her!"* and the pressure abruptly eased; Becks staggered and almost fell before catching herself against the balustrade. She backed rapidly down the steps, out of sight of all three of them, then broke and ran, not caring where she was going. A full-grown, adult Flinger—no, she wasn't going to be anywhere where he could *see* her again—

But they didn't try to pursue her, or if they did, they couldn't catch her. Becks thought the first was more likely; after all, they had their son back now. She was still painfully glad for Fierce, though, and both glad and sorry for herself—it had been an added complication in an already complicated life, trying to secretly care for a little kid—but it had been something, to have a person around who was even a little bit like herself, and not having to hide herself away always, in every way there was to hide.

At that thought, Becks stopped running and finally looked around. Her feet had had more wits than her head because she was back under the docks now, where there was another entrance into the Labyrinth. She edged toward it, keeping a sharp eye out for the smugglers that most often frequented this one—but it was hard, because her thoughts were in a sudden mad tumult. She hadn't had time to process it before; first she'd been fighting for their lives, then she'd been making her way through a less-familiar part of the Labyrinth and then further into the city proper than she'd ever gone aboveground before.

*I do got a Spark.*

*I'm a Mech-Mage.*

Becks stared at her hand, resting lightly on the trapdoor leading down to the Labyrinth: her home; the only home she'd ever known. The half-rotted wood was inert under her palm and dead to her mind's eye. She wasn't twice- or thrice- or whatever-number-magicked Fierce was, nor likely ever to be so powerful as his father, able to reach out and just effortlessly *hold* a person motionless from the crown of her head to the soles of her feet without even breaking a sweat. But—

She thrust her other hand into her pocket, where she'd stuffed her hand lantern after they'd left the Labyrinth. At the first brush of her fingers against the cool metal, a shudder rolled up her arm and she could *see* the lantern, every hinge and striker and the tiny, beating heart of ambergris buried deep inside it—it was a little frightening, how quickly and easily it came to her now, as if the battle in the Labyrinth had torn off a cover deep inside her mind that she hadn't even known was there.

*Mech-Mage.*

She could hardly fathom it.

She had considered, more and more often as the years had passed, abandoning the Labyrinth for the city above it. She had hit upon the idea trying to win a place as an engineer's drudge in one the great foundries on Sparrows Point—once she'd settled in with Sal's crew, she'd come to realize just how valuable all her Mole lore in particular, and how rare her knack with machines in general, was. Before then, her main interest had only been in survival, raw and brutal; actual *satisfaction* or even more shocking, *happiness* had not seemed like goals worth striving for, as distant and unachievable as the Moon.

Her casual obfuscation of her gender, though, while serving her well enough below the city, likely couldn't have withstood a more constant scrutiny aboveground. Women seldom set up shop in the city proper as engineers or mechanics, and the few who did, certainly hadn't begun life as nameless Labyrinth waifs—what use was there in learning more machine lore if she'd never be allowed the chance to use it? Better to stay where she was, live however she could, figure out something else someday…

But she had more than just simple mechanic's lore to lurk and spy and glean for, now. And if she could master *that*, somehow—learn what all a true Mech-Mage could know and do and be—

The trapdoor beckoned, familiar and repellent. She didn't have anywhere else to go, anyway…not now. Not yet.

Becks straightened her spine and pushed the trapdoor open, slipping back down with the ease of long practice into the darkness beneath the city.

*Lisa Short is a Texas-born, Kansas-bred writer of fantasy, science fiction and horror. She has an honorable discharge from the United States Army, a degree in chemical engineering, and twenty years' experience as a professional engineer. Lisa currently lives in Maryland with her husband, two youngest children, father-in-law and cats. She is a member of the Horror Writers Association and a Futurescapes 2021 alumnus.*

# Scourge of the Airways

## *Karina Steffens*

In retrospect, booking first class passage on an Averly Airship was hardly the cleverest way of accomplishing my escape.

The deluxe stateroom on board *RMA Helios* occupied square footage akin to my shoe closet back home. Hiding away inside it, with my dog-eared penny dreadful for company, may have seemed the prudent course of action, but in truth would have set off a dangerous ripple of raised eyebrows and wagging tongues. Instead, I resolved to come down to the gondola and blend in with Society in the first class lounge.

So there I was, sat next to the panoramic window with the French countryside gliding below, partly obstructed by gathering clouds. At a nearby card table, some of my fellow passengers engaged in a game of Whist and Gossip. I heard a familiar name mentioned, and my pulse quickened, anxious for news-crumbs from home. Sadly, the rest was drowned out by Widow Theodosia Billinghurst, whose husband must have passed away from an incurable ear condition.

"Disgraceful," the old woman was saying, "how little they spend on heating the communal areas, do you not agree, Miss Walden?"

"Indeed I do, Mrs Billinghurst," I said with an equable little smile.

She hadn't the slightest notion how unfeasible it would be to keep the brass-and-wood gondola as warm as our cabins in the dirigible's hull. A deficiency quite to my advantage, as both temperature and air travel etiquette favoured practicality over style. In contrast to my usual sunny attire, I had donned a brown, high-collared bodice and a matching skirt. My pale hair hid under a dark bonnet, its wispy veil shading my eyes. Nothing about this mousy ensemble would betray the identity I hoped to leave forever behind.

There was no refuge, however, from Mrs Billinghurst's hawk-eyed scrutiny under the brim of her fortress of black lace. I fidgeted with my collar and complained, once again, about "that wretched girl" missing our flight.

I had not been previously acquainted with Widow Terror-dosia or any of the others. The newly commissioned Royal Mail Airship's third voyage had begun in Edinburgh, and the only passenger scheduled to join *RMA Helios* on her brief layover at Averly Airfield, south-east of London, had found his reservation mysteriously misplaced. In the ensuing confusion, a certain "Elizabeth Walden" had boarded in his stead.

No sooner had I stepped onto the gangway than the tongue-wagging commenced. Neither God nor the Queen approved of a young woman travelling unaccompanied in first class. Mrs Billinghurst *most certainly* disapproved, and had made it abundantly clear until I broke down and asked her to chaperon. I should have expected it, really, in this floating bubble of Victoria's England, but would the Republic of Venice be any different? The Americas, Africa, Canton … How far must I run to find freedom?

"My dear, this will simply not do," Mrs Billinghurst proclaimed. "As soon as we disembark in Constantinople, we must find you a new maid at the consulate."

"You are too kind." I resolved to slip away well before that.

A clockworker steward rolled up. The latest model, as the fine detailing on its brass mustachios and faux-jacket revealed to the discerning eye. A hatch opened in its midriff, and a tray slid out; articulate arms flexed to deposit a porcelain tea set and a transcript of the latest news bulletin received by the onboard wireless.

She reached for the paper, leaving the teapot to me.

"No sugar," she said as I poured the steaming, black brew she had insisted on ordering despite my hopes for exotic tisane. "It wreaks havoc with digestion."

I stirred milk and two sugar cubes into my own cup and tried not to stare at the back of the transcript. I sipped the sickly-sweet tea and watched a peculiar, whale shaped cloud drifting our way.

"Well!" the shrill voice cut through my cloud gazing. "Of course, in *my* day we would not have dreamt of postponing a wedding due to a headache or sneeze. Today's youth have no stamina."

"*Postponing* a wedding?" My teacup rattled in the saucer's groove.

"Yes, yes, the impending Averly-Carmichael nuptials, do keep up." She tapped on the paper. "It says so right here: The aviation magnate's daughter, Miss Estelle Gwendolyn Averly, was unexpectedly taken ill, and the wedding is postponed until her complete recovery."

Warmth drained from my cheeks and awoke a dangerous glow in the gossip's eyes.

"Miss Walden, you seem quite affected! Are you acquainted with the bride?"

"Oh, no, not at all … It does sound rather worrying, though, the poor thing."

In truth, I was in perfect health, although the mad-doctors might diagnose me with hysterical affliction for fleeing the prospect of marital bliss. But if Father had his way, neither Society nor the Carmichaels need ever learn the truth. Should I "recover" in a timely fashion, then the wedding, business alliance, and expanded production of Averly Airships could still be salvaged. I had been a fool to expect otherwise.

"Oh, piffle." She sniffed. "I doubt it is anything too terminal."

But wait – what if it *was*?

Under the table, I reached into my reticule for the reassuring touch of metal: my portable, galvanic analytical engine, the very same I had recently employed for spiking into the local booking office to switch reservations and create the "Walden" identity. By connecting it to the ship's wireless, I could spike into the telegraphy station at Averly Hall and relay the sad news of my demise to the London Times.

If the public and my prospective in-laws assumed I had passed away, Father would have to call his men off the search or risk igniting a scandal. Mother might disagree but would, as always, comply in the end.

With the message and spiking instructions pre-encoded into the Analytic, it would only take a brief connection to send a rapid burst of Morse code. But first, I had to gain access to the wireless room in the control car.

"I wonder, Mrs Billinghurst, can passengers arrange a tour of the *Helios*? I should like to see the bridge, oh, and those new Solar-Steam turbine everyone speaks of and –"

She blinked. "Why yes, though I cannot see the appeal. I shall accompany you, of course. My word, young people are so easily distracted."

Indeed, distraction was quite the thing. If I could prompt Terror-dosia to engage our escorting officer in a barrage of advice on the proper running of airships, neither would notice me plugging a portable device into the wireless.

With midday-dinner soon to be served, my scheme had to wait. I sipped from my cup and looked out the window just as the large, whale shaped cloud decided to behave in a most uncloudlike manner.

An airship swam out of the cloud, as bizarre a contraption as ever to have sailed the skies. Its gondola, for want of a better word, was the reclaimed hull of a shipwrecked brigantine, cobbled into something that could be dangled from a semi-rigid blimp on high tension wires.

It began to turn about, revealing the name *Leviathan* painted on the envelope. Below the keel, three hooks lowered to release a sphere each; three pairs of wings unfolded, and the ornithopters hovered mid-air. Over the stern, a black flag was hoisted, with two white wings under a grinning skull.

Airwaymen colours.

Our alarm bells went off, scattering people, clockworkers, and Mrs Billinghurst in a panicked frenzy. I ought to have followed suit: run, hide, anything but stay and watch pirates attack from the sky. But my limbs had chosen that very moment to turn into lead. My eyes were glued to the panoramic window with the best views afforded on board.

The *Leviathan* finished turning and matched speed in parallel with us. From the railing, a swivel cannon swung towards us and fired. Below it, a row of gun-ports opened and launched harpoons into our envelope. The gondola shuddered as both airships were pulled closer together, and leather-clad Airwaymen bridged the gaps by zipping over the lines.

One of the ornithopters flew close to the window, and I stared at the gleam in its pilot's goggles.

That finally broke through my paralysis. I grabbed my reticule, sprang out of the chair, and pushed my way out of the lounge.

Somehow, I had to get to the wireless room and telegraph for help.

Cyrus J Averly had never encouraged his disappointingly female child to follow in his footsteps. But he had not anticipated my insatiable curiosity and prodigious talent for snooping, undetected, into his business. White nights had been spent poring over schematics by candlelight. Although I had never set foot on an Averly Airship, I knew my way around even this, the latest model. At least my fingers did: on paper, without the milling bodies of passengers, crewmen, and befuddled clockworkers.

My progress towards the bow was painfully slow. Judging by the surrounding pandemonium, most passengers of both classes had already come down to the gondola for midday-dinner, but the stomping of feet still reverberated from the ceiling, accompanied by muffled screams and gunshots.

After what seemed like eons, I reached the control car and opened the bulkhead door. To my relief, it was as yet unoccupied by pirates. Through its corridor I could see part of the bridge with the back of a helmsman wrestling with the rudder wheel, an elevatorman struggling to control the pitch and altitude, and an ornithopter hovering beyond the glass panes.

Neither man could have left his post since the attack began; those pirates had timed it impeccably, with most of the ship's officers going off duty for dinner. Moreover, should a crewman literate in Morse code endeavour to transmit an SOS, he would only send it to the French Authorities, who would hardly take the attack quite as personally as the proud, private owner of the airship fleet.

Or the less-than-proud owner of a runaway daughter.

His men in Lyon would launch a swift, decisive response, but should the local Gendarmerie receive my distress call, I might still slip away unnoticed ... if they ever arrived at all.

A hand grabbed my shoulder, followed by a flustered voice in my ear. "Miss!"

I spun toward the red-faced steward, speechless with shock. How dare he touch me in this fashion?

The wretched man flinched at the look in my eyes and snatched away his hand. "Miss, you should not be here!"

"Indeed I should! Kindly keep your hands to yourself and allow me to save this airship."

The steward blinked but the idea of a woman saving an airship did not quite sink in.

"Please, you must find shelter. The Airwaymen will be here any –"

His jaw snapped shut as a pair of booted legs appeared on the ladder coming down from the hull.

Not waiting for the rest of the Airwayman to materialise, I shoved the steward back into the gondola and slammed the bulkhead behind us.

My heart was pounding out dots and dashes. I had failed. I was too late.

Perhaps not yet. "Where do you keep the spare?"

"Spare?" The useless man mumbled.

"Yes, the portable, emergency wireless. You *must* have one of those."

"Oh." He pointed weakly towards the stern. "In the storage room behind crew's quarters, but … you can't use it."

I drew myself up. "I am perfectly capable of tapping out an SOS."

"I wouldn't know, Miss, but don't you see? It's backup in case of shipwide galvanic failure, right? Small enough to be powered by a stationary bicycle – back in the control car!"

Abruptly, the *Helios* shuddered and stopped dead in the air, sending us floundering against each-other. The

*Leviathan's* swivel cannon must have hit the main propeller.

I disengaged from the steward and dove back into the bedlam, employing my elbows to good effect. Eventually, I reached the gondola's aft ladder mostly intact, apart for some scratches and an elbow – not mine – in the chin.

But how could I be certain no one would be waiting on the other side?

Renewed screaming behind me meant some of the Airwaymen had made their way from the control car into the gondola. I had to take a chance. But before I could do so, a burly male passenger pushed me aside and clambered up the ladder.

*The cheek!* Whatever happened to women and children first?

I followed him up, poked my head through the hatch, and immediately ducked down again. Some grunts and a thud later, the urge to look got the better of me. I hazarded another peek, in time to see a dazed Airwayman getting up to stumble after the man.

With thanks to Mr Burly-and-Boorish under my breath, I slipped out of the passengers' quarters towards the storage room.

The dimly lit keel corridor was blissfully empty of Airwaymen. On either side of me lay the crew's tent-like quarters. Enormous hydrogen gas cells loomed overhead, each wrapped like a puffed sleeve around the axial corridor. They shielded me from any watchers from above, except for the sparse gaps in between, where brass ladders joined the two walkways together.

As I neared the first of those gaps, a sudden stomping of boots on brass sent me scurrying for cover. I ducked into one of the tents, stumbling over layers of petticoats. One of my shoes came off and I barely had time to nudge it into the tent before pulling the flap behind me. Frozen, I waited for the steps to come the rest of the way down the ladder.

"*Attandez!*" a boyish voice called out and continued in French-flavoured English. "Did you hear that, Jack?"

I looked frantically around me for cover, but any movement would only generate more noise.

"Hear what, Simone?" The reply came in an American accent and a deeper pitched voice.

"Ah, never you mind," said Simone. A *female* Airwayman? "I will be jumping at my own shadow next."

The Jack fellow laughed. "You? We'll both be strung up on the gallows before I live to see the day."

Simone chuckled with an air of easy camaraderie. "*Alors,*" she said over the rustle of unfolding paper, "we came down too soon. My blueprints show the Solar-Steam turbine further to the aft, see? You will stay there to secure it while I go on to patch up the tail propeller. *D'accord?*"

"Aye, aye, Chief!"

Could this be? Far from being the Airwaymen's doxy, this woman, Simone, was their *chief engineer*!

I stayed frozen in place until their footsteps faded away together with my hopes of connecting the spare wireless to the turbine. I would need to find a galvanic cell instead.

When at last I dared to move, I discarded the other shoe. Next went the pesky skirt and petticoats, exchanged for a pair of breeches found hanging over the edge of a hammock. My skin crawled at donning a garment another – a man! – had worn before me; a scandalous behaviour to be sure. I wondered if Simone wore breeches while mucking around propellers and turbines. An outlaw had the luxury of choosing her own attire.

With the leg cuffs rolled up and a borrowed belt tightened, I ventured back into the corridor. The cold metal floor reached through thin stockings to bite into the soles of my feet, but those could now tread softly to the storage room.

The spare wireless did not take very long to locate, but my search for a galvanic cell had proved fruitless among the assorted bedding, cleaning supplies, and distressingly non-galvanic spare parts. I could hardly waltz back to the control car and ask the Airwaymen to kindly allow me the use of the stationary bicycle.

With Jack the Pirate guarding the Solar-Steam turbine, only one option remained: cannibalising my own Analytic for the miniature cell powering its galvanic valves.

This course of action seemed less than ideal. Without a working analytical engine, I lacked the means to calculate the airship's coordinates and would have to tap out the SOS by hand. At least, with the *Helios* dead in the air, Father's men could extrapolate the location from our itinerary.

As I gazed longingly on my Analytic for one last time, the floor shuddered. Simone must have brought the tail propeller back on line, turning a perfectly disagreeable plan into an ill-conceived flop. Clearly, sending a handful of messages was of no use if we could be anywhere when the rescue arrived.

Something rattled out in the corridor and the flap was pushed aside. I clapped a hand over my mouth to prevent a scream from tearing out.

A clockworker whizzed into the storage room and headed for one of the shelves stacked with blankets. Only a stray clockworker, following daily routine without countermanding orders.

One mobile galvanic cell, with its own analytical engine for a brain.

#

*Bleep, crackle, whizz,* said the clockworker's head, wedged between my crossed legs upside down on the floor. Its prone torso twitched next to me in response. Around us scattered an assortment of cogs, wires, and makeshift tools.

"Patience, we are nearly done."

I threaded the last of the wires into the tea tray compartment, jammed the portable wireless into the cramped space, and reacquainted the torso with its head. Having plugged my Analytic into the clockworker's brain, I encoded the SOS, coordinates, repeat broadcasting instructions, and caught myself short of signing the message with STRLNG instead of Estelle.

My secret call sign, used for moonlight liaisons with fellow Spikers in the aether, would not do at all. The other, my birth name, ensured an immediate response – and placed me back inside the gilded cage.

A rescue or a ransom bore the same result: Father would station a small battery of nurses and bodyguards to see to my continuing "health", while he signed me over to Edwin ... or was it Eugene? I could never properly recall. Regardless, I was expected to wed him and bear his child. The very idea of his hands – any man's hands – on my body brought bile up my throat.

I could endure such a fate, but apparently the Carmichaels did not abide galvanic frippery on their estate. The nearest telegraphy station to their glorified hunting lodge in Norfolk was miles away in the village; my concealed Analytic and any wireless I could devise would have to be powered by lamp oil and hope.

Whatever happened, the Republic of Venice now seemed as unreachable as the moon.

My finger only trembled once as I signed HLOS. The *Helios's* call sign should be quite sufficient to mount a prompt rescue without broadcasting my name.

But first, I had to get the signal outside. I hid the Analytic inside my reticule at the back of a shelf and left the storage room with a wad of blankets and one noisy hulk of metal in tow.

The network of cargo platforms stretched on either side; just as well, since I did not dare stay too long in plain sight. The clockworker's articulate arms extended to clamp onto the ladder, and we climbed up to one of the platforms with bundles and crates packed against the hull.

I left it there covered in spare blankets, with its arms gripping the nearest metal strut. From this point, the signal would spread through the mesh, reach the wireless antenna, and escape into the aether.

Rather pleased with my work, I endeavoured to distance myself from it as far as possible. Draping the last of the blankets around my shoulders like a shawl, I crawled over the cargo platforms, past Royal Mail envelopes and parcels, slowly inching away from my Wireless Clockworker. Occasionally, footsteps or voices flattened me down to the platform, with the blanket thrown hastily over my body. Each time, I lay quietly as a mouse, trying not to shiver or breathe long after the sounds faded away.

When I could go no further, I wedged my aching body between packages under the blanket and waited for Father's men.

Of course, the Airwaymen found me first.


Two pairs of footsteps approached.

"Would you check out this parcel?" Someone whisked away my blanket.

"Wakey, wakey," said a second voice. Quite unnecessarily, as it happened.

Two grinning faces loomed over me. The bearded one wore flight goggles over a leather hat flapping about like a spaniel's ears. The younger man wore a ship officer's cap over his brush cut – backwards.

I shuddered and tried to burrow deeper into the bundles.

Spaniel-Ears laughed. "Now I know what they *really* mean by 'stowing away cargo'."

"Hey there, little stowaway." Back-Cap reached for me.

I swatted his hand off. "Get away, you louts! How dare you touch me?"

"Louts, are we?" Back-Cap gaped and grimaced in mock offence.

"Well, I say!" Spaniel-Ears' attempt at posh would have been amusing under less terrifying circumstances. "Lady Stowaway, might I extend an invitation to join the others in the lounge?"

"Yeah, I hear they're serving champagne and hores doors … um, cucumber sandwiches."

Despite my protests, they lifted me off the cargo platform as if I were another bundle and did not put me down until we were back in the keel corridor. Even then, Spaniel-Ears grabbed my arm from behind to steer me along.

"Unhand me!" I wrenched my arm from his grasp, ignoring the spasm of pain. "I can walk perfectly well on my own."

They both laughed at that. "By all means, Lady Stowaway. As long as you don't run."

Run? After the first step, I doubted my stated ability to walk. Muscles and joints with whom I had not been previously acquainted had cramped up and were now protesting their treatment. I ignored their impertinence and walked ahead, straightening my back one vertebra at a time.

To my immense lack of surprise, they were not serving champagne nor hors d'oeuvres of any kind in the first class lounge. I wished they had, since by now, my stomach was emitting an unladylike grumble. Instead, the lounge was crawling with Airwaymen, who added a hitherto unknown variegation of colour with their manifold complexions, facial hairstyles, and a patchwork of leathers, denims, and wools. Everything a well-dressed Airwayman required for a day out zipping across grappling lines above the clouds.

For a moment, an odd sense of wonder subsumed the dread, as I fancied myself stepping into the pages of a penny dreadful.

Somewhat drab by comparison, first class passengers huddled together with the ship's officers. The latter could be recognised by their uniforms, perhaps not quite as impeccably turned out as before, and the fact that their caps, where not missing, were the right way around. They had also been relieved of all weaponry, thus adding to the Airwaymen's growing collection of firearms and blades.

Captain Barringer of the *Helios* stood apart from his crew, facing off a tall, trim figure garbed in a most outrageous manner.

Even from the back, the Airwayman's tricorne hat was certainly unmissable, possessed as it was of a flagrant shade of cobalt blue with copper trimmings. The brass epaulets on his tailcoat nearly compensated for the narrow shoulders, yet sadly lacked a perching clockwork parrot to complete the ensemble.

"I wouldn't tell you if I knew, *pirate*," Captain Barringer was saying. "Why would I? It's the only thing that can save us now."

"Really." The Airwayman's voice sounded mellow despite the dry tone. A curved sabre and a pistol slung from either hip; gloved hands brushed their hilts with almost deceptive lightness.

Almost.

"Hey, Skipper," Back-Cap called out. "Look what we found stowed away in the cargo!"

As the skipper turned towards us, I realised my mistake.

"Did you find the source, Mick?" said the Airwaywoman.

"No luck there." Back-Cap – Mick – shrugged. "It could be coming from anywhere on the ship. But look here, we caught ourselves a stowaway!"

"A Lady Stowaway." Spaniel-Ears grinned.

I found myself wilting under an arctic-blue gaze, a stark contrast to her raven hair.

"Skipper?" my nitwit tongue blurted out, "but you are a –" *woman*, I did not say, but they all heard it nonetheless.

Her icy stare did not waver while the rest of the Airwaymen laughed.

Spaniel-Ears bowed with a clumsy flourish, which would have earned him disdain in polite society. "Lady Stowaway, might I introduce our esteemed Captain Maeve O'Malley?"

O'Malley, of course! It all made a peculiar kind of sense: the O'Malleys had been terrorising the seas since the notorious Pirate Queen Grace, and now must have followed in ancestral footsteps up into the airways. And down to the gallows if I had my say.

"Enough!" O'Malley snapped, and the lounge promptly stilled to a hush. "We may have to abandon our prize airship, and yet you allow yourself to be distracted by a *girl*?"

Mick appeared uncomfortable. "Well, Grizzly and I thought –"

"You did not think, did you now?" She sighed and flicked a perfectly manicured hand. "Just put her up with the Second-Class passengers and keep searching for that bleeding wireless."

The wireless? *My* wireless?

This time, I did not struggle when Grizzly and Mick started herding me out of the lounge, glad for the excuse to turn my face away.

"Miss Walden?" A shrill voice put halt to my near-escape. "What do you mean wearing a man's breeches? For shame!"

Theodosia *blasted* Billinghurst.

The arctic stare swung back in my direction. An eyebrow was raised.

"Indeed, Miss Walden, for shame." Captain O'Malley flicked her fingers, and an Airwayman with braided side whiskers and a bowler hat rushed over with a sheaf of papers.

"Ah, yes. Miss Elizabeth Walden, passenger, first class. So, now we have the full set."

I shivered under her smile.

"You two" – she rounded on Grizzly and Mick – "why are you still here? Go, search for that infernal wireless!"

The pair slunk away.

O'Malley handed the passengers' roster back to Side-Braids. "What are you worth, Miss Walden?"

"Worth?" I pretended ignorance.

"Do not play coy with me. How much will your family pay for your safe return?"

A fortune, of course. Widow Billinghurst and the entire first class complement paled in comparison to what Father would pay for my safe, *confidential* return.

He would pay for "Estelle".

"Nothing," I said. "'Elizabeth Walden' shall not receive a penny in ransom."

That eyebrow shot up again. "And why is that?"

My upbringing took over, composing my lips into a serene smile. "Because she does not exist."

Mrs Billinghurst gasped. "I knew it! This, this ... *woman* is a confidence artist, a flimflam woman. I suspected as much from the very start."

Never in my life had I been more grateful to such an odious personage.

I flourished a gentleman's bow. "Flimflam woman extraordinaire at your service, Captain O'Malley."

"You are a poor liar if you expect me to believe such a thing."

"Believe what you will, Captain, but I am quite certain your Spiker can verify no such person as Elizabeth Walden exists. She is merely my latest identity, a fabricated name on my reservation."

O'Malley's eyes narrowed. "And what do *you* know of Spikers?"

Too late, I bit the inside of my lip. If I had prattled away my Spiker identity, O'Malley would surely infer me capable of encoding wireless distress calls.

"Oh," I said with deeply unfelt airiness, "I have engaged their services once or twice. Lately, to create the 'Elizabeth Walden' identity. Though if you ask me, the man has done a shoddy job of it."

There. Would this be enough to throw this bloodhound off my scent?

"Ha!" Side-Braids grumbled. "'Course he has. That's Spikers for you, the louts. Can't wait to get pissed to their eyeballs and bugger –"

"That's enough," the captain cut him off. "Corral her in with the others. We will sort the question of her identity at our leisure, which we do not currently possess. In fact, I have wasted enough time here to warrant speeding things up a notch."

The Airwayman took me by the elbow and "guided" my way into the huddle of first class passengers and officers, until I found myself back near the table where, only that morning, I had taken tea.

"Captain Barringer" – O'Malley unsheathed her sabre – "Unless you give me what I want, I shall commence slicing your passengers in half … starting with *this* blabbermouth."

She pulled Theodosia Billinghurst away from the others and held her in front of her, with the blade to the old woman's throat.

Mrs Billinghurst let out a squeaking sound through her nose. Her face contorted in horror, her mouth opened and closed and opened again like a fish out of water.

"You are bluffing, O'Malley," Captain Barringer said. "She is worth more to you alive."

"Bluffing, am I? All these wealthy toffs combined would not fetch the price of an Averly and that new-fangled engine of yours."

Evidently, these pirates were not content to plunder our cargo and hold passengers to ransom; they were hell-bent on taking the *Helios* as a prize.

Unless Father's men got here first.

"I told you before," Captain Barringer said, "I do not know from where the wireless is broadcasting."

"One of your officers would know. *Someone* in this room has sent out the signal."

"Ask them yourself." Captain Barringer's voice carried contempt.

"I am asking." O'Malley's tightened her hold. Was that a drop of blood glistening on the blade? "Which of you misguided fools knows where the wireless is broadcasting from?"

"I do!" Someone cried out. In the hush of the announcement, I realised it was my voice.

The blade moved a fraction away from Widow Billinghurst's throat. The cold blue stare returned to chill the pit of my stomach.

"You do? Lady Stowaway Flimflam?" O'Malley's lips curled in contempt.

*Why?* Why did I have to speak out? For the insufferable biddy who had named me a conwoman, for her I endangered everything. Those perfect lips were right to mock me.

"If you are trying to con *me*, Miss Walden, you are spectacularly out of your depth."

I stood up straighter, jutting out my chin in a possible attempt to stab her with it in the chest, or something to that effect. "Elizabeth Walden is not, in fact, my true name."

What was I doing?

"So you have already informed us, and yet I cannot imagine what bearing this has on the matter at hand."

"Then allow me to enlighten you, Captain. My *true* name is STRLNG."

Not Estelle, not Gwendolyn, nor Averly – a string of names to conjure up a pirate's treasure. The name I had chosen on joining my Spiker community, my international, wireless tribe.

'Starling … A call sign!' A quick, lopsided grin transformed O'Malley's face. 'Are you a Spiker, girl?'

I flourished another bow. "Starling, at your service." The name rolled easily off my tongue, though spoken that way for the first time.

"So you sent the distress signal to the French Authorities?"

The honeyed words contained both a trap and a way out. I could still allow her to "catch" me at a lie and pretend this was all a confidence trick.

I met Theodosia's pleading eyes. What would stop this pirate from slitting her throat as soon as she thought I was lying?

"No," I said. "To Averly Hall, where I am certain good old Cyrus would take your hijacking of his airship somewhat more personally. Surely you must have some inkling of his men's reputation? Leave us be while you can."

"Very well. Let us say I believe you." She lowered the sabre and pushed Mrs Billinghurst out of the way. A split second later, the point was tickling my chest.

"Now then, Starling, will you tell me the whereabouts of the signal's origin, or should I carve it out of you one slice at a time?"

How could I ever refuse such a polite request?

"I shall not," I said with bluster I most certainly did not feel.

Light as a feather, the point of her sabre brushed up the length of my throat and sideways to my cheek. "Such lovely skin. Should I sign my name on it?"

I trembled at the frosty touch. "Kill me, and you will never find it. His men are coming, so you had better take your *Leviathan* and run."

"Why kill when there is a better motivator?"

Torture! Her words buzzed in my ear. I had no way of knowing how long I would last, and hardly relished the prospect of finding out.

"When the Averly forces arrive," she said, "how well do you think you'll fare? If I don't kill you myself, *if* they win – will they thank you, pin a medal to that lovely chest, or arrest you for the criminal you are?"

My chest was lovely? I blinked away the irrelevant thought.

Her lips twitched in a ghost of a smile as she lowered the sabre and stepped closer. Too close. Tiny, caged wings fluttered inside my abdomen. I flushed or paled – not quite sure which – almost wishing for the blade to return and restore a modicum of distance.

"I like you, Starling, you have gumption. Give me the signal's origins, and you can come with us. We could use a new Spiker."

I gaped like a flounder out for a stroll in the fresh air. The Airwaywoman Captain had just offered me *employment!* The very idea.

"A new Spiker?" My voice thickened from passing through a tightening throat. "Whatever happened to your old one?"

"That lazy son of a seagull?" Side-Braids huffed. "Didn't I tell you? Got pissed to his eyeballs and buggered the hell off."

How easy it would be to embrace a life of crime rather than wait for Father to collect me. Just tell them where the wireless was hidden, betray my family, my airship, and every passenger and crewman on board.

Why did O'Malley have to stand there, far too close to allow any coherency to my thoughts? With nowhere to move, I turned my face away from her and looked out the window, wishing I could turn into a real starling and simply fly away.

The *Leviathan* loomed outside, tethered by grappling lines to the *Helios*. Two of the ornithopters buzzed a short way down, with the third out of view. Below them, the idyllic French Countryside peeked through puffy, lavender clouds. I searched through the patterns as if they had the oracular power to inform my choice.

In truth, the prospect sounded shockingly ... tantalising. Father would never search for me among Airwaymen; he would scarcely entertain the thought. Except, of course, I would be consorting with criminals. Not merely Spikers in the aether, but true, hardened criminals. The kind that would not flutter an eyelid at capturing an airship and holding the passengers hostage. Or turning me in for a hefty ransom should they ever discover the runaway heiress of Averly in their midst.

Further on the horizon, something glittered in the sun. Could it be ...?

I stifled a smile and schooled my expression into utter innocence before turning to look into the Airwaywoman's eyes.

"Captain O'Malley, I accept your invitation."

As I blabbered away the precise location of my Wireless Clockworker, I wondered how long I could spin this distraction before she realised it no longer mattered in the least.

When the airship's alarm bells sounded while the Airwaymen searched for my pesky transmitter, I knew they were too late: Father's forces had arrived.

The Airwaymen did not quite trust me yet, and so they left me corralled among the passengers and officers, whose dirty looks made their thoughts perfectly clear. I turned my back on all of them to watch one corner of the battle waging outside.

Ornithopters and biplanes zoomed past, exchanging gunfire with the *Leviathan* and each other. Both sides aimed to avoid us with varied success. The Averly flyers outnumbered those of the pirates and had not travelled here on their own steam. An aerodyne carrier hovered nearby: a rigid airship with a bellyful of heavier-than-aircraft and cannons it did not hesitate to discharge.

Untethered, the *Leviathan* might have outrun the rescue squadron. With its harpoons firmly buried in our hull, the Airwaymen could not cut the lines without abandoning captain and crew.

Huddled in the first class lounge, all we had to do was wait, with the scent of fear palpable in the air. My nerves screamed each time the *Helios* shook, or a successful shot from the *Leviathan's* swivel-cannon brought down a rescue aerodyne. Mrs Billinghurst's silent pallor appeared to be catching.

"You there, Spiker!" Mick the Pirate entered the lounge, his demeanour no longer jolly. "Skipper wants a word with you."

Back on the bridge, Captain Maeve O'Malley stood at the helm, with both hands planted on the wheel. Beside her, an elevatorman struggled to keep us level, and a third man hunched over an array of gauges.

"More thrust to the engines, Chief! Me ole' Nan can hobble faster than this," O'Malley spoke into the mouth of an acoustic bullhorn whose brass piping relayed her commands to the ship's public address system.

"Here she is, Skipper." Mick thumped me on the shoulder. "Our newest recruit."

"Ah, Starling. Li Cheng, take the helm." She ushered us into the wireless room, the one that only hours ago I had been so desperate to reach.

"What do you want from me, O'Malley?" I raised my chin with hauteur I did not feel.

Mick frowned. "Is that how you speak to your captain, Spiker?"

O'Malley emitted an indelicate snort. "Did you really think our confidence trickster was quite on the level accepting our commission?"

I opened my mouth and closed it, lost for words. She had known all along! What *else* did she know? I struggled to breathe in a room too small to contain the two of us. Oh, and Mick, though his presence did not affect me as much.

Her chuckle had a bleak undertone. "No matter. This time, I would like to engage your specialised services."

"Do you mean … you still wish me to join you? Even *now*?"

For all her arrogance, she could hardly have failed to realise the Airwaymen were about to lose both airships and their freedom, likely to be hanged at Newgate for piracy. I imagined the coarse rope tightening around her neck and found myself no longer relishing the prospect.

"Consider it more of an audition," she said.

"You wish to parley," I realised. "And you would like me to send the message to Fa … French authorities?"

O'Malley narrowed her eyes. "The French? These are Averly's men, as well you know. And now I need you to use the frequency of your last transmission to send another one from me."

I took the wireless operator's seat and turned up the dials. With the gauges pointing to the right frequency, I placed my finger on the telegraph's key, ready to transmit my dots and dashes.

AVRL AVRL DE HLOS QSL? – *Averly, Averly, this is Helios, do you acknowledge?* – I tapped out a mix of call signs and abbreviation codes. I did not know the aerodyne carrier's official call sign, so Averly would have to do.

HLOS DE AVRL QSL – *Helios, this is Averly, I acknowledge* – beeped the reply through wireless receiver. They did not bother to correct me.

"We have their attention," I said. "What are the terms of your surrender?"

"Surrender?" O'Malley raised an eyebrow. "Oh, I have no intention of surrendering."

I did not like the grim cast of her voice. "But I thought ..."

"Here are my terms, Starling. Instruct them to stand down, or the hostages will suffer the consequences."

I willed my finger not to tremble as I relayed her message.

After a long pause, the reply arrived: *Release the hostages or else.*

Unlike the even rhythm of Analytic-generated Morse code, human operators are irregular at best, in tune with their character and state of mind. This message felt hesitant and somewhat nervous, in stark contrast to its terse content. Someone was standing over the operator's shoulder and dictating the reply.

As I translated the beeps, O'Malley interrupted. "Oh, I will release the hostages, all right." Her half-smile at my surprise informed me she could well have communicated without my help. "If they do not disengage, the next heavier-than-air object they observe will be a passenger in mid-flight. Tell them *that*, if you please."

"No!" I snatched my finger away from the key, aghast at her thirst for blood. I searched for a glimmer of humanity, but her gaze could have frozen a volcano.

"But, Skipper!" Mick broke up our glaring duel. His face had turned ashen. "Maeve, that would be –"

"Cold blooded murder?" Doubt flickered in O'Malley's eyes before they hardened with resolve. "I will do what I must, little brother."

Her brother? Now that I looked, the resemblance became apparent, as did the fact that I had misjudged her. This was no thirst for blood or money, but the simple, raw need to protect her family and crew. She would never surrender because promises to pirates held no value. And by calling for help, I had left her no choice.

Unless, of course, I revealed my identity. Father would pay any ransom for my safe return and her continued discretion, as long as he could avoid a scandal and sell me off at the altar for a higher price. With that kind of leverage, O'Malley stood to gain everything without harming a soul. What else could I do but trade my personal freedom for lives?

I drew myself straighter in the seat. "Captain O'Malley, I –" my resolve faltered at the glimmer of a new idea. "Perhaps there is another way."

Her countenance did not invite elaboration, but I pressed on regardless. "Supposing you promise to release the hostages – everyone, passengers and crew – and they give their solemn word to cease pursuit?"

O'Malley glared. "Do you take me for a bleeding fool? We would need to land first and, no matter what they swear, never be allowed to take off again."

"Not so," I said. "The hostages can all depart on the lifeboat, mid-flight, increasing buoyancy and lift as a result, since we are currently overloaded with your crew."

"A lifeboat?" She scoffed. "One large enough to accommodate all passengers and crew? Hogwash! There is no weight allowance for such a thing on board."

"I beg to differ, Captain. I happen to know … through my Spiker associates … that not all parts of this airship are quite as integral as the Solar-Steam turbine. And that is your true target, is it not?"

Perhaps, in the ensuing chaos, I might evade O'Malley's crew and Father's men and make my own escape.

Mick kept me company in the wireless room while O'Malley saw to the arrangements. It had taken extensive back and forth negotiation with the nervous operator on the other side, but we were given two hours' head-start.

The Captain had insisted on that – she would not release the hostages anywhere near the rescue squadron.

The door opened and Grizzly entered the room.

"Howdy-do, Lady Stowaway. Skipper wants to know if your thingamajig is ready."

"Thinga …? My *Wireless Clockworker* would have been ready sooner if you oafs hadn't damaged it." I placed a screwdriver back into the toolbox. "But yes, it should now transmit on contact with the hull. Watch."

Almost as soon as the clockworker's arm touched the metal wall, a message beeped through the receiver, demanding to know why the previous SOS signal had been renewed.

*To help guide you to the lifeboat,* I tapped out.

With the signal continuing to broadcast from the lifeboat, the rescue team would be sure to focus on the passengers, and leave both *Helios* and *Leviathan* be. At least, for a while.

*Understood, Helios. Over and –*

The message was interrupted in mid-beep, and when the Morse code resumed, it had a clipped and authoritative tone, containing more fully spelled-out words than abbreviations: *Now see here, Pirate. I am a man of my word today, but I shall see you all hanged for piracy tomorrow.*

The pit of my stomach constricted. All warmth drained away from my face.

DE? I barely managed to tap out. *Who is this?* But I knew the answer already. His Morse code sounded just like his voice.

DE CJ AVRL, came the inevitable reply. Small wonder the operator's code had sounded so nervous; Father must have stood over the poor man's shoulder the whole time. But how did he get here so quickly? No airship could have carried him from Averly Hall in mere hours; he must have been in France already, searching for me.

"He is here," I answered Mick and Grizzly's questioning stares. "Cyrus J Averly *himself* is on board the aerodyne carrier."

They shrugged, not nearly as affected by his presence, and Grizzly took the clockworker away.

I had been so incredibly naive to believe in the fairytale of my escape. Should I somehow slip away into the gondola, should Widow Billinghurst and the others refrain from denouncing me as a traitor, a confidence woman, a *pirate* – I would now be stepping into the welcoming arms of my father.

If he knew of my presence on board the *Helios*, he had kept it to himself. More likely, my distress call had brought him here to save a beloved airship from Airwaymen. But even in my current state of attire, he would hardly fail to recognise his runaway daughter. He would whisk me away discreetly, keep me safe and sedated before escorting me down the aisle with bodyguards in tow. And afterwards, those guards, nurses, "companions" would remain constantly by my side until I began manufacturing little Averly and Carmichael heirs. There was nowhere left to run.

"All hands, prepare for separation." O'Malley's voice over the public address horn interrupted my spiralling thoughts.

"We must maintain wireless silence from now on," Mick said.

He opened the door, and I stepped out into the narrow corridor. The bulkhead door to the gondola lay on my right; Captain Maeve O'Malley stood on my left.

"Well, Starling, do you want that job or not?" she asked.

"Did you mean to say … I have *choice* in the matter?"

My head fizzed with giddiness and a dash of trepidation. All my life, every facet of it had been dictated by the rules of Society, except for the brief moments of freedom I had stolen away. Even this feeble attempt at escape had pitted me against the expectations of my class. And now, this woman I had fought, whose plans I had disrupted, was offering me a *choice*.

"Of course," she said, as if free-will was as indisputable as gravity. "Well, do you?"

"I do," I said and followed my captain to the bridge.

The *Helios* – no longer RMA – shuddered and shook as the gondola separated, crammed to capacity with passengers and crew. Not overloaded though, since it had been designed to serve as a contingency lifeboat. Only the control car remained attached to the airship's hull.

My heart skipped a beat as I watched the gondola float wingless in mid-air. If something had gone wrong, if the propellers had not engaged, it would plummet to its doom with everyone on board. So many lives.

When the gondola-lifeboat reached a safe distance from the envelope, its propellers, thin as gossamer, unfurled from the roof into the helix form of Leonardo's aerial screw. Such a contraption could never keep the loaded gondola in sustained flight, but it had enough lift to float it safely to the ground. The gondola's descent stabilised, its trajectory taking it away from the *Helios* and the *Leviathan*. And with my clockworker broadcasting their location, Father and his men could rescue everyone on board while we, the Airwaymen, made our escape.

Side by side, our airships chased the new moon rising underneath, scattering a skyful of stars in their wake. What adventures lay beyond the ever-shifting horizon? We might never catch that moon, but perchance the Republic of Venice, even Africa or Canton, would not be entirely out of reach for a Starling's wings.

*Karina Steffens began her love affair with fairy tales as a young girl in Soviet Ukraine, quoting Pushkin at anyone who'd listen. It followed her to Jerusalem, where she picked up a degree in Journalism, and to Dublin, where she consults as a web designer and writes SFF. Her work has appeared in Enchanted Conversation, Empyreome, and Gathering Storm. She tweets @KarinaSteffens*

# Twelve Essential Things Found in Commander Scarlett Archer's Spacesuit Pockets (And Some Which Were Not)

*Dawn Vogel*

**Thing the first: In which Commander Scarlett Archer discovers the problem, with the help of her Sextant**

Commander Scarlett Archer, Chief Engineer of *The Gasket*, rarely put in an appearance on the bridge. She preferred working in the "guts" of the ship, as it were, getting her hands dirty. The bridge was far too clean, clean enough that she was certain every individual currently on the bridge was looking down their respective nose at her filthy uniform. Certainly the cleaning drones bumping up against her boots seemed dismayed by the grease and other stains covering her uniform that they were unable to clean.

Or perhaps the other crew members were observing how her uniform looked both hand-crafted and somehow more flattering than all of theirs. When Space Command had first informed her they didn't have any uniforms in her size, she'd made do with belts and pins to make the uniform work. But when no uniforms in her size were forthcoming after months, she'd taken matters into her own hands and made her own, with a special enhancement: quantum pockets.

Utilizing quantum theory, she'd linked the corners of her pockets to locations in her workroom back on Earth. She knew the location of every item there, so if there was something she'd neglected to grab from Engineering, she could reach back to her workroom to retrieve it, all through the pockets she'd sewn into her handmade uniform.

Captain Enoch Belcher stared at Scarlett, and she knew it was not because her uniform looked particularly fetching today. It was likely because she hadn't answered his question yet.

Clearing her throat, she removed a sextant from her pocket. The unwieldy device was larger than pocket sized, but Scarlett had accounted for that possibility when creating the quantum pockets, making them large enough for anything that fit into a rather oversized handbag.

As soon as she surveyed the expanse and located a pair of guide stars, Scarlett saw the problem. "I am neither a navigator nor a pilot, Captain, but we appear to be listing somewhat off course."

"Thank you for the confirmation, Commander Archer," the captain said, his voice a rumbling baritone. "Now the question is: what are you going to do about it?"

Scarlett looked toward the pilot and navigator, twin sisters who she could never tell apart, but recalled their surname as Letchford. "Lieutenants Letchford, any ideas?" she asked.

Both women shook their heads. One of them spoke up. "We've tried everything we can, but she keeps listing back to this same heading."

"Well, then I suppose I'll have to see what I can figure out."


**Thing the second: In which Commander Archer gets to work, with the help of her Multi-tool**

Deep within the bowels of the ship, Scarlett thanked the heavens that she had purchased a multi-tool with a light attachment. Headlamps had proven impractical, as the variety of axles and tubing within *The Gasket*'s inner workings were always just at the right level to take a headlamp clean off, often tugging out strands of her hair as well.

She'd narrowed down the problem to the rotors that kept the ship's gravity as close to Earth normal as possible. Somewhere, there was a gear out of sync, and while gravity was still maintained, it had given *The Gasket* the equivalent of a limp, the very listing off course she had identified on the bridge.

Scarlett identified a faint thumping sound coming from one of rotors, somewhere to her left. She shone her light in that direction, took note of the location of the nearest axles, and wound her way amidst the tubing to get closer to her destination. She stopped now and then, waiting as a cleaning drone passed (she'd reprogramed the cleaning drones here to take no interest in stains on uniforms), listening again, trying to pinpoint the location.

The rotor in question was tucked away behind several of the thicker axles, the ones requiring feats of contortion to move amongst. Scarlett could either call a request to the bridge for permission to shut down the rotors, thus pausing the force of gravity onboard, or signal one of her junior engineers to flip the switch.

"Better to ask for forgiveness than permission," she said, giving the signal.

The rotors and axles wound down, and Scarlett's feet left the floor. Swimming through the air, she made her way between the axles to the troublesome rotor.

Locating the appropriate portion of her multi-tool to dismantle the apparatus holding the rotor in place, she swiftly replaced it with a spare rotor she had tucked into her pocket.

Before she got a good look at the malfunctioning rotor, the replacement began to spin. Now Scarlett was between a wall and a turning rotor, blocked from her view of the junior engineers by yards of whirling metal. Clearly, her order had been countermanded, and even her presence amongst the rotors had not been enough to overrule the captain's order. She would have words with him later. Once she figured out how to get out of this mess.

**Thing the third: In which Commander Archer realizes there's more than meets the naked eye, with the help of her Loupe**

The wall panels in this section of the ship had been snapped into place, rather than bolted down, so with a few nudges from Scarlett's feet and shoulders, she popped one of the panels out and tumbled into the adjacent hallway. No other crewmembers were around to witness her ungraceful landing, just a handful of cleaning drones, who sped out of her way and continued to vacuum the hallway. And the rotor was safe, pressed to her chest.

She located the nearest communications panel and opened a channel to Engineering. "This is Commander Scarlett Archer, reporting that I am, in fact, still amongst the living, and I would like to have a word with whomever countermanded my order immediately upon my return."

One of the juniors replied, "Affirmative," before disconnecting the call.

Scarlett glared at the communications panel, certain her look could penetrate through the ship's systems and strike the appropriate level of fear into that crewmember. But the panel did not power back on. She would have to stare them down in person.

She headed down the passageway toward Engineering, turning the rotor over in her hands as she walked. The dull metal surface did not appear to be pitted or scratched, the most likely reasons for a rotor to wobble and cause the ship to list off course. But there was something there, in the gear surrounding the center hole.

Scarlett reached into her pocket and felt around until she located her jeweler's loupe. Placing it in front of her right eye, she examined the gear.

There was the root of the problem. Five of the gear spokes were missing. Now the question was: how had they been removed?

**Thing the fourth: In which Commander Archer finds evidence of sabotage, with the help of her Chalk**

"We can't live without gravity, Commander Archer," Captain Belcher said.

"I cannot begin to explain to you the multitude of ways in which that is an incorrect statement, Captain," Scarlett replied. She mentally patted herself on the back for not flat out telling the captain he was wrong, but getting her point across nonetheless. "That being said, I am no worse for the wear, and I have identified the problem. Now, if you don't mind, I need to inspect this rotor to determine how the fault was introduced. It will do us no good to continually replace the rotor with additional rotors that will fail in the same way."

Captain Belcher blinked a few times, then nodded. "Then I'll be out of your way."

Once the captain was out of earshot, Scarlett wheeled on her juniors. But rather than glare or snarl at them to determine who had abruptly cut off their earlier communication, she announced, "I will be in my office, undisturbed. At least once someone has brought me my tea."

Scarlett set the rotor in the center of her desk, turned on a bright lamp, and re-examined the spot on the gear missing its teeth. The surface there was textured, though even with the help of her loupe, she could not quite get the sense of the pattern.

She reached into her pocket and this time extracted a piece of chalk. She rubbed it across the broken portion of the rotor, then sat back with a gasp.

One of the junior engineers entered with a tea service, but Scarlett was already out of her seat.

"No time for tea, my good man. We've been sabotaged."

## Thing the fifth: In which Commander Archer finds a way to return the ship to its course, with the help of her Cork

Scarlett returned to the corridor where she had exited the inner workings of *The Gasket* previously, relocated the panel she had removed, and pried it off the wall, a feat that was, it seemed, easier once a panel had been removed once.

The rotors continued to spin, but there was the thumping sound again, coming from the exact place she had found it previously.

Leaving the panel off the wall (much to the apparent chagrin of the nearest cleaning drone, which had to reroute its path to avoid this new obstacle), she approached the communications panel and opened a line to the bridge. "Captain Belcher, sir, this is Commander Scarlett Archer. We have another problem in the rotor room, and I need to suspend gravity yet again for a short time."

The captain sighed across the channel, but said, "Very well. Will you at least allow me to make an announcement to that effect so everyone may be prepared?"

"Of course, Captain. Will five minutes be sufficient for everyone to prepare?"

"I should hope so."

"Excellent." Scarlett closed the channel and opened a new channel to Engineering. "In exactly four minutes and forty-five seconds, please turn off the rotors for a space of two minutes and forty seconds."

As she waited for the rotors to stop, she prepared a fresh rotor, her multi-tool, and one final item--the cork from a bottle of Old Earth Merlot. The bottle the cork had come from held no real significance; it was the first cork in her workspace on Earth she had laid hands upon.

She checked the time on the communications panel, and then prepared to go to work.

## Thing the sixth: In which Commander Archer prepares a trap, thanks to her Tarred Hemp Line

"Blast!" Scarlett announced as she continued to pull tarred hemp line from her quantum pocket. "Is there no end to this?"

"Thirty seconds," the junior engineer who had opened a channel to the hallway to report in on the remaining time before the rotors, and thus the ship's gravity, would be reactivated.

"No time like the present, then," Scarlett murmured. She tugged about a foot of the line out and fashioned it into a constrictor knot around the center of the cork. Then she impaled the cork on the screw that held the rotor in place.

Everything where she needed it, she stepped back from the rotors and replaced the hall panel, taking care to keep the tarred hemp line away from the rotors, but still dangling out of the panel.

The remainder of the line she pressed into the gaps between the panels all the way to the utility closet where she planned to wait. The moment someone moved either the panel or the screw to sabotage the rotor, she would know.

## In which Commander Archer is presented with new problems, no thanks to Mineral Spirits

"Commander Archer?" the voice came over the communications panel just outside the utility closet.

Scarlett poked her head out, tapped the panel, and snarled, "What part of complete silence did you fail to comprehend?"

"The captain just called to let us know the ship is still listing, and he wanted to speak with you directly."

With a frown, Scarlett replied, "But that's not possible. Let me investigate."

Leaving the safety of the utility closet, Scarlett followed the tarred hemp line, which still lay where she had placed it, wedged in the crevice between the panels all the way back to the location of the rotor.

The next panel down, which she had not previously disturbed, now jutted off the wall at a rakish angle.

Prying the panel off the wall, Scarlett poked her head into the space where the rotors were. There, to the right, was the cork, the tarred hemp line still tied around it, impaled on the screw above the rotor. The line, however, was frayed and split at the level of the rotor, and the whole space had the faint scent of mineral spirits about it.

"Blast!" Her well-orchestrated plan had been foiled with a simple solvent, which now marred the surface of the rotor, as well.

There was something else, though, on the floor beneath the rotors--something the saboteur had left behind. Scarlett couldn't identify it from her current angle, and it was too far within the space to reach with her arm, but already she was concocting a new plan.

**Thing the seventh: In which Commander Archer solves one problem, with the help of her Chewing Gum**

Scarlett reached deep into her pocket to find the small stash of chewing gum she kept in her desk drawer on Earth. She popped a single stick into her mouth as she removed the remainder of the tarred hemp line from between the panels and then removed the panel she had previously used.

The captain marched down the hallway. "What are you doing to my ship?"

"I'm trying to fix it, sir." She beckoned the captain closer and lowered her voice. "We've been sabotaged. Thrice, now. But I've found a clue, if you'll permit me to continue what I was doing."

The captain nodded, and Scarlett removed the wad of chewing gum from her mouth, wrapping it around the frayed end of the tarred hemp line. Gauging her throw cautiously, she pitched the end of the line forward toward the item she'd spotted.

Her throw fell short, but remained clear of the rotors. She pulled the line back in and prepared a second throw.

"What is it you're doing, exactly?" Captain Belcher asked.

"Trying to retrieve the clue, sir."

Captain Belcher squatted beside her, craning his neck to try to see into the rotor space. "I don't see anything."

"Give me another moment, sir." Scarlett tossed the line toward the item again, and this time the chewing gum landed atop the clue. Letting out a slow breath, she reeled the line in, hoping the chewing gum would stay adhered to the clue and not obscure it.

## Thing the eighth: In which Commander Archer takes matters into her own hands, along with her Self-Adhesive Cellophane Tape

The clue was nothing more than a small piece of glossy polystyrene, now with a wad of chewing gum stuck to one side of it. Scarlett frowned, but as she lifted the tarred hemp line to bring the clue closer to her eyes, she spotted something on the other side of the polystyrene.

She raised the polystyrene to get a better view, and then exclaimed, "I have it!"

"What do you have, exactly?" Captain Belcher asked, squinting toward the piece of polystyrene. "That looks like garbage."

"It may have been, but there are fingerprints on this garbage." She handed the tarred hemp line to Captain Belcher. "Hold this a moment." Then she dug into her pockets for her self-adhesive cellophane tape.

Captain Belcher was still squinting at the underside of the piece of polystyrene when Scarlett measured out a length of tape and applied it to the fingerprint on the polystyrene.

"Perfection," Scarlett announced as she held the tape up to the light. But where she anticipated swirls and whorls, she instead saw miniscule numerals. "Hmmm, well, this may put a slight wrench into things."

## In which Commander Archer finds a glimmer of hope, after a nice spot of Tea

Commander Archer made her way back to her office, still scrutinizing the piece of self-adhesive cellophane tape. She paid no attention to the fact that her cup of tea from earlier was no longer steaming, and she took a deep sip from it, sputtering when the cold liquid reached her lips.

"More tea," she shouted. "Hot, please."

She placed the self-adhesive cellophane tape across a discarded headlamp on her desk, turned on the light, and examined the numerals there with her jeweler's loupe. It was a brief sequence of numbers. "Zero, one, one, two, three, five, eight," she read aloud. "A Fibonacci sequence? But to what end?"

One of the junior engineers brought in a tray with piping hot tea, which she set in front of Scarlett. "Anything else, ma'am?"

Scarlett beckoned the junior engineer to the side of her desk and handed the young woman the jeweler's loupe. "You see this sequence of numbers on the tape across my headlamp? Can you make out what is right there at the leftmost edge?"

The engineer examined the tape. "Where did this imprint come from?"

Scarlett took a sip of tea, then reached into her pocket for her sugar bowl and the small piece of polystyrene, from which she had cleaned the chewing gum. Placing it in front of the engineer, she scooped an extra lump of sugar from the bowl and stirred it into her tea.

"Tea," the young woman said.

"Yes, it's quite nice now, thank you," Scarlett replied.

"No, that's the letter at the beginning of the numerical sequence. A 'T'."

Scarlett took the jeweler's loupe from the junior engineer and examined the fragment of polystyrene. The cellophane tape had not copied over the full detail of the letter present there, and, as the young engineer said, it was a portion of the letter T. "Well, then, that narrows things down a bit, as I had identified the font used on *The Gasket* for labeling of all equipment. And there is only one department that uses a letter sequence ending in 'T'."

"Maintenance," they said in unison.

**Thing the ninth: In which Commander Archer valiantly defends *The Gasket*, with the help of her Rubber Cement**

"We seem to have a malfunctioning cleaning drone aboard *The Gasket*, Captain," Scarlett reported. "It has twice now broken a fragment from a rotor due to overzealous cleaning, and then used mineral spirits to sever the tarred hemp line I intended to use to suss out the saboteur."

"So the saboteur is a drone?" Captain Belcher asked.

"It is unclear at this point whether the malfunction is intentional or incidental, sir. We need to isolate the cleaning drone and examine it. If Maintenance disables drone MNT0112358, we can have our answers."

"One moment," the captain replied. Nearly a minute passed before he came back on the line. "Maintenance reports that drone MNT0112358 is not responding to commands."

Scarlett frowned. "Then, sir, I may need to take matters into my own hands."

"Permission granted. Just warn us if it means we're going to lose gravity again."

"Yes, sir," Scarlett said, trying to refrain from rolling her eyes. She switched off the communications panel and returned to the access panel nearest the malfunctioning rotor.

No cleaning drones were in the vicinity, but they scuttled around other parts of the rotor room. The rotor wobbled, but rather than reach into her pockets for a replacement, Scarlett instead seized a small jar of rubber cement. The rotor could be replaced once and for all after this malfunctioning drone was stopped.

And what better way to stop a ground-based drone than literally stopping it in its tracks?

Scarlett poured the contents of the jar of rubber cement onto the floor surrounding the rotor axle.

## Thing the tenth: In which Commander Archer makes sense of it all, with the help of her Hatpin

Scarlett had sufficient time for a second cup of tea before she returned to the rotor room to see the results of her handiwork.

As anticipated, a cleaning drone had fallen afoul of the rubber cement. It continued to run its wheels, but they made no progress against the sticky and viscous substance. Its electronic chirping had taken on an agitated tone, as though it was expressing emotions in a very un-dronelike fashion.

Scarlett looked the drone over before approaching. Several pieces of polystyrene had broken off it in various locations, but some of those gaps had been covered by other materials, including two pieces that looked remarkably like the rotor teeth that had been snapped off.

"Well, that explains a few things," Scarlett murmured. "Now to figure out how to get you out of there and repair the damage to your chassis."

Scarlett reached for the cleaning drone, and its chirping grew smoother and louder, like a tiny scream. It raised a pair of limbs with rotating brush attachments and wielded them in her direction.

"I'm trying to help," Scarlett said, holding up her hands.

The drone did not seem soothed by her words.

Scarlett slid her hands into her pockets to consider other options, feeling around her workspace to see if anything there gave her a good idea. She seized upon a misplaced hatpin and paused. Though the drone might perceive it as a weapon, it was just the thing to accomplish her goal.

She extracted it slowly, sliding it up the sleeve of her uniform to keep it out of sight. Then she looked at the cleaning drone with fresh eyes until she identified the switch on its back, as it were, that would deactivate it temporarily.

As Scarlett moved toward the drone's back end, it tried to follow her, but the rubber cement kept it fixed in place. The rotating brushes raised to attempt to intercept her, but the limbs to which they were attached could not extend so far back.

With a delicate lunge, Scarlett pressed the drone's button with the tip of her hatpin, and the whirring brushes and agitated electronic noises cycled off.

**Thing the eleventh (and twelfth): In which Commander Archer rights the course, with the help of her Cyanoacrylate Adhesive (and her Parasol)**

"There are two problems to be solved in order to keep the ship on course," Scarlett explained to Captain Belcher. "We must repair the rotor, of course, but we must also repair this cleaning drone."

"Why can't we just deactivate the drone?" Captain Belcher asked.

Scarlett pressed her lips together in a firm line. "While I suppose that is an option, I see no reason to do so, since it is simple enough to repair the drone. Its outer shell is broken, and it simply wants to be whole again. Would you suggest that an injured crew member be 'deactivated' for the length of the journey, or would you have the ship's doctor patch them up and allow them to return to duty as soon as they are fit for it?"

Captain Belcher chuckled. "Well, you certainly have strong feelings about cleaning drones, it seems. Very well, do what needs to be done so we can get back on course."

Scarlett left the bridge, already rummaging through her pockets for a solution to the drone's broken shell. She seized upon a bottle of cyanoacrylate adhesive--the most potent adhesive she had found to date--and returned to her office, where the disabled drone sat on her desk.

Replacing the fragment of polystyrene the drone had left behind, bearing its designation number, was easy enough to accomplish. She applied the adhesive, slid the polystyrene into its proper spot, and clamped it into place with the use of some over-large paperclips.

The drone was missing other fragments, though. It had replaced them with bits of the rotor teeth, held on with what smelled like a paste made of mineral spirits and something Scarlett could not identify. She loosened those pieces and re-adhered them using the stronger adhesive.

As she worked, Scarlett noticed the cleaning drone's shell was flimsy all around, cracked in several places where the polystyrene had not fallen completely away, but nonetheless was in danger of developing more problems in the future.

"Well this won't do at all," she said, looking at her repair jobs, held together with most of the paperclips from her desk at this point.

Scarlett reached into her pocket again, and this time extracted an old parasol, one that had been awaiting mending when she had a moment of time to spare. The lavender fabric had faded from its time in the sun, and she wondered if perhaps she should have the entire parasol re-covered, rather than attempt to patch the tear.

With a firm nod, she was decided. She pulled scissors and a mending kit from her desk drawer and set to work on a protective dust ruffle for the drone, one that would buffer its shell from anything that might further damage the inadequate polystyrene.

## In which Commander Archer is lauded for her accomplishments and presented with a Handkerchief

Commander Scarlett Archer presented her handiwork on the drone to the Maintenance staff to thunderous applause. Already, the crew chief was taking measurements of the protective dust ruffle and drawing up specifications for additional ruffles to protect all the drones. At least, she said, until the shells could be replaced with something stronger in the future.

Captain Belcher joined in the applause for Scarlett, though his face gave the impression he was thinking very hard on something. As the din died down, he beckoned Scarlett to his side.

"Sir?" she asked.

"You've fixed things, much as you said you would, and in such an inventive way. I believe this means I'm obligated to present you with an award of some sort."

Scarlett blushed crimson. "Oh, sir, that's not necessary. I'm simply doing my job." In truth, she did not want to be made a spectacle of, especially as such would require her to don a clean uniform and do something elaborate with her hair. And she would, after all, rather be in the guts of the ship, keeping a closer eye on the cleaning drones now that she understood them better than before.

"It's nothing elaborate," Captain Belcher said. "I'll have to check the regulations manual, but I believe you're entitled to a handkerchief bearing the seal of *The Gasket*."

Scarlett was now certain this award would not require an elaborate hairdo, nor a clean uniform, and she found herself underwhelmed by the reward she was to receive. "Well, then," she said. "I suppose you can have that dropped off at my office."

*And then*, she thought, *I will pitch it through my pocket into my workspace on Earth, and never think of it again.*

*Unless, of course, I need it in a pinch.*

*Dawn Vogel learned everything she knows about "micrometer accuracy" from listening to and editing reports for the archaeologists she works with in her day job. When she's not working, she's usually writing, crafting, gaming, or herding cats. Visit her at http://historythatneverwas.com or on Twitter @historyneverwas.*

You can follow us:

on **Twitter** (@WyldbloodPress)
on **Facebook** (www.facebook.com/WyldboodPress)
on our **website** (www.wyldblood.com)
by **email** (contact@wyldblood.com)
or by subscribing to our **newsletter**
(http://eepurl.com/haa4Zn).

# WYLDBLOOD